The Weight of Gold

JS Gariety

Stained Glass Publishing

To my grandmothers: Brita Rose, Sherilyn, and Carlene
To my mom. The angels never left.
And to my Emily-Rose.

May these stories honor you.

Copyright © 2023 by JS Gariety

All rights reserved.

No portion of this book may be reproduced in any form without written permission from the publisher or author, except as permitted by U.S. copyright law.

Contents

1

A Sawdust Moon

Rose, 1971

I buried my sister under a sawdust moon. It cast a rusty glow on the treetops and thirsty grass as the world sunk deeper into darkness. The peach tree was as still as death, without even the whisper of an evening breeze to coax its leaves to life. My chest sparkled with sweat—a black shroud wrapped around my body like an unwanted blanket you kick off in your sleep. But I remained outside in the sticky warmth of an Alabama summer dusk—for the first time this was preferable to being in the air conditioned indoors. Close friends and extended family, who had all gathered in my parents' home after the funeral services, slowly took their leave, until only my parents, Lenny, and the kids and I were left. I listened from the back porch steps as the last of the car engines sputtered to life, fading away down the road until the cicadas' cacophonous drone was the only sound left to the night.

"Rose." Ma opened the back door, and the sound of a crying baby drifted out from the kitchen. "Please come help me with the baby." Her voice was tight and desperate.

I turned away from copper moonlight towards a new reality. My older sister, my best friend, was gone.

I walked up the old porch steps—the white paint almost glowed in the fading light. Inside, a rush of cool air greeted me and goosebumps spread across my forearms. I took my wailing niece in my arms, who was naked except for a diaper. Her tiny black dress lay crumpled on the floor by the staircase, damp with a milky vomit. She smelled like sour milk, but I didn't mind. I was grateful for her cries, they drowned out the shouting of angry men from the next room. But being in my arms calmed her almost immediately. Besides her late mother, I was the only other person she had bonded with in the handful of days she'd been alive. I had been there by my sister's hospital bed only two weeks earlier, unaware that she wasn't out of the woods when the baby arrived safely.

"Thank you, Rose. She wouldn't settle with me." Ma's eyebrows were furrowed, and she looked at me like she'd had a question and I'd just answered it. A door slammed, and she started as Pa stormed from his office where he and Lenny had been arguing.

Pa leaned against the stair banister, next to the crumpled newborn dress. Ma went to him, first glancing at me again with that significant look.

"I won't let this happen," he said, in an attempted hushed tone. But I still heard him easily. "He's a good fer nothin' drunk."

"Richard." Ma titled her head towards my nephew, Eugene, who sat at the kitchen table, until then invisible to all the grownups.

It was true, Lenny was a drunk. Though not a *good fer nothin' one*, just a sad one. My sister had married for love, not security. They'd been high school sweethearts, and on her eighteenth birthday, she'd dropped out of school to marry him. I was fourteen at the time, and in awe of her wild romanticism.

"You'll understand someday," she had said, as I'd helped her zip up the white dress she'd worn to the courthouse. It was the dress she'd bought the summer before for the garden party of an important colleague of our father's. It was a simple, sleeveless sundress with a fitted waist and full skirt. The top of the dress cut inward into a mock neck, almost like a halter, exposing more of her collarbone. It was her loophole in Pa's stringent modesty regulations. She was always finding little ways like that to infuriate him. His lawyer mind was obsessed with the letter of the law, and she used that against him. She could've been a lawyer, herself.

"Is it worth it?" I'd asked as she'd done her own bridal makeup. It wasn't anything different from her normal makeup, except for dark red lipstick. Pa had threatened to cut her off if she got married that day. He'd pulled out every argument of logic he had to convince her not to marry Lenny Howell. He didn't approve of the boy—who offered little in his eyes by way of security and absolutely nothing by way of blood. Lenny had no trust fund, and his career aspirations were deemed unacceptable—he'd wanted to be an actor. But he got a job right out of high school waiting tables at a seedy dinner theater and had been working there ever since. Pa was humiliated by this, so despite his threats to cut her off on her wedding day, he'd funded their lives these eight years to keep up appearances. Although, I always suspected Ma was the real reason he'd changed his mind. She would never openly defy her husband, but when she needed to she could be persuasive. She wasn't necessarily thrilled about the marriage either—she wanted her daughter to finish high school and go to college. But she didn't mind Lenny, and she would never cut her child off. Not if she had any say in it.

"How do you know if it'll be worth it?" I'd asked again, after a long pause while my sister checked herself up and down in the full-length mirror of her walk-in closet.

"I don't," she'd answered, grabbing her red cardigan off the door handle. It matched her lipstick exactly. "But I want to find out. What is life without a little risk, anyway?"

Eight years later, I still didn't have an answer to that question. I'd never had the courage to do what she'd done—carve her own path.

The baby was drifting off, so I took a blanket from the diaper bag that sat on the kitchen table, wrapping it round her. She snuggled in with her head against my chest. She had thick, dark hair and golden skin, inherited from her papa. But her lips and nose were distinctly her ma's. *What was she gonna eat now? Do babies drink cow milk if they have no mother to nurse 'em?*

I caught Ma and Pa surveying me, watching how I wrapped my niece up and held her close to my body—the way my sister had taught me with Eugene when he was a wee thing. I'd visited her a lot back then. When I met my parents' eyes, they turned away and lowered their voices. But it was a quiet room.

"We can't. Not with your health." Pa took on a more tender tone with his wife.

"But Rose is just a young thing. Practically still a girl. Not to mention unmarried—it wouldn't be proper."

"She's a full-grown woman, Annabel. Not your little girl anymore. And as for the issue of marriage, I've already spoken to Thomas."

A chill arose in my chest. Pa had pulled Thomas aside at the funeral for a lengthy stretch, shortly after which Thomas had left with a hurried farewell kiss on my cheek and mumbled promise to check on me tomorrow. My stomach went cold as I considered the possibility Pa was implying. He'd been pressuring Thomas and me for some time to get engaged. I was twenty-two, *a good marryin' age*, as he said. But Thomas and I had agreed to wait. I was going to graduate from the University of Alabama and get myself a job in journalism. Thomas was going to get an internship and pass The Bar. Then, after we were established in our careers, we would start talking about engagement. What exactly did Pa mean, that he'd already spoken to Thomas? I imagined them bartering over me, like I was a bushel of the season's first strawberries for anyone to get their hands on. I hoped Thomas had stood his ground. I hoped he'd said he wouldn't discuss it a moment longer without me. But Pa was a terrifying man, and there was a sense of finality in his voice, like he knew it was a sure thing.

Pa believed the only good reason for a woman to go to college was to find a husband. He couldn't understand why I wanted a degree, and didn't like the idea of his daughters working. *Women's education is for the home, not the workplace*, he would look to Ma to endorse his wisdom. She would smile, meekly, and say, *of course dear.* That submissive smile would fill me plum up with uncharacteristic anger.

Lenny was my dream; a fancy journalist career's yours, my sister would have said. *It's worth it, Rosebud. More worth it than gettin' up 'fore first light an hikin' Wellington hill to see the sunrise. Besides, you can't possibly make them any more angry than they were when I up and married an actor. And I'm still welcome at Christmas and Sunday dinners, am I not?*

But she wasn't here to be on my side anymore. There would be no more Christmas and Sunday dinners with her.

Pa returned to his office where Lenny had remained and the shouting resumed—Pa's shouting, anyway. The sun had fully set some time ago, and the long windows in the kitchen were dark and lifeless. Even the lightning bugs were hiding tonight.

Eugene sat at the kitchen table in silence, where he'd planted himself since we'd got home from the cemetery. Still in his suit, his dark, wavy hair was damp from sweat and humidity. It'd been hotter than a fresh apple pie at the cemetery, and that little black suit was probably suffocating. Every so often, a small sniffle pierced the emptiness in front of him. I wanted to go to him, kneel by his side, wrap him up in my arms, and tell him it was all gonna be ok. But I didn't know how to tell him something I didn't believe myself. Instead, I helped him out of his suit coat, then silently hung it on the back of his chair.

Like I'd been there for my niece's birth, I'd been there for Eugene's. I'd watched him grow all these years. When I'd started college I'd had less time for him, and I wasn't sure we had the same bond that we used to. We used to do puzzles and capture lightning bugs together. I didn't know if he still enjoyed those things. I wanted to be there for him now. I wanted to want what I suspected my parents had in mind for my niece and nephew's future. But I was scared. Despite how it may have appeared to Ma, I had no earthly clue what I was doing when I interacted with those kids.

The baby was finally in a deep sleep. I put her down in the living room, in the portable bassinet Ma had brought out earlier. Then I paced by the living room's bay windows, trying to find something in the darkness outside. I don't know what, but whatever it was I didn't find it. Eventually the arguing in the office ceased and the house went quiet, which was somehow worse.

We all gathered in the kitchen at Pa's command, cooling off with Ma's sweet tea and avoiding each other's eyes. Lenny lowered himself into the chair directly across from me, the defeat radiating from him. This man, who I'd come to associate with life and passion, had been broken.

"Now son," Pa addressed Eugene. "Cryin' 'bout it won't do a damn thing. God needed your ma more than you did. A'cept his will."

Eugene's sniffles slowed and then stopped, but when I stole a glance his way, I saw that silent tears continued to fall from his listless eyes. Those tears burned into my heart, and something roared up inside me. This was a child. A newly motherless, innocent, vulnerable child.

"Leave him alone, Pa." The vibrato in my voice shocked me and everyone else at the table. The words came out as if from a schoolteacher scolding a child. Pa shot me a look that could've turned Medusa herself to stone, and the roaring thing inside of me shrunk back, overshadowed by a familiar cold dread and regret.

"I beg your pardon." Pa dared me with anger bubbling under the surface of his controlled voice.

Ma sat wide-eyed in alarmed silence, her eyes flitting between Pa and me. Then she spoke quietly, "Richard, we're all grieving. Rose didn't mean any disrespect. Right, sweetie?"

She turned to me expectantly, her eyes pleading. My heart softened—she was right after all, we were *all* grieving. Including her.

"Sorry, Pa." But the apology wasn't for his sake, it was for Ma's. And I imagined my sister standing behind our father, her eyes joyfully chaotic, proud of my brief moment of insubordination. I lifted a hand to my mouth to cover the smile that tugged at the corners of my mouth. She'd felt so close since she passed.

Like she was reluctant to leave me. It felt almost like she wanted something from beyond the grave and was guiding me to it.

"Let's continue then," Pa said.

She faded from my mind and my heart sank with her. I stared into the wood grains of the table, willing them to spell out a message, giving me the answer to an impossible situation. The key that would rescue me from all this. I wished the defiant courage of my sister had lingered a little longer.

"Lenny." The way Pa said Lenny's name reminded me of the time he'd caught my sister sneaking out late as a teenager.

Lenny started, then turned his gaze on me. In his brown eyes were stories of pain and reluctance. I returned to my wood grain, yearning for a different story. He finally cleared his throat, "I 'spose congratulations are in order, Rose." So, it was already decided. My hopes in Thomas's loyalty melted away like the ice-cubes in my tea. My breath whistled a little as I inhaled through my nose. Lenny looked to Pa as if unsure he'd said the proper thing. Pa nodded.

"And—" his voice cracked, "I'd like ya'll, you and Thomas I mean, to take care of the kids fer me." My heart snapped and shattered at the pain in his voice. I'd seen it coming, but hearing it from Lenny's mouth was worse than I could've imagined.

Lenny slid something across the tabletop. The sound of metal skimming across wood made my breath catch. He lifted his hand to reveal a family heirloom. My stomach churned as I recalled the last time I had seen it—earlier that day, adorning my sister's cold, stiff finger.

2

The Witch

I drove without a destination, but with a clear direction: away from him.

Outside the windshield, the world looked as though every surface had been coated in sugar crystals. My hands were numb—maybe from the cold, maybe because I clutched the steering wheel like it was the edge of a cliff I was hanging off of. Despite the dangers of the icy road, I kept my foot glued to the gas pedal. My mind was made up, and I wasn't going to let some ice-storm stop me.

I checked the rearview. Niles was wrapped up in blankets, tucked around him in the car seat. Tiny, closed eyes and a little nose poked out from the covers. He was slumbering peacefully, sighing every so often. His lips suckled like he was sleep-eating. He seemed warm enough.

The heat was broken in my old Nissan sedan. My dad had bought it used for me when I got my license three years ago. The heat gave out a year later. In the Alabama climate, I had never cared much about the broken heat. But now I was shivering in this freak-of-nature ice-frenzy that for some reason waited until spring to make its dramatic entrance.

The icy sleet transformed into thick, puffy snowflakes, and darkness wrapped itself around our little car. I'd never driven in snow before. The danger, the escape—they were thrilling. The rush had started back at home as I threw things into the car, hurrying to beat the 5pm arrival of my ever-punctual husband. The exhilaration had only increased on the journey. I'd woken up that morning with this momentum, this sudden and inexplicable courage. I'd let too many chances pass me by. And now it seemed like all consequences had lost their power, and mountains had become molehills.

I slowed to an easy crawl, my left knee bouncing like those jumping beans they show you at school when you're a kid. Niles shifted sleepily behind me. My arms ached, and I tried to soften them. But the adrenaline pulsed through my muscles, hardening and flexing them from shoulders to fingertips. The road was empty except for the eerie headlights' glow reflecting off the bright snow. It was ghostly how the landscape disappeared under a layer of white. The snow and ice insulated the world with an oppressive silence broken only by the crunch of my tires and sighs of my infant child. And we were utterly alone. No one else was crazy enough to travel in this weather. Maybe I was crazy. Don always said I was. It was what kept me with him for this long. I believed him. My track record was enough evidence; I'd never conformed and was prone to moods of impulsivity—like the one I was in now. He'd tried to keep me in check. He actually had me thinking I deserved it—like a disobedient dog that needed a good kick. But then I realized—I'd never kick a dog.

I looked in the rear-view mirror to assess my eyes. The right one was still blue and purple from last week. I was grateful it hadn't affected my vision too much to drive. A small cut sat inside my left brow, almost over the bridge of my nose. In the mirror, my face reflected a glistening dew. Crying was a normal state of being for me. It might've started at the exchange to highway 20. Or even all the way back on 243. I honestly didn't know. But they weren't tears of sorrow. They were tears of relief.

The snow slowed it's fall and soon everything was ice again. The car slipped around as I climbed a slight incline then steadied at the top of the slope. Over the hill, the highway began to decline. I lifted my foot from the gas and pressed the brakes. The car lurched, jerking to the left as the tires slid across ice. I tried to steer back on course, but it was out of control, and my efforts only threw the car around even more. I should've been afraid. Terrified. But I watched myself as if I were in a movie, with the same concern I'd have for a fictional character, hoping for a good outcome but numbed to any real terror. I let go of the steering wheel and the car spun all the way around, then sideways. Through the windshield, the side of the road came into view. I spotted a slushy snowbank and released the brake. The car slid into the shoulder of the road and stopped in the slush.

We were finally still.

I turned around and checked on Niles. He was still asleep—oblivious to the peril he was just in. I stared down at my hands resting in my lap. I was calm. Detached. Strangely unaffected by the near tragedy.

I put my hands back on the wheel, but when I pushed the gas, the tires spun beneath me, the car unmoving. They spun faster as I pressed harder on the gas. I switched gears. No luck. I thought for a moment we'd run into something. But there was nothing but the slush, glowing through the fading light. I lifted my foot from the gas and sat in silence while I processed. I tapped the gas again, gently this time, as if performing brain surgery with my toe. The engine revved angrily, and smoke drifted up from the front tires, accompanied by a burning rubber smell.

I shifted to park and opened the car door. The front tire was wedged in ice and slush. What I had thought was a wet snowbank was actually a shallow ditch. We were stuck. Stuck hours from where we had started, and who knows how far from where we would end. Another obstacle from the universe. Another force trying to stop me.

"I knew it, your dad's a witch." Even if Niles had been awake, he wouldn't have been much of an audience for my humor.

There were still no other cars in sight, or any kind of habitation visible through the freezing rain that obscured the air beyond the car lights. And absolutely no sign of life. Not even the birds dared travel. I turned off the lights and killed the engine. I didn't need to run out of gas in an ice storm. I stared at the freezing rain as it clinked on the windshield for what felt like half an hour. Naked trees slumped under the weight of ice on their branches. In the absence of the engine's hum, my ears picked up the faint whistle of winter wind. The ice was beautiful. Formidable. The danger inherent made it all the more striking.

What now? I drummed my fingers on the steering wheel, waiting for divine intervention or a stroke of genius, I didn't know. For the first time that day, a small but icy thrill of fear crept into my heart. If Don was following me, he could catch up any moment. And Niles—what if he freezes to death?

"Oh *God*." I rested my elbows on the steering wheel and covered my face with my hands. Does that count as a prayer? To say *Oh God* when you're in distress?

Minutes passed and the car grew colder. The freezing rain had become a wet snow again, flakes landing and immediately freezing on the sheen of ice that covered every surface. I sat motionless in my seat, thinking through my options, not convinced by any of them. *I suppose I could get out and try pushing...*

A distant shout startled me and I gasped. The cold air hurt my lungs. Was it in my head? I listened carefully. Another shout, louder this time, came from beyond the road. I turned the ignition to the first click and switched on the lights and the wind shield wiper. I used the arm of my coast to wipe away the fog on the inside of the glass. A man appeared a dozen or so feet ahead, emerging from the white fog. He carried a sack on one shoulder and waved with his free hand. With relief, I opened the car door and stepped out.

"Do you need a push?" The man approached, smiling warmly. He was bundled up, but I could see the crow's feet around his eyes. His teeth were yellow compared to the white backdrop behind him. There were no vehicles, and I was sure no residential accommodations for miles around. He'd emerged from wherever or whatever this road passed by. Perhaps there was a farm or something further off I couldn't see.

"I'm stuck," I answered lamely. He smiled in response, hoisting the sack down to open it. He started spreading a sandy substance around the front tires. Outside the snow was only an inch or two deep. It seemed too little to get stuck in, but then again, my experience with snow was limited to movie screens and a single high school ski trip.

"Where's your car?" I asked.

"I try not to drive in this weather." He situated himself in front of the car. "I'm gonna push you out. Start it up and hit the gas, gently." I wanted to find out where he'd come from, but the car was the more pressing matter.

"Aye-aye, captain." I climbed back in and started the car, putting it in reverse. He pushed from the front, and I eased on the pedal. After a few pushes, the tires caught and the car lurched backward. I drove a couple feet back, turning to face forward on the road again, then stopped. I looked at the ditch of ice where I'd been stuck. The man approached and I cranked down the window. He offered his hand and I shook it, dazed.

The man smiled. "Get you and your boy somewhere safe for the night. The ice is far more dangerous than snow. Remember, don't go too slow. You don't want to win any races by any means, but if you go too slow, you'll lose traction. And if you start sliding, don't break, just steer." He let go of my hand and turned away, dragging his now empty sack beside him. Something crumpled in my hand. A $50 bill. I couldn't believe how kind this stranger had been.

I realized I'd forgotten to thank him and threw the door open, stepping out into the winter. But he was gone as mysteriously as he had appeared. I climbed back inside the car and pushed gently on the gas. After a small slip we gained traction and started moving once again. This time I kept a steady pace.

I searched the twilight for somewhere to stop. An hour passed. And another. I stopped a couple times to nurse Niles. Soon all had gone dark, and all I could see was the glow of ice ten feet ahead where the headlights reflected off glittering ice crystals. Niles was contentedly cooing behind me, but I knew I needed to get him somewhere warm and safe soon. The cold gripped my chest and steamed up my breath.

I squinted through the glowy, white haze. My bruise throbbed as I over-worked the muscles in my face. Finally, I caught a glimpse of a faint yellow glow in the distance. My heart lifted, the light bringing hope like some cliché. *Please, someone be home.*

At first all that was visible was the glow, but each minute forward increased my confidence that this was some kind of residence; the light divided itself into small rectangles—windows. A house, most likely occupied given the light. Soon I made out a shadowy silhouette. It was a small rambler. The light from the windows illuminated the snow around it, keeping the darkness of midnight at bay. Smoke billowed up from a red brick chimney. Nearby sat a large barn, closed up for the winter. Fighting the dark with my eyes, I found the highway exit and made my way down a short road up to the house.

As I drove up the slippery driveway, the front door opened. A woman appeared, hand over her eyes as she strained past the glaring headlights. Relief flooded my whole body from limbs to core. I stopped the car then opened my door, preparing to ask for her hospitality.

"Finally, you're here." she called out before I could open my mouth.

I stood in the snow, shocked into a momentary silence. I racked my brain, but her face brought no recollection. I didn't think I knew anyone this far north. Then sudden fear grappled at my chest. Did Don figure out what direction I'd gone in and somehow contacted this woman*? No, that's impossible...right?*

"What do you mean?" I stuttered.

"Just that I've been expecting you. Come in and warm up."

She turned on her heel, leaving the door open. I hesitated for only a moment before a wall of warmth enveloped me, drifting on the wind from the open door. It was more enticing than a bottle of Patrón. I collected Niles from his car seat and trudged as quick as I could up the snowy walk towards the inviting sanctuary ahead.

Maybe she'd murder me. But what other options did I have at this point?

Immediately inside was a small kitchen that smelled of beef broth and freshly baked bread. The kitchen opened to a sitting room with a fireplace, holding within it a blazing fire.

"I'm Amanda," the woman introduced herself, taking my wet, snow studded coat and offering a soft, thick blanket in its stead.

"Lillian." I wrapped the blanket around Niles and myself, gratefully. "The crazy girl driving in the snow. And this is Niles. All you really need to know about him is that he poops a lot."

Amanda chuckled, then went to the stove and ladled stew from a large stock pot. "Please, sit—make yourself at home." She set the stew on the table and pulled out a chair for me. I sat, eyeing the stew hungerly, but still cautious of this bizarre stranger. She reminded me of the witches in children's fairytales—the real fairytales, not the watered-down ones. But my soul was somehow at ease. She had long silver hair, the kind only dark hair can become when it goes gray. One small piece in the front was braided all the way down with colorful string weaved into it. She looked straight out of the seventies. Around her neck she wore two leather cords tied around rocks. One was a clear, shimmering crystal. The other bright blue, with veins of gold running through it. Around the room there were more rocks, in various colors and shapes set on virtually every surface in sight.

She left briefly and came back carrying a folded bassinet.

"You have kids?"

She set the bassinet up in the living room. "No, never could. But I used to run a child-care center before I took on this little farmstead." She took Niles from me and laid him down in the bed. "I still have a few things in storage."

"Ok, so how did you know I was coming? You realize how freaky that sounds, right?"

She smiled and joined me at the table with a bowl of stew for herself. "God works in mysterious ways," she shrugged. I stared at her, probably gawking. "I'm teasing," she laughed. "I wasn't expecting you, specifically. I knew there'd be travelers coming this way, and most folk round here don't know how to drive in this weather. I waited up in case someone needed shelter. And good I did." She looked at my untouched bowl. "Please, eat." Her eyes were sincere and kind. She tucked into her own bowl, blowing lightly on the broth before bringing it to her parted mouth, lips closing around the spoon.

"A midnight snack?" I asked.

"Nothing like a warm stew on a cold night," she said.

I took a spoonful. It was warm, not just in temperature. I couldn't recognize all the spices, but it was earthy and slightly bitter. The carrots were the most flavorful I'd ever had. The beef melted in my mouth, the warmth filling my core. Amanda sliced up a loaf of the bread, steam billowing up in clouds as she cut. She handed me a slice. I almost burned my tongue shoving it into my mouth. It was soft and pillowy, tasting of butter.

Halfway through the bowl of stew, I shed the large blanket, the chill from my journey now thawed. When there was only a bit of broth left, I used another slice of bread to sop it up. Then Amanda took my bowl and filled it again.

We ate in silence until I had filled my belly enough to bother with conversation.

"So," I ventured, "you're religious then?"

She swallowed a bit of potato, then cleared her throat. "Oh, religion has nothing to do with God, dear—or the divine, higher power—whatever form people might choose to believe in. Human-constructed rituals only serve as pathways to connect to that higher self."

I stared at her, blankly. This gal was wacky. She reminded me of how George Harrison got all spiritual after the Beatles traveled to India. I imagined her swaying and singing to "My Sweet Lord"—the long version with all the Krishna stuff.

"Do you believe in a higher power?" she asked.

I pondered the question, unsure if being forced to attend each Sunday growing up counted. "My parents do."

"I asked about you." She raised her eyebrows.

"I haven't attended a service in..." I tried to remember the last time I'd went. "Five years?"

"And do you believe in a god? A higher power in the universe?"

"If there is one, he certainly enjoys watching me suffer," I laughed. She smiled politely in response. I continued in seriousness, "I used to pray a little. I guess I believe in some kind of power. But I'm not going to pretend to know anything about what that power is, or who I'm praying to. That power could just be physics as easily as it could be some god. I mean, there's no real way of knowing, is there." This was an opinion I'd defended many times.

But Amanda did not argue. She smiled knowingly. "Ah, now that's where faith comes in. But religion isn't faith. Religion is only made meaningful because of faith."

"So, you *are* religious?"

She chuckled again, as if enjoying a private joke. "I'm what some might call spiritual. The sight of my crystals and magic books might incite some pearl clutching in your parents' congregation." She fingered the blue stone that hung from her neck. I laughed, partly at the thought of my grandmother and her church friends witnessing this conversation, and partly because this woman had, in all seriousness, admitted she was a witch. Apparently my witch-radar was pretty good.

She laughed with me before continuing. "Regardless of what you call it—physics, the universe, a god—there is *something* there. Something powerful that surrounds us. Connects us. It brought you here."

I considered her words. If anything had brought me here besides my own physical being, it was—

"Hope?"

She reached across the table and took her hands in mine.

"Yes, hope." She stared earnestly into my eyes, unblinking, and I locked back into them like I was feeding on her energy. She lowered her voice, continuing to search my eyes like they were revealing my history. "Hope brought you here. Hope for something better."

I didn't know if she knew where I had come from, or what I was running from, but somehow, she knew what I was running to: safety.

"I don't know where to go," I whispered, tears blurring her image. I turned to blink them away. All the emotions of the day, of leaving my husband and setting off alone, came bursting through the dam I'd somehow built to keep them locked away.

She released my hands and stood, going to the kitchen counter. She picked up a newspaper clipping and returned to place it on the table in front of me. It was a listing for apartments available. She circled one in bright pink gel pen.

Studio apartment with private bathroom and kitchenette, bed and mattress included. 500 square feet. $400/month plus electric. Stove, fridge, and microwave included. Coin laundry in building.

"It's in St. Louis." She stood over my shoulder, as I read the advert. "Only a few more hours north of here. You could be there tomorrow."

"St. Louis," I mused. How different St. Louis must be from Jasper. Or Tallahassee. In school as a kid, we'd done projects on other states. I was assigned Missouri. Ever since then, I'd wanted to see St. Louis. I was free now; I could go if I wanted to. I could move there. In fact, it seemed ludicrous in this moment that I hadn't thought of going there a long time ago.

"Any job leads in that paper for an unskilled high school dropout?"

"You'd be amazed how many people are willing to pay someone to clean their houses for them." She picked up a pink stone from the windowsill above the kitchen sink and rubbed it between her fingers.

3

To be...or not

Eleanor, 2017

S ilence pulsed in my head. I longed to turn on the TV for some background noise to fill the empty numbness in our small apartment. But the sick, clawing weight of anxiety glued my hand to my belly, held back from the simple act of reaching for the remote. Even with the sound down so low that I needed subtitles, the neighbors complained of a "constant buzzing" from our shared wall. I knew their expectations for apartment living were unrealistic, but the threat of confrontation froze me in place, and so I reclined on the couch in a silence that throbbed in my head.

I was on partial bedrest because of early contractions, and so far, it had been the most boring couple weeks of my life. I considered eating, and the thought put a lump in my throat, sending woozy waves through my head and stomach. Morning sickness was a misnomer. It really lasted all day. They said the second trimester would be better than the first, but so far it wasn't. Sometimes Danny had to force feed me pieces of breakfast cereal, one golden nugget at a time, concern and fear in his eyes. I knew I had to eat something—for Danny. And for the baby, of course.

My stomach ballooned up over my line of sight, cutting out a lumpy crescent from everything in front of me. It wiggled and bubbled, and I swore I was growing a giant gelatin monster. How was I already so large? I couldn't imagine getting any bigger. My doctor said they weren't concerned because it was my first—and on account of my short stature. I planned in my head how to get off the couch, then rolled to one side to let the weight of my protruding midsection give me momentum. As always, it went much smoother in my head than in execution, and I was sure I could be mistaken from a distance for a sand-dried whale struggling to flop its way back to the salty blue comfort of home.

Determined to find something to eat that wouldn't send my stomach churning, I wobbled to the kitchen at baby turtle pace, as if using those puffy flipper feet for the first time, steadying myself with sausage fingers and aching wrists. What was wrong with me? I had yearned for this. I thought back six months, when I took the pregnancy test. Peeing on a stick wasn't as easy as people joked it was. Didn't the people who designed these things realize women's pee didn't come out in a straight, thin stream? It was more like a waterfall, and I always got pee on my fingers and on the part of the stick you weren't supposed to get wet. But the test had worked anyway—so maybe they really were foolproof. Two little pink lines had faded into view, and I'd shouted for Danny immediately. I didn't even have to tell him; he knew when he saw my face. We'd embraced, spinning and tumbling to the floor in breathless elation, my panties still at my ankles. I'd clutched onto that pee covered stick while he kissed me, his hand placed protectively on my abdomen. I longed to taste that rushing bliss again. I longed to long again. Now, it felt like a mistake. I didn't know how much it would hurt. How deformed I would be. How lonely I would feel. How completely unready I was to be a mom. But honestly, how could I have predicted the bed rest? Or the hyperemesis gravidarum? No one had ever warned me that such a thing existed. Everyone I'd known who'd ever been pregnant always talked about how magical it was. And when I was so tired in the beginning, the nurses had kept telling me about the energy I'd get when the second trimester finally came. But like the sickness, things only got worse and worse. I'd been ill-prepared.

Still, I felt a fool for wanting something so badly at first, then hating it so much now. I reminded myself, as I had many times before, that this was simply the temporary and necessary evil to bring my baby into the world. A baby I still wasn't convinced existed. Something between the Jell-O wiggles of my belly and the facts of procreation disconnected in my head.

It was almost ten at night. One hour until I could pick Danny up from work. He'd been working second shift—paying his dues. I surveyed the kitchen cabinet and grabbed a few saltines to nibble on. At least I could tell Danny I ate *something*.

The silence was suffocating. I wanted to call my grandmother, but she would already be asleep. I know she would've answered anyway, but we'd already talked for a couple hours that day. I would wait until tomorrow. These days, we talked several times a week. Not going to a workplace every day was lonelier than I'd expected.

My laptop sat at the kitchen table where I had been filming some American Sign Language transcriptions. My eyes ached in the bright glare of the computer screen, and I waddled over to check on it. The upload to my agency was finished so I shut the lid, the relief to my eyes immediate. But as I bent over the table a pang tore through my abdomen. This contraction was different than the others, and it was getting stronger, fast. I cried out and doubled over, clutching under my belly. Bits of cracker crumbled to the floor from my fist. Stumbling onto my knees, I bent forward and pressed my forehead against the cool linoleum floor, breathing through the forceful waves that tore through my abdomen and back. When it finally passed, I pulled out my phone and started a timer like Dr. Farris had instructed. I waited there on the floor, watching the numbers go up. One minute passed, and I attempted to control my hyperventilation. I willed the pain not to come back. The intensity of that contraction frightened me. Two minutes passed, and I wanted to call Danny, but I didn't want to worry him if it was nothing, so I decided to wait and see if I got to five minutes. The time ticked upwards, baiting my breath as I waited for the two to become a three, but before it could, the pain returned, even stronger.

The fluorescent lights in the hospital room were giving me a migraine. I squeezed my eyes shut.

"Let me dim the lights for you, sweetie," a nurse said. I couldn't remember what she said her name was.

"Thank you," I breathed out slowly.

Another contraction was coming, and I tried to concentrate on relaxing instead of bearing down.

"Don't bear down," the nurse reminded me. A flash of irritation faded to gratitude when I realized I had been bearing down, despite my efforts.

It felt like we'd been waiting hours for the on-call doctor, though it'd only been thirty minutes. The contractions were two minutes apart, each one over a minute long. Every time the pain began, I silently cursed whoever was on-call for making me endure another one. In between contractions, I tried to think of a pleasant memory and pretend I was there.

Sunshine and pizza on the pier. Danny laughing as I try to stretch my arm out and take a selfie that includes both our faces. I ask him to just take it for me, and he rolls his eyes, but does it without complaint. I smile for the camera, placing my hands on my bump. We walk and talk hand in hand, the sun glistening off the river in ripples. It's easy. Right. Complete like a brand new thousand-piece puzzle before the pieces start going missing.

Another contraction set my body aflame, and I shut my eyes to breathe through the pain. My back and pelvis ached. I was already exhausted. *It's too early.* I stubbornly resisted my body's efforts to birth this baby. After an eternity, it passed, and I opened my eyes. Danny was on speaker phone with his parents. The three of them were all praying in Korean. Danny hadn't prayed since his parents were in the country for our wedding, at least as far as I knew. They each spoke their own, unique prayers aloud and at the same time, and with my limited Korean I couldn't understand the different words spoken simultaneously. But I could hear the strained emotion in Danny's voice. *It's just another false alarm*, I told myself despite knowing I was already five centimeters dilated—they had checked before admitting me almost forty-five minutes ago. But I held out hope that they could stop the labor and send me home. Another contraction came, and my womb hardened. I tried not to bear down but I swore my body was doing that of its own accord.

"Relax," the nurse reminded me. The request was completely ludicrous.

Danny squeezed my hand in response to my own tightening grip. He and his parents had finished their prayers, and he told them he'd update them soon—that I could understand. They said *annyeong, Dae-hyun*, in hushed tones before hanging up, using Danny's Korean middle name. I thought of his name, trying to keep my mind occupied and distracted from the pain. Christian names were fairly common in South Korea. Being devout Christians, my in-laws had given Danny the Biblical name. But they still always used his Korean name.

The contraction finally subsided.

"That one was two and a half minutes long." The nurse glanced at me, then went to a phone on the wall next to the door and dialed.

I wanted to scream. Did OBs rush around when they were on call late at night, wasting no time knowing their patients were frightened, exhausted, and in agony? Or did they saunter lazily about in their duties, wishing they could be home sleeping instead?

"Is the doctor coming?" Danny asked, after the nurse hung up the phone.

"Not yet," her tone was apologetic. "But we're going to give your wife a steroid shot."

"Why?" I asked.

"Babies this early don't have fully developed lungs. The steroid shot helps strengthen them."

The worry etched in Danny's features was evident. "Does that mean—"

"It's just a precaution. Whatever happens, we're going to take good care of you. Try not to stress."

As if that were even remotely possible.

Another nurse arrived with an injection sitting on a tray. They waited for the next contraction to come and go, then turned me over to my side. The injection went into my left buttock. I felt a slight sting, but it was quick.

"That's it?" I asked.

"Yes, that's it."

"So, if the baby comes tonight, she'll be ok?" Danny asked.

The nurses exchanged meaningful looks. "The steroid will better her chances."

I closed my eyes and tried not to think about viability rates at 26 weeks. I searched my memory for a happy place.

Pillows on pillows on recliner, nestled in my space, surrounded by books and small craft projects. I stare out the window, the spring had brought flocks of birds to our feeders, and I lived for the minutes watching them flutter to and from the perch, pecking away at tiny specks. A feast for them, a show for me. Zebra striped wings and white burglar masks of chickadees dance past my line of view. If a rainbow were made of shades of brown, they would come in the form of house finches, colorful and uncolorful all at once. The goldfinches are my favorite. A bright yellow that cannot be replicated with a 24 box of crayons. The black accents look sharp against the lemon feathers.

I longed go back there—to the bed-rest I'd despised. I had been so fed up with being pregnant, but now I needed more than anything to stay that way.

The door to the room opened and finally, the on-call doctor entered. His eyes were tired, and he squinted blearily at the computer while the nurse filled him in. He nodded as she spoke, his bored expression not matching the urgency in the nurse's voice. Danny looked at me in a way that said my annoyance was unhidden on my face. But he didn't admonish me with his eyes. They were too preoccupied with concern. There was no room in either of us for politeness or tact.

The nurse had kept her demeanor calm so far, but now that the doctor was here her façade crumbled. She, too, seemed frustrated by the doctor's nonchalance, and was putting little more effort in hiding it than I was.

"Ok, Mrs. Sun," he started to speak as another contraction gripped me. I tried to listen through the involuntary moan under my breath. He stopped and waited, looking down at me with disinterest. This one was particularly long, and the silence in the room taunted me. I was too aware of each pair of eyes fixed on me, waiting for my body to finish with its rude interruption so the doctor could speak.

When the contraction began to deescalate, I hissed through gritted teeth, "stop the labor."

He answered like he was a waiter, reporting that the restaurant was all out of tiramisu. "It's probably too late for that, Mrs. Sun. You're progressing rapidly."

Without warning, he lifted my gown and shoved his fingers into me. I gasped.

"Whoa," Danny shouted, his eyes wide as he grabbed my shoulder. He looked at the doctor in disbelief. The doctor ignored him.

The pressure was terrible. As he finished the exam, another contraction began. He nodded at the nurse. She looked at us, poorly veiling apprehension with a small smile before going to the phone. When the doctor's back was turned to her, I caught her glaring at the back of his head.

The doctor looked between Danny and me. "You're having this baby tonight." I couldn't find any compassion in his eyes or tone, only apathy. Or if not apathy, slight annoyance even. Like *I* had inconvenienced *him*. If he had seen me as soon as I was admitted, would it still have been too late? Another contraction surged up on top of the last one.

I looked pointedly at him and huffed, "get me a different doctor."

"Now," Danny said.

4

Promises

Rose, 1971

Light filtered through the white, gossamer curtains of the upper east room in the Strawberry Grove plantation house. The house belonged to family friends, the Habershams—it wasn't one of those plantation houses rented out for anyone. The Habershams lent it only for the weddings and baptism receptions of family and close friends. Every year they hosted New Year's Eve there, so I was familiar with the rooms and the grounds.

A goldfinch landed on the balcony balustrade outside and the song of another called to it. It sang back, then flew away into the glare of the sun. I turned away from the picturesque window and back to my reflection in the vanity mirror. For a few minutes, I could be alone. Ma had gone off somewhere, bustling about managing flowers, food, or whatever other last-minute wrinkles needed ironing out. But hair and makeup would arrive any moment, so I took a tissue and dabbed away the tears that had appeared in my moment of privacy, then blew my nose. I reached into my bag for a small glass jar of face cream. The cream was cool on my skin, and I hoped it would bring down any puffiness that would give my emotional state away.

I was now a college graduate. I had spent the summer finishing school early. But instead of walking across a stage at commencement, I was about to walk down the aisle. I don't know how Pa was convinced to let us postpone the wedding until I finished my degree, but I wasn't going to question it. Perhaps it was a concession. I was the first woman in my family to earn a degree. That accomplishment made today easier to bear.

I avoided the mirror now and gazed at the door. On the back hung the dress. It was stylish and easy, like those trendy prairie dresses, but with a touch of old southern class. It was going to be a dream wedding—someone's dream anyway—orchestrated carefully by Ma. And no expense had been spared.

Pa's money was older than this house. His wealth did not come from plantations like so many of his associates, but traced all the way back to London. Our family came from a long line of lawyers and politicians, descended from Lords and Ladies who lived off the backs of serfs. So not all that much better than a plantation, I suppose. Ma's ancestors, however, were plantation owners. And the engagement ring that I now wore on my finger, that had once been my sister's, was an heirloom from that era. I twisted it around my finger. It felt like I had stolen it; that at any moment my ma or grandmother would burst in and catch me with it—then lecture me about playing with things only meant for grownups.

I stood up from the vanity and moved to the bed. Atop the comforter all laid out were my shoes, stockings, and veil. I picked at the lace edge of the veil.

Someone knocked at the door.

"Come in," I called, surprised when my voice sounded hoarse. I cleared my throat.

A rich brown, curly afro peaked out from behind the door.

"Celiah?" I stood and met her halfway between us, embracing. "I thought you weren't coming?"

"Flew in this mornin'," she laughed. "I asked another TA to cover for me. I wanted to surprise you." Celiah had been at the University of Alabama with Thomas and I until she transferred to Howard University. She was starting a job as a teaching assistant this fall.

"I don't have a bridesmaid's dress for you."

"Baby, don't stress. I'm here for you, I don't need to stand up there all gussied up." I laughed with her, more relaxed now than I'd been all day. Celiah didn't like wearing dresses anyway. She was wearing a burnt orange bell bottom suit with a white mock neck blouse. A silk, floral scarf was tied around her head, at the base of her short afro. She had decided before transferring to Howard to cut off the hair that she'd been getting relaxed since she was ten and start growing her hair natural. She said it was a movement.

We made small talk. Celiah joked, and I laughed. *Nice weather for a weddin'. I'm glad you could make it. I bet Peavy's only thinkin' about tonight.*

"I can't believe you're gettin' married here," Celiah mused as she made her way to the bed and laid down on her back, propping herself up on her elbows.

"What do'ya mean?"

She watched me a moment, her eyebrows pulled together as if considering if it was worth it to answer. "Well I'm not real fond of plantations, Whitfield."

I gaped stupidly for a moment. "Oh Lord, I'm so sorry, Celiah. My ma planned everything, including the venue." I fidgeted with the ring again.

Celiah nodded, but I thought I caught her eyes roll a little bit. Her tongue worked over her teeth as she continued to look around the room. I joined her on the bed, still twisting the ring around my finger.

"What's with the nerves?" Celiah rolled over and slid down next to me. She could read me too well.

"Just prenuptial nerves, I guess." We must've looked a pair, her in her pressed suit and pumps, me in nothing but my satin slip. "Come on, distract me. What've you been up to at Howard? Are you still playin' tennis?" Celiah and I had played tennis together at Alabama. It was how we met. After discovering our shared passion for second generation romance poets, we became inseparable—Celiah was a bit of an anglophile. When Thomas and I started dating, he and Celiah bonded over her interest in social justice. But since she'd transferred to Howard the phone calls became less and less frequent, and after a time had ceased entirely.

"Jus' intramural. I played on the team for a semester, but it was a time vortex. I need to focus on my five-year plan."

"I see," I paused, searching for a direction in the conversation. "What else are you up to?" I was going in circles.

Celiah grinned. "I've made some friends. And some lovers," she winked. "Nothin' serious." Her eyes suddenly lit up like a light bulb. "Hey, did you hear about what happened with Swann v. Charlotte-Mecklenburg Board of Education?"

My cheeks flushed. Celiah had been keeping me apprised of the case up until she left for Howard. After she'd left, I'd forgotten all about it. "No," I answered weakly.

Disappointment briefly crossed Celiah's face but was gone in half a second. "Well, they made the ruling. Schools have to actively integrate now."

"That's wonderful."

"It's got me feeling like I can make a difference. I know my path now; I wanna change the law. I wanna do something real."

"That's beautiful, Celiah."

"Yeah, well, we can't leave all the work to white people. They'll never care as much."

My stomach dropped. "I'm real sorry, Celiah. I've had so much—"

Another knock at the door interrupted me, and two women entered carrying a big black bag and a plastic tote. Hair and makeup.

Celiah kissed my cheek. "Don't worry about it now, focus on Thomas." She wished me good luck and slipped out.

There was a large, copper-framed mirror in the hall. Ma led me to it before we descended the stairs. The woman looking back at me through the glass was unrecognizable. The dress, the hair, the face—they were made for someone else. My usually unruly and carelessly pulled back waves were smoothed into perfect ringlets and gathered atop my head like some kind of nest. The veil fountained out the back of the updo, and I felt strangely like a show pony. I was frosted in white, like a Christmas angel or a French pastry topped in cream. I did like the dress. It had a simple elegance. But with all the ensemble together, even it felt too much. I imagined my sister on my other arm. *Make way for the snow queen*, she would've said, poking fun at the fussiness of it all.

The tiered layers of chiffon in the drop shoulder trembled—I was shaking. Ma stood next to me, her hand placed protectively on my back. The smile she wore was not one of joy, but of sympathy. She didn't like this either, but she was ever obedient to her husband. And she had become even more submissive since losing a child.

I studied her reflection in the mirror and recalled when things had been easier.

"Kevin Dordin is an egg-suckin' ass." My sister's voice reverberated in my head. They were the words she'd spoken as she and I laid side by side on my bed. Kevin Dordin was on the boy's tennis team at Jefferson Academy, and I had had a huge crush on him.

I had been on the court, playing doubles with Rebecca Conners. The boys were practicing on the court next to us. He was supposed to be running a lap for being late, but he was watching Rebecca and me. My skin was hot under the scrutiny. I became hyper-aware of what my body looked like with every lunge and jump to get the ball.

"Hey, Rosie," he'd called out. My heart lurched. I looked at him lean against the pole between the nets on the boys' and girls' sides of the court. My palms started to get sweaty and I was worried my racket would slip out of them. I smiled shyly, then tried to refocus on the practice match.

"I was thinkin' about homecomin'," Kevin continued, loud enough for everyone on both courts to hear.

I stopped breathing. Could this really be happening?

"You wanna go?"

I stopped my match and he waited for a response, grinning at his teammates, who'd also paused to watch. Coach was on another court, unaware of the cease-play on ours.

"Sure," I squeaked out. I wanted to pinch myself.

Kevin laughed. "Well that's fine. I've been looking for a chauffeur. Your daddy's new Aston Martin will do just fine. Me and Rebecca will wanna leave at seven."

I thought I would throw up.

Kevin and his buddies roared with laughter. Rebecca looked as dumbfounded as I felt. She regarded me with pity. Then something hard thwacked me in the back of my head, making me stumble and trip over my feet. I crashed to the ground, humiliated and my head smarting.

"Whoops," Kevin shrugged. "I thought you were ready." I looked down at the tennis ball that had hit me. It had, *give me a ride* written on it in sharpie.

"Kiss off, Kevin!" Rebecca yelled at him. "You could make a preacher cuss with that backwards behavior. An' I'd never go out with a skuzz bucket like you."

Kevin and his buddies continued to laugh.

At home that evening, I stared up at the ceiling while my sister invented new insults for Kevin. I had called her when I got home from practice. She'd left Eugene with Lenny and come over for girls' talk.

"He's just flappin' his gums 'cause Pa won that big case 'gainst his daddy." She turned to me suddenly. "We should egg his car or somethin'."

"What's that now?"

"Or we could dump a load a' tampons in his gym bag! You said he was goin' to that party straight after practice, right?"

"Yea, but come on. Get your head on straight."

Ma cleared her throat from the doorway and we both jumped.

"How long you been listening?" My sister asked.

"Long enough."

We all paused, waiting to see who would make the next move.

"It's past curfew," Ma said.

My sister sighed heavily and rolled her eyes. "I know, Ma. Don' worry, I'm not gonna corrupt your precious *Rosebud*."

Ma smiled, like she'd remembered an inside joke. She peeked down the hallway. "I'll cover for ya'll. But you better hurry."

A grin that exactly mirrored Ma's crept onto my sister's lips, like they were in cahoots. I was dumbfounded.

After telling Pa I was going to bed early, Ma got a carton of eggs from the kitchen and sent us out the backdoor. "And ya'll better not get caught," she called out after us. "If Mr. Dordin finds out, nothin' in heaven nor hell will stop your father hearin' 'bout it."

We went to the party, eggs in my purse. It was the first and last high school party I ever went to, but my sister knew how to navigate. She led me through a crowd of kids I'd never said a word to before. It smelled like beer and grass. They didn't notice me, as usual. We found the bedroom where everyone had left their coats—Kevin's gym bag was sitting next to the bed.

"Ready, Rosebud?"

She opened the carton and dumped all twelve eggs into the bag, then zipped it closed.

"Jump on it," she instructed.

I stared at her wide-eyed.

"Like squashin' a junebug." She stepped onto one end of the bag, grabbing my arms and pulling me onto the other side. The music blared through the house, and even with the bedroom door closed, I could hear it clearly. No one was going to hear us.

She jumped. "Come on, Rose. Show all the Kevins of the world they won't get away with pissin' on all that's good in God's green earth." She pinched my chin affectionately.

She jumped again, and I stepped into the center of the bag. I felt an egg crunch and break beneath my foot. We held hands, laughing and stomping until the bag was all squish and no crunch.

Ma was still up waiting when my sister dropped me at home. She sat at the kitchen table sipping sweet tea.

"Your pa went to bed. Can I fix you some?"

"Sure, Ma."

She poured me a glass from the pitcher in the fridge. "How was it?"

I grinned, blushing. "He's gonna need a new gym bag."

"Well God knows the Dordins could buy a new boat when they get the other one wet," Ma chuckled. "Losin' that case 'gainst your father hurt Mr. Dordin's career like a feather 'cross the face. He's just sore to lose." She returned with the tea and sat back down.

"Why'd you cover for us?"

She smiled at me in a sympathetic kind of way, then reached over the corner of the table to touch my arm. "You're tighter strung than a fiddle 'bout to snap. And I feel rather certain that someday, you'll look back on tonight and remember that your sister stood up for you. And that you stood up for yourself. And I wanted you to remember I was on your side, too."

"Thanks, Ma." I smiled.

"Besides, it felt good helpin' ya'll get revenge on that low-belly."

Looking back now, on my wedding day, I wondered where she had gone—that mother who showed me she was on my side. I watched her reflection in the mirror. Her smile didn't reach her eyes.

After we couldn't keep the guests waiting any longer, Ma led me down the staircase. Pa waited for us at the bottom, and she handed me over before heading out the front doors to find her seat. The ceremony was set up in the front garden. Rows of heads and hats were framed by the piano room window, which sat just to the right of the front entrance. A string quartet stood at the ready. In response to a cue invisible to me, the chatter outside subdued and the quartet began to play Pachelbel.

Pa led me outside and between the rows of white chairs. I was distant from myself, as if in a dream. I searched among the guests. Celiah was sitting in the back—the seats were assigned, so she sat in the extra row meant for last minute guests who didn't RSVP. She was the only Black person there in a sea of white. Out past the side yard, fields extended out beyond the house. I imagined someone who resembled Celiah—a great-great grandmother perhaps, standing in those fields. I looked back to Celiah. She smiled and waved at me when our eyes met. My stomach felt hollow. I hadn't thought twice about getting married here. But now the whole thing started to sicken me.

Bracing myself against Pa's arm, I surveyed the front rows where mine and Thomas's families sat. Lenny was not in attendance, I had expected that. Still, a prick of pain in my heart reminded me that the gathering was incomplete. It was like having less of my sister there, somehow. Ma had taken her place in the front row with Eugene next to her and Carol in her arms. Carol wore a tiny, pastel pink dress that poofed out like a cupcake. Eugene was the only one in the audience not standing, despite several relatives nearby urging him to get up. He sat facing forward, away from me, and I didn't blame him. He was young, but he knew as well as I did what today meant. I cast my eyes downward, deciding I was safest looking at the bundle of peonies in my hand. One of the leaves was crumpled and dead.

The aisle felt much longer than it should have been, but finally we were nearing the front and I found the courage to look at Thomas. He stood smiling, his eyes fixed on my face. His smile was soft, comforting.

The day after my sister's funeral we had talked. He'd confirmed my fears that Pa had spoken with him about marriage, and that he had agreed to move up our life plan. At first, I was certain I'd never forgive the betrayal.

He'd found me sitting on the front porch steps of my parent's home. He sat next to me, close enough to feel his heat, but far enough that I felt alone.

"If I'd said no he would've arranged for someone else," he almost whispered. "There was no way I was gonna risk losin' you." Being pressured to marry was difficult enough, but having Pa arrange an engagement with someone other than Thomas would've been unbearable, even if I didn't go through with it. I knew how ridiculous it was, doing something like that in this day and age. But Pa was old-fashioned. And he had power. He had the power to destroy Thomas's career. And power over me he'd held since the day I was born. I wanted Thomas to be the strong one. To do what I couldn't. But it was an unfair expectation, even though I longed for it. I longed for someone to defy Pa as my sister had.

The sun had been hot, and a slight breeze carried the smell of ripened peaches from the small grove behind the house. The sun reflected off of Pa's Aston Martin parked in the round about driveway. He always left it there instead of in the garage, which annoyed Ma. She said it was prideful.

I sat in silence, scratching at the white paint on the wooden planks of the porch.

"Please, Rose," he continued after waiting a long minute for me to respond. "Say something, will you? This silence is gonna put me in an early grave."

"Tell me what he promised you."

Thomas paused.

"In exchange for making me a married woman, what did he promise you?" My voice cracked. I focused on his chest, unable to meet his eyes yet.

"Rose," he started. The pain in his voice alarmed me, and I lifted my head. His face was blurry behind the mist in my eyes, and his expression difficult to read through them. I hated myself for crying.

"He never lets a favor go unpaid. Tell me," I pushed, more gently this time.

Thomas looked down at his black, leather Fosters. There was a small scuff on the side that gave away his unfamiliarity with nice things.

"Judge Douglass offered me a clerkship." Judge Douglass was a justice on the Alabama supreme court.

When I remained silent, Thomas looked up. The tears had stopped. My lips pressed together. I knew there would have been recompense. It was how Pa operated, how he worked people. But hearing Thomas confirm it aloud hit harder than I anticipated.

"I got a call the day before the funeral. I accepted immediately." He glanced at me to gauge my reaction. I tried to keep my face blank. "I didn't even think to question it. I should've. Gettin' an offer I never applied for—I should've seen it. I didn't want to tell you until after the funeral. It wasn't the right time. When your pa took me aside after the wake he told me, *I've made sure you can take care of her proper.* That's when I put it together that he'd set it all up."

I breathed in sharply and closed my eyes. He hadn't even known it was a bribe. I opened my eyes into his and found sincerity and shame. His pride had been wounded. He'd always wanted to make something of himself without my pa's help. He was the first in his family to go to college, let alone law school. Pa had tried to interfere before, and Thomas had already turned down other offers—or bribes—throughout our courtship. But he'd have been a fool to pass a chance like this up even if he'd known Pa was behind it. He must have been crushed, thinking he'd earned such a prestigious clerkship on his own, only to discover he was a pawn on Pa's chess board. Pa had been tricky with this one. Thomas couldn't retract his acceptance now; snubbing Judge Douglass would kill his career before it had even begun.

When I'd seen all of this in his eyes my walls melted away. I'd whispered that it was ok and held him as he wept.

Now he stood waiting for me at the altar, and in each other's eyes we communicated the things we'd struggled to say out loud to each other the past few months.

I'm sorry, his said.

I know, it's ok, said mine.

We arrived under the white-painted trellis adorned with white roses Ma had picked out herself. Pa gave Thomas my hand, then leaned down to kiss my cheek, brushing away a stray baby hair.

Then we were standing side by side, Thomas and me. My boyfriend—fiancé. Almost husband. Warmth emanated from him, hotter than the sun. The minister stood before us, but I didn't hear the words he spoke. I only felt the fire.

5

Grace

Lillian, 1992

I 'd stayed overnight and well into the next morning at Amanda's, catching up on sleep. After a breakfast of eggs, sausage, and biscuits, I called the landlord for the St. Louis apartment, arranging a deposit and immediate move-in. It was all rather kismet.

Amanda directed me to a tiny gas station, sending me off with a little pink stone.

"For unconditional love," she said.

I didn't really know what she meant by that. But I took the rock anyway. It was polished and felt nice in my palm.

The little apartment was grey, overcast like the sky outside its single window. I took everything in: a faded and stained rug, scuffed linoleum, and peeling wallpaper. The kitchenette was only a few square feet, with a gas stove and rusted sink. A card table sat nearby, accompanied by single folding chair. The metal looked cold in the grey window light. On the other side of the apartment was a metal twin bed with a bare mattress that dipped in the middle. A shower curtain hung around a corner from one wall to the other, like those curtains at the doctor's office. I assumed that was the bathroom, but I was a little scared to pull it back to see. A metal cord hanging in the center of the room controlled a single naked light bulb—the apartment's only source of light aside from the grey haze through the single window. I tugged the cord, and a yellow glow illuminated tiny dust particles in the air. The place needed work, that was clear, but I wasn't afraid of a little work.

The studio apartment was smaller than Don's master bedroom. It wasn't even much bigger than his walk-in closet. But I didn't care. In this room there was hope. Hope for freedom—for a better life. And it was all mine.

I was born in Alabama, my family's home for generations, but I did most of my growing up in Tallahassee. My parents moved there to start fresh. I didn't remember home being anywhere besides Florida. I didn't even catch the Alabama accent. But when I was thirteen, my grandma got sick and we moved back to be closer to her before she passed away. I went from a typical, suburban, middle-class neighborhood to living in my grandparent's old mansion among the elite of Alabama. I rejected that elitism on account of it stifling my freedom. What I hadn't realized at the time was that the same privilege I'd been born into was exactly what allowed me room for rebellion without suffering dire consequences. I rejected society, but my parents wouldn't ever have cut me off, so I always had a safety net to ease the consequences of some of my more idiotic choices.

But now, I had cut myself off. I didn't tell my parents I left Alabama, and I had no plans to contact them. The church frowned upon divorce. Plus, I couldn't risk Don finding me. The less anyone knew, the better. I called my brother to tell him I was alive and ok, but I didn't leave a return number or address. In St. Louis, I had no one. For the first time my rebellion hadn't left me unscathed, and I was loving every minute of it.

I took out a small, hand-quilted baby blanket and wrapped Niles up in it, laying him gently in the middle of the sagging mattress. I hoped to get a crib soon, but he wasn't rolling yet, so this would do for now. I took a brass pig out of my suitcase and put it in the middle of the card table—a place of honor. Don hated that thing. It had been a gift from his mother, so every time she came to visit he'd bring it out of hiding and set it on the mantle. I loved that pig, and not only because it exasperated Don. It was cool. Plus, Don's mother had always been kind to me. So I stole it when we left—from the floor of the coat closet under a pile of shoes. He wouldn't notice it was missing until the next time his mother visited. Then he'd look everywhere for the stupid pig, and look in vain. I grinned at it. Even the smallest revenge was sweet.

I moved a few grocery bags from the floor to the table. Two were filled entirely with cleaning products. I'd pawned off my wedding ring to cover the deposit, first month's rent, and to buy some necessities. I used the fifty from the stranger on the road to buy an ad in the local paper. I pulled a phone from one of the bags and plugged it into the phone jack. It was an old phone—bought at the same pawn shop where I'd sold the ring. There was a card taped to the wall with the number for the apartment's line. I called up the paper and relayed it to them. With all the required information, the ad would run tomorrow and again next week —all I had to do was wait for the phone to ring.

My business took off. Two months after leaving Alabama, I was cleaning houses six days a week. Many of my clients were the kind of people who lived in my grandparents' neighborhood—trophy wives with old money, unwilling to stoop to that level of menial work. Some of the others were new money workaholics and their impressive careers left little time to waste on housekeeping. There were some regular folks, too. But they didn't have as much work for me. I'd barely kept up with the phone calls, surprised at how many people wanted to pay someone else to clean their houses for them. Once I had a couple clients, more kept pouring in by recommendations from their friends. My rates were lower than the average, and there's no penny-pinchers like millionaires.

Plus, I knew how to clean nice, old houses, and my clients quickly realized that. I never thought I'd be grateful my parents never hired housekeepers. They'd insisted my brother and I learn hard work in the home. That was literally paying the bills now. I had some cash leftover from selling my ring, but after having to pick up and leave once, I stored it away for a rainy day.

It was usually the wives who hired me. They would give me a house tour and give meticulous instructions regarding things like polishing silver or laundering drapes. Many of them never tipped. And every one of them bristled at the sight of Niles, the snap judgements flashing across their eyes when they inspected my ringless left hand. They must've thought they were subtle about it. Or they didn't care to be. I never gave them the satisfaction of an explanation. I just worked with a baby strapped to my back, content that they didn't turn me away for bringing a child with me.

One time I overheard one of my clients, the newly married Mrs. Glowski, talking about me on the phone. "—I dunno, not even a year I don't think. No, I haven't seen if he can walk, she keeps him on her back." She chuckled, "Because her rates are so cheap. Just don't tell Mom I hired a maid who brings her bastard to work with her."

I strode into the kitchen, and Mrs. Glowski hurriedly changed the subject. At the end of my shift, she came to give me my check while I was packing up.

"By the way, next week my rates are going up fifteen percent," I said as I pocketed the check. "Gotta feed the bastard. We don't want Mr. Glowski robbing another cradle." I smiled and winked at her. She turned redder than that bitch Susy Fischer when her leotard ripped during dress rehearsal for Swan Lake—she'd cut a small hole in mine but didn't know I'd seen her do it, so I'd switched them.

The next week, Mrs. Glowski paid the extra 15% and pretended as if nothing had ever happened.

There was one man who hired me. Mr. Davis. He told me the old housekeeper had quit and that his wife was too busy with medical school to deal with these matters. I ran into the wife only a couple times. She was tall and athletic, and despite myself I was intimidated by her. She was always rushing from one thing to another, never staying in one place for long. She had a lot of girlfriends that she went to jazzercise and other extracurriculars with. I don't even know if she ever saw Mr. Davis hardly at all. But Mr. Davis was always home, it seemed. He was one of the old money ones and only stepped into an office a couple times a week to make sure things were running smoothly. I didn't really know what he did, I only knew he owned whatever it was.

He would watch me when I cleaned his office, sitting at his leather chair smoking a cigarette and drinking dark liquors. He had blonde hair that was so thin he might as well have been bald, and was tall and stocky like a football player. Maybe he was one of those big-shots who played in high school.

Today I'd let Niles sleep on a blanket in the living room while I cleaned the office. I was wiping down a window, scrubbing at a smudge that didn't want to come clean. It was almost dusk, and I felt fatigue in my eyes. I longed to close them and drift away with the sun.

Then arms wrapped around my waist. I shrieked and spun around, pushing Mr. Davis off me.

"What are you doing?"

He grinned. "No need for that, Lillian. Now, have you ever wondered what it's like being with an older, more experienced man?" He reached out and touched my arm with the backs of his fingers.

"Don't touch me."

Mr. Davis's eyes narrowed as he took a step back.

"You see I had an arrangement with our last housekeeper."

He went to his desk, opening a drawer and pulling out a thick envelope. He held it out.

I stood with my back against the window, unmoving.

"I'm not going to touch you. Come take it."

I stepped forward just far enough to take the envelope. It was thick and didn't close all the way. It was filled with cash. Lots of cash.

"I compensate for *all* services."

I wasn't proud. But it paid better than half my jobs combined.

Five months since I had made my journey across state lines, I'd taken on as many clients as my days would allow. With steady cash coming in, padded significantly by my secret side gig, I got some real furniture for the apartment. I shopped exclusively at thrift stores but was still choosy. Little by little, it started to look more like a home. More like me.

I got a brand-new crib to replace a used one. And a highchair, a real table with real chairs made of wood, and two folding screens to replace the shower curtain for the bathroom corner. One of my clients had tipped me extra to run a box of donations to their church, and I swiped a rug and a big decorative vase that were in there.

But the most important items were the lamps. I had six of them now: four floor and two table-top ones. The light made such a difference. The apartment became cozy, a refuge from the condescending women I interacted with all day, every day.

I ate a lot of TV dinners and Campbell's soup. The kitchenette wasn't much, and there wasn't really any way to improve upon that. So cooking was limited. But I would dump the dinners out of their paper containers onto a real plate and eat them with a glass of boxed wine. I kept the harder liquor for special occasions.

Niles was growing rapidly and I struggled to keep clothes that fit him. Often what I found at the thrift shops were too big or too small. I would get out my sewing machine and make little onesies out of old t-shirts, or tack in clothes that were too big—but never cut the extra fabric so I'd be able to let them out again when he grew. I took the clothes he'd grown out of and sewed them together into a thin quilt. I imagined that someday I'd look through a chest of keepsakes, like the one my mom had, and pull out the baby clothes quilt, smell it, and reminisce about this time. That image kept me optimistic, and I held to it like it was a lap bar on a roller coaster.

But despite all this, the days grew mundane and exhausting. I hated most of the people I worked for. Mr. Davis most of all. Most times I refused his advances, but every so often I was stretched a little too thin, and the extra cash was too tempting.

I hadn't met anyone here I had a shred of respect for—and honestly I didn't even respect myself.

Then Grace Bird hired me.

Her house was huge. I suspected old money, for one because she was a college professor with a college professor's salary, and two because the house looked like it hadn't been redecorated since the 1920s. Grace was somewhere in her upper thirties, I think, and her modern and clean personal style was at odds with the archaic home.

She lived alone in the big house, except for a sour faced cat who ignored my existence—and hers. Sometimes I wouldn't see it for weeks. Then it would randomly wait for me by the front door when I arrived, scaring the shit out of me.

I assumed Grace must've been pretty lonely. On my first day she'd thrown her arms around me like we were old friends. It'd shocked me so much that Niles sensed my alarm and started crying.

"Oh no, I'm so sorry. I didn't mean to frighten him." She stepped back, her forehead crinkled in worry.

"No, that's ok."

"I'm just so glad you're here. The Fredricksons had nothing but glowing recommendations and I worried you'd be all booked up."

I'd been surprised the Fredricksons had recommended me so highly. They'd barely spoken three words to me. Ever. They were a stiff old couple that lived down the street from Grace. Mrs. Fredrickson was hard of hearing, so sometimes when I spoke to her, I'd say something completely ridiculous like, *now I'm going to drink all your booze and set the rose bushes on fire.* She'd smile and nod. I never did anything untoward. I had a soft spot for old folks.

"I was able to squeeze you in." I replied.

"Well thank the Lord. I moved in here from a little apartment. I don't even know where to begin. It's too much house for me."

"It's a beautiful house," I probed, curious why she'd moved in if she felt that way.

"Thank you. It was my grandparents'."

Old money. As I suspected.

"Part of my inheritance," she smiled wryly.

"That was very generous of them."

"They had ulterior motives." Her eyes glittered mischievously. "I'm the only grandkid left who's unmarried with no kids. They were trying to nudge me in the right direction." She laughed, and I got the sense that she found the whole situation rather humorous. "But I'm moving in, anyway. Out of spite. I'll stay here unmarried without having any man's babies until the day I die."

I laughed with her. She must've been one of those anti-marriage feminists. Despite how much I loved Niles who was indeed created with a man, I related to her sentiment. She went on to tell me about her job—she taught psychology at Washington University, and in the evenings, she offered counseling in her private practice. Her specialty was *mood and personality disorders in adults and adolescents*. I didn't know what that entailed, but it sounded like serious stuff. She was the smartest person I'd ever met. Smarter than Mrs. Davis or Don. Even smarter than my eleventh-grade biology teacher who never passed up an opportunity to brag about his PhD.

Niles played in the living room when I worked at Grace's. She was ok with it, and for that I was grateful. It was so much easier than cleaning with him strapped to my back. As he was getting bigger, he not only got heavier but was becoming less and less thrilled with being confined most of the day. I had started to bring toys with me. I'd found these little toys that had clips on them for attaching to a stroller or car seat. I sewed a ribbon across the inside edge of the hoods on my sweatshirts, tacking them in one-inch increments across. I would attach the clips to the ribbon and wear the sweatshirts to work, hood down, with all the little links, squeaky soft toys, and rattles tucked inside it where Niles could reach them. Sometimes I even threw some loose cheerios in there, tossing them over my shoulder as I worked. I'd started taking longer nursing breaks, letting him out to roll on the bathroom floors—newly cleaned by me—for a while after every feeding. As long as I got all my work done, my clients didn't pay much attention when I took breaks. Some of them even invited me to use a guest room when I needed to nurse. Grace was one of those, of course.

Grace's home wasn't the largest or the most grand of my clients, not by a long shot. It had four bedrooms and three bathrooms. It was two levels, plus a root cellar that I never went in—Grace only planned on using it as a tornado shelter. But it was still an impressive house. A chestnut staircase adorned the front hall, polished weekly by my own two hands. Wood floors sparkled with my elbow grease. It was a beautiful home, with good bones. I finally understood what adults meant when they said that—real adults, not like me.

Grace worked a lot, but she did manage to do daily cleaning herself—sweeping, dishes, laundry; she only had me come in once a week for a deep clean. Some of my other more modest clients were like that, too. Those were my favorite jobs because I like the deep cleaning more than the little chores.

Grace was easily my favorite client, and I wasn't bashful about it. For Christmas I made her a quilt. It was small but carefully hand stitched by the light of a desk lamp in the early hours of December mornings. Grace was also the only one to get us any gifts, besides cash bonuses—which I certainly didn't mind, but the sentimentality of Grace's gifts were something special. She gave Niles some sets of store-bought trendy clothing—better fitting than anything he'd worn since he grew out of the clothes we left Alabama with. And she gave me a small pendant necklace, which I could tell was real gold. The pendant was a thin circular plate with a tiger lily etched into it.

"A lily. Like for Lillian."

It was so intimate. I'd tried to hide the misting in my eyes. She had no idea what it meant to me.

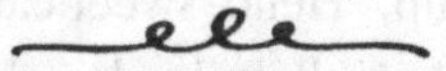

The day after New Year's Day Grace wasn't home when I arrived for my shift. Thursday was her grocery day since she only had classes in the mornings. I assumed she was running late at the store and used the hidden key to let myself in. Christmas decorations were still up, and a single empty bottle of champagne in the kitchen was the only evidence that New Year's Eve had come and gone.

About twenty minutes into my shift the garage door hummed and screeched open, signaling her arrival. I went to the side door to help carry things in, but before I could open it she burst in, panting. She had sweat across her forehead and was bending down to catch her breath. Her pale, yellow hair fell over her collarbone, and I resisted the urge to reach out and brush it away.

Instead, I placed a hand on her shoulder. "Whoa, are you ok?"

She straightened and embraced me. "Never better, Lillian."

I was stiff in her arms, surprised by the sudden affection. We'd become familiar and casual with each other, but Grace hadn't hugged me like this since the first day we met. I think she could sense I wasn't the most touchy-feely person. But this, I didn't mind.

She released me, her eyes apologetic. She stepped back and caught her breath a moment. When she'd collected herself, she waved a hand dismissively. "Don't worry, I'm just not as young as I used to be." She walked down the hall.

"Ok, weirdo. I'll go get the groceries."

"I didn't get any," she called back.

I followed her. "Oh. Do you want me to go pick some up?" I wasn't in the habit of offering extra services, but Grace was basically a friend.

"Don't worry about it. We're ordering in for dinner."

"We?"

"You and me." She stopped and looked back at me. "And Niles. What are you in the mood for? Chinese? Pizza?"

I stared at her, blinking in confusion. She laughed at my stunned silence. That beautiful sparkling laugh that always brought a smile to my own face. She was always charismatic, but right now it was like staring into the sun. No—the moon. Bright but soft.

"You don't have work?" I asked.

She shook her head. "I rescheduled my clients. We're celebrating." She winked, then continued down the hallway to find Niles. He was playing in the living room. She picked him up, "Hello, sweet cakes."

"Grace. What's going on?" A small smile played at my lips—I couldn't help it. She was eccentric.

"Let's order, then I'll tell you."

I looked at my watch. I was supposed to meet Mr. Davis in an hour. His wife was on a hospital rotation and working a night shift. He'd hired a babysitter for Niles and everything, so we could go out. We'd never done that before. He'd been getting his way, lately, more than I liked. The holidays were hard, and he'd offered extra cash to do a date. He was treating me more and more like a mistress instead of a casual affair. For Christmas, he'd given me a diamond necklace and some lingerie. I was planning to sell the necklace if I could find a fake one that looked identical. I knew he'd get mad if I didn't wear it.

Grace snuggled Niles as she spoke into her cordless phone, holding it against her cheek with her shoulder. She caught my eyes, smiling at me as she recited a pizza order. I wasn't mad that she assumed I didn't have plans. I kind of liked it.

She shifted Niles onto one hip to free a hand and covered the receiver. "What's your favorite kind of pizza, Lillian?"

In a split second, I made a decision—one more significant than pizza toppings.

By seven o'clock we were sitting at the breakfast bar in the kitchen with two large pies—one with my favorite toppings, and one with Grace's. Niles was on my lap, chewing on a crust I'd torn off for him.

"Are you finally gonna tell me what we're celebrating?"

Grace grinned and held up a finger while she finished chewing a particularly large bite of veggie pizza. After what felt like an eternity, she swallowed. "I got a book deal."

My mouth dropped open stupidly.

"I know." She reached over and touched my arm. My skin tingled.

"You wrote a book?"

"*Going* to write a book," she corrected.

"Congratulations." My admiration was evident.

She beamed.

"What's it about?"

"Oh, you know, boring psychology stuff," she took another large bite of pizza.

I reached over and took a slice of her pizza choice, four-cheese with chicken and bacon.

"Give me the sneezing trees version?"

There was this *Calvin and Hobbs* comic Grace showed me once that she liked to use with her graduate students. In the comic, Calvin asks his dad where wind comes from, and his dad says the trees are sneezing. Kids are taught the *sneezing trees* version of a lot of things. It's a way to describe something complex so younger minds can understand. It's not necessarily accurate, but it'll do to get the concept across. But in college and graduate school, you finally learn the complicated truth. Or something close to it, anyway. It had become a sort of inside joke between us whenever she tried explaining details of her lectures. It was a kind of code for when I needed her to speak plain English.

She laughed, snorting a little, and the sound made me almost choke on a chunk of chicken.

"Ok, sneezing trees version," she put her slice back down and took a swig of beer. "It's going to be about something called mixed episodes that can occur in bipolar disorder."

"Bipolar disorder?"

"Manic depression."

"Oh—is that the one where you're like super happy one minute and really sad the next?"

"Not really," Grace went into professor mode. She was a soft-spoken person, but when she talked about her work, she donned this awe-inspiring confidence. I imagined her teaching one of her classes, eyes full of life and wisdom, her smile slowly growing wider as she got excited about the topic. I pictured male graduate students staring at her body as she wrote on the chalkboard. I shook off the thought.

"Bipolar is episodic. It's not one minute and the next. Mania usually has to last at least a week to be considered a true manic episode. Depression can last even longer—months. And mania isn't equivalent to happy, but we can get into that another day."

I nodded.

"Anyway, a mixed episode is when mania and depression happen at the same time."

"That sounds rough," I wanted her to believe I was following, though I was honestly still confused by what exactly mania was.

We chatted and ate cooling pizza until Niles was fighting to stay awake. When we finished cleaning up, she leaned back against a counter, studying me with her big eyes.

"Do you like it?" she asked. She was looking at the necklace around my neck.

"I really do." I instinctively reached up to finger the lily pendant.

She smiled and there was something new in her eyes. It was unexpected, and unclear.

Grace walked us out to the car, carrying the leftover pizza that she'd insisted I take home. She put the boxes in the passenger seat while I buckled Niles in the back. Then she came around and stood next to the driver's door.

"Thanks for celebrating with me, Lillian."

We stood facing each other. I shifted my weight from one leg to the other, suddenly overly aware of my hands and where to put them. Before I could figure them out, Grace reached out and pulled me into her. Her arms wrapped around me, my breasts pressed against her narrow torso, and I was suddenly self-conscious of their size and shape. Breastfeeding had altered them dramatically. We stood there for moment, our cheeks brushing, chins on each other's shoulders. Grace was shorter than me, and slender. Though she had initiated the hug, I was enveloping her. Her blonde hair brushed against my face, and I smelled lavender as the wind tousled the strands. It must have been quite the picture: her delicate, light features wrapped around my Amazonian frame with my wild, dark curls carelessly thrown up in a bun.

The wind was bitter, and a shiver in my arms prompted Grace to release me.

"Do you have any plans Saturday night?" she asked, while opening the car door for me.

"I think I'm about to," I flirted. My cheeks burned hot.

Grace's eyes smiled like starlight. "How about a girls' night out."

I turned my head slightly to look at Niles, now asleep in the back seat.

"I have a niece who babysits. I'm told she's good." Grace winked, playfully. "She could watch him here."

I nodded. "Yeah, ok."

"Ok. It's a date."

As I drove away, she grew distant in the rearview mirror, standing in her driveway. She grew smaller and smaller, but even when she was out of sight, something told me she was still there.

At home the light on my answering machine blinked on and off like those lights that show airplanes where buildings are at night. I knew who it'd be from. I picked up Amanda's pink rock from beside the phone and fidgeted with it, squeezing it against my palm with my fingers, then I pressed play.

Lillian, where are you? I've never been so disrespected. Do you know how humiliating it was for the sitter to sit in my living room waiting for you to never show up? I have half a mind to—

I deleted the message.

My daybook was sitting open next to the phone. I turned back a few pages to a client list with their schedules written neatly under their addresses and contact information. I scanned down to the Davises.

M-Th 10-11am; F 5-7pm.

I crossed them out.

6

Two Years Later

Eleanor, 2019

eavy heart. People say that when they're sad. I wished my heart was heavy, instead of empty.

The waiting room was warm—sticky warm like a lemonade that sat on the porch all afternoon. A woman sat across from me reading a book. The title was partially obscured, but I caught a "q" somewhere in there.

Queen. Question. Quiet.

Silent. Except for the low hum of the A/C unit, working too hard in the 90-degree evening.

The room glowed with pink-yellow light painted by the late afternoon sun. The light seemed tired from a lazy day. Like me. Tired and still, the very act of wakefulness too exhausting for productivity.

The woman put down her book and checked her watch, sighing before folding her arms in front of her and turning her head to look out the window. Her foot tapped against the ground, making a soft *putt putt* sound as the thin sole of her loafer hit the carpet. The hem of her dress pants swished around her ankle with the movement. I caught a glimpse of the book now sitting next to her. It was upside down, and the back cover had a picture of a woman with big hair. The author I presumed.

A boy, maybe twelve years old, walked in from the back hallway. The woman with the book stood to greet him.

"Ready?" she asked.

He nodded and they exited together.

Now I was alone. Except for the voice that tells me I'm a failure. A failure for having to be here. Whispers of doubt invaded my mind, and I closed my eyes trying to quiet them. Quiet. Qualm. Quit.

"Eleanor?" The voice jolted my senses like an alarm abruptly pulling me out of REM sleep.

I stood, almost groggy.

"I'm Aliza." She reached out and shook my hand.

She was tall and lean with long, wavy hair—a metallic white silver-gray that I imagined was once black. Her eyes were a pale brown, slightly lighter than her skin. She had crow's feet around her eyes and smile lines framed her lips. Her smile exuded confidence and joy. In my hasty first impression, I resented her—for her beauty, her thin waist, her cheerful demeanor. And probably on a deeper level for the exposing details she would soon know about me.

I followed her down the back hallway to a small office. There was a desk with a closed laptop computer and a leather-bound planner. Pictures of what I assumed were her family lined the back of the desk. In one photo, she and three young girls of various ages were all wearing colorful saris and adorned with ornate golden jewelry. Henna bloomed in vines and floral patterns on their arms and faces.

A purple suede sofa sat across from the desk with a floor lamp next to it—the only light in the room that was on. It was soft and unobtrusive, creating a calm and warm atmosphere. A swamp cooler hung in the window; gratefully it was cooler in here than in the waiting room. It smelled like a warm vanilla air freshener, good enough to eat. My stomach rumbled, reminding me I'd skipped both breakfast and lunch.

"Take a seat," she invited, and sat herself in the swivel chair in front of the desk. She took a legal pad and set it across her knee.

I sat on one end of the couch, acutely aware of how much space my hips took up on the cushion.

"So, Eleanor, what brings you here today?"

I hated vague questions like that.

"Um..." I rubbed my thumbs together. "I just had a baby and I'm not doing so well."

She started jotting notes on the pad. "Tell me what not doing well looks like for you."

I described the usual symptoms of depression and anxiety that had come and gone since I was a kid. Trouble getting to sleep, sleeping in too long, isolating myself, panic attacks...

"When were you diagnosed with anxiety?"

"As a teenager. I think fifteen."

She wrote in her notebook.

"Have you talked to your doctor about post-partum depression or anxiety?"

"I have, I'm on medication."

She nodded and continued to jot notes.

"A medication safe for breastfeeding," I added. "I want to breastfeed for at least a year."

"Sertraline?"

"Yeah."

She put the notebook in her lap and smiled at me, her body language became conversational. "What's your baby's name?"

Tension in my shoulders I didn't know was there released.

"Marc."

"A lovely name."

"Thank you."

There was a pause while she watched my eyes.

"What's going well?" she finally asked.

The question took me aback. I'd rehearsed and prepared for talking about all the things wrong with me. Not for chatting about happy things.

I considered for a few moments. "I'm alive," I laughed, dryly. She smiled, but the smile didn't reach her eyes. My dark humor didn't always land with everyone. Or maybe she simply wasn't indulging my attempt at deflection.

I moved on. "Marc, I guess. He's healthy. He's happy. My husband Danny—he's been great. Really supportive. He even takes care of all the nighttime diaper changes so my sleep isn't interrupted so much. I pump and he feeds Marc bottles when I need a break." I listed in my head all the reasons Danny and I weren't ok right now. He at least would've laughed at my joke. That was something.

"What are your anxieties about? Are you belaboring the past, or fantasizing the future?" She was probing now, and I didn't like this question—a question I'd been asked in so many words by various therapists over the years.

In the short pause she read my face. "What bothers you about that question?"

I stared at my hands again, already feeling the waves of emotion rise up, feeling myself forcing them back down.

"It's hard. Hard to talk about I mean."

She nodded but said nothing. Her eyes were kind and patient, waiting. It was an opportunity to tell her about what happened two years ago, but I didn't want to. I focused instead on the present.

I stumbled on my words. "I...well I guess...I've been having these thoughts. And I've been doing strange things. I dunno. Sometimes it scares Danny. And me too, I guess."

"What kinds of thoughts?"

"Bad ones."

She nodded, not pushing it further.

"What are some examples of strange things you've done?"

I steadied my voice. "Pulling my hair out. That one scares Danny the most. And lining up my shoes in the bathroom for no reason at all. But I can't stop myself. Checking on the baby every four minutes while he sleeps. It has to be exactly four minutes. And I never trust if I've locked the front door or changed his diaper before bed. And...and some other stuff."

All the crazy poured out of me. I hung my head and pressed my hands against my eyes, trying to stop the embarrassing waterworks. But it was good to finally tell someone. This was a big reason I'd made an appointment in the first place.

"I promise you this isn't anything new to me," Aliza consoled. "Are you ready to talk about the thoughts?"

"I think about him dying." I blurted before I could over-think. "Getting hurt. About...me hurting him. Not on purpose, but from doing something stupid like falling asleep while he's in the bathtub. Or dropping him in the driveway. The thoughts come and I can't make them stop. Not until I check on him. Or wash my hands. I'm afraid I'll make him sick. Or..." I trailed off.

She smiled at me sympathetically, clearly unphased by what I'd admitted—what I'd never told another soul before, not even Danny. It was my deepest fear and shame.

"That's hard," she spoke softly.

"I feel...crazy."

"You're not crazy, Eleanor. Trust me, I'm an expert." She winked.

I smiled half-heartedly—my turn to underreact to humor.

"Do you enjoy spending time with Marc?"

I chewed my lower lip. "I'm having a hard time connecting with him. Or feeling like I'm really his mom."

I stared at a filing cabinet next to her desk. On top sat a wooden sculpture of two abstract figures intertwined. One figure was a dark wood, the other lighter, like oak. The figures were plated on the edges in gold.

She followed my gaze. "Ah, do you like it? A local artist made it for me. It symbolizes the duality of mental illness." Her eyes returned to my face, steady, but kind. I couldn't help but look back into them. "There is great pain, but with great pain comes a greater potential for joy. They are inseparable."

I believed her. It felt impossible not to. She spoke with an authority that was undeniable, but not intimidating. I felt she knew me. That she was certain this joy was somehow already inside me.

"So, you're saying there's meaning to all this?"

"Not always inherently. Bad things can happen to us for no reasonable purpose at all. But you have the power to create your own meaning. It comes at a cost: hard work. You have to reframe the narrative—rewrite the trauma. Like gold, meaning can be a heavy burden, but it's also precious."

I jumped a little when she said *trauma*. Could she know, just from my answers to those questions?

She swiveled in her chair and opened a drawer in the filing cabinet, flitting through paperwork.

"Here," she said, pulling out a packet. "I want you to take this screening for obsessive compulsive disorder. I think you might have post-partum OCD. Just answer the questions as honestly as you can. This won't diagnose you, but it'll help me to know if this is a possibility as we continue sessions."

"Post-partum OCD?" I asked, incredulously. "That's a thing?"

"PPOCD is usually temporary," she reassured. "Your hormones have changed a lot, but they'll level out eventually. That will help. In the meantime, we can work on some coping strategies and help you find ways to connect with Marc."

It was starting to rain when I left the clinic. The sun still shone through the clouds, drifting down towards the earth. I loved a summer rain. I climbed into my Toyota RAV and texted Danny that I'd be home soon.

Post-partum OCD. This was uncharted territory. My mental health history included general anxiety and major depressive disorder—the common colds of mental illness. Obsessive compulsive disorder...*that's like having cancer or something, right?* Admittedly I didn't know much about it.

I was simply afraid of the unknown. I told myself this, falling back on an exercise I had done as a teenager in therapy. The assignment was to make a list of three things I was afraid of then research and learn everything I could about those three things.

Confidence is knowledge. Fear is the unknown, my childhood therapist had said.

I just need to do a little research.

I considered what Danny would think. Or my mom. My mental health status was no secret as far as my mom was concerned. After all, she was the one who took me to therapy as a teen. She was the one who first noticed when I was in pain, who helped me understand it wasn't my fault. She was the one who understood because she'd struggled too. Looking back, I wasn't sure how she knew what to do. There was still such a stigma about going to therapy, even then.

But I didn't know how to tell her about *this*. It felt so much more serious. Would she feel like she failed me?

I pulled into our driveway. Danny and Marc were in the front window of the condo unit we rented. Danny was holding Marc and talking to him, pointing at the car. I smiled and waved. Danny held Marc's hand up and waved it for him. Marc's eyes moved around, not focusing on anything. He was only two months old, and probably couldn't even see out the window. I rolled my eyes dramatically so Danny could see, but a familiar wave of relief washed over me, the relief I always felt when I saw them after a separation, alive and healthy.

When I walked through the front door Danny didn't waste any time.

"Did you tell her?"

"Tell her what?" I played dumb while I hung up my raincoat in the front closet, annoyed he didn't even let me breathe before interrogating me.

"Don't do that." He followed me from the front door, to the coat closet, to the kitchen, Marc balanced on his narrow hip.

I sighed. "It's not relevant. She thinks I have post-partum stuff. It's probably all hormones. She didn't ask about traumas or anything." I didn't mention the OCD. He was already so on edge. I'd wait until there were more concrete answers.

"And why would she ask about trauma if you didn't tell her there was trauma." It wasn't a question.

"It's not connected, Danny." A lump started to form in my throat.

"Like hell it isn't."

"I don't want to talk about it."

"I think you need to."

"Leave me alone." I raised my voice.

Danny paused, then sat down at the table. I heard him breathing, bringing down the level of his intensity. With each inhale my body tensed tighter. He was actively trying not to trigger me. And ironically, that was triggering me.

"Eleanor," he spoke softly. "We lost a baby. That will never not be relevant. You *have* to bring it up next time."

When he spoke the words aloud, it hurled me back to that hospital room. Blood, sweat, and a lifeless bundle being taken from my arms. Desperation. I need to get out, out of that hospital room. *Put her back. Put her back inside me. She was safe there. She was alive in there.*

"I don't want to talk about it." I repeated. I opened the freezer, still in my rainboots, hoping the cold air would ground me.

"I need to talk about it," Danny said.

I stood in front of the fridge silently. The words fell on my ears, but I couldn't process them.

"Eleanor, you can't just not say anything."

Couldn't he see this wasn't a good time?

"Please just say something." He stood and walked to me, reaching over to put his hand on my shoulder. I pushed it away.

"Leave me alone." I left the freezer open and tore back through the kitchen to the front entrance, grabbing my keys from their hook by the door. I ran to the car, sprinkles of raindrops pricking my arms, and climbed in. I backed out of the driveway into the street.

Danny ran out after me, Marc still in his arms. He was yelling. I kept driving. I wondered what the neighbors would be thinking, if they were watching him waving and running barefoot in the street holding an infant. I saw him stop in the rearview and hold his phone to his ear. I'd left mine in the pocket of my raincoat, hanging in the coat closet.

I drove aimlessly, hyperventilating until I sobbed. The panic attack tore through my stomach, my chest, my limbs. My arms ached from gripping the steering wheel too tightly. I needed to go somewhere I could be alone. I found myself on the highway, westbound.

Motherhood was supposed to be joyful. You're not supposed to go crazy. You're not supposed to feel sad every time you look at your baby. You're not supposed to be afraid of holding him. *You're not supposed to bury a child.*

I drove until the Rockies emerged ahead of me, splendidly purple against the darkening sky—back lit by the sliver of sunlight sinking behind them. The shadows of trees painted the ground, and I was convinced they were reaching out to grab me, to stop me. I sped up, racing them as they lengthened in the dimming light. I turned on the headlights to chase them away.

Danny's face, panicked and confused, burned in my mind. I was hurting him with every mile I conquered. But I couldn't stop, not until I'd outrun what was chasing me.

Soon the mountains were lost in darkness. My breathing regulated. Then my chest started to ache, my breast heavy with milk. I began to feel anxious about leaving my phone. And my wallet for that matter. The gas was under a quarter of a tank. I needed to turn around now if I wanted to make sure I got home.

Lights from a gas station appeared at the next exit and I pulled over. It was a rundown place with only two pumps and a small convenience store. I parked, sitting back and looking out the window at the misty rain falling in the light of the streetlamps. My breathing slowed, and the familiar exhaustion of a panic hangover slowly crept over me. The rain picked up. The patter on the windshield was comfortingly hypnotic. I got out of the car. Rain splattered across my bare arms. But I didn't mind it. It was cleansing—almost baptismal.

I entered the store. It smelled foul and I almost regretted walking in.

"Can I borrow a phone?" I asked the kid behind the counter.

He was wearing a black polo with the gas station logo on it, disinterested in me or anything else. I was the only customer and he the only attendant in sight, so I guessed this gas station didn't get much traffic through it. He lifted an old landline phone off its base and handed it to me.

"You have to include the area code," he said.

"Thanks," I dialed Danny's number.

The kid sat down on a tall stool behind the cash register and pulled out his cell phone. Thematic music played from some kind of game app.

"Feels like being in elementary school again, calling my mom from the office," I said while the phone dialed. He looked up briefly before choosing to ignore me. Zero for two today, I guess.

"Hello?" an anxious Danny answered.

"It's me."

He exhaled into the receiver, and I knew he was trying to compose himself. "Where are you?"

I recalled which exits I had passed. "Somewhere before Colorado Springs."

Danny's breathing slowed and calmed. We camped a lot in Colorado Springs, and Danny backpacked and rock climbed there regularly. It was familiar. "Do you need me to come get you?"

"No," I almost spoke over him. "No, I'm heading back home now."

"Ok."

The drive home was exhausting and felt longer than the drive there, but I eventually turned onto our street and pulled into our driveway. Rain pounded on the top of the car sounding more like a rockslide than hypnosis, now. Danny ran out to meet me, opening my door and pulling me into his arms before I stepped out of the car. I let my head sink into his chest.

"I'm sorry," I whispered.

The rain battered against my back. Danny reached up and stroked my damp hair.

"I'm just glad you're safe."

My strength was gone, used up by the rush of adrenaline triggered by my flight response. Danny recognized the look in my eyes, so he wrapped his arm around my waist, helping me into the house. It wasn't really necessary, but his arms were warm and comforting, so I didn't protest.

He helped me to our room and sat me down on the bed, taking off my boots and leaving them muddy on the floor. I pushed away the thoughts about the mud getting all over the carpet, and about my wet clothes on the comforter.

Danny sat on the edge of the bed, his torso twisted toward me.

"Eleanor?" I met his eyes. They were full of fear. "It's fine if you need to get away. Go for a drive, a walk, whatever. But next time, could you please bring your phone?"

I nodded. But in that moment, it was like I was looking at a stranger. The cold distance that had emerged between us since Marc was born grew wider, and I didn't know how to close the gap.

7

Seventeen Days

Rose, 1972

There was no honeymoon. But we weren't in the mood for one, anyhow. Eugene and Carol had been living with Ma and Pa since the funeral, and Ma had struggled keeping up with two young children, so they moved in with us the day after the wedding. The adoptions were finalized before Christmas. It wasn't that laborious a process with Lenny's voluntary relinquishment of his parental rights. And then there was Pa's connections speeding up the proceedings. Still, adoption day was tense and exhausting. It felt to me like we were burying her all over again.

Thomas and I moved into a house that Pa bought for us—much to Thomas's dismay. But even he admitted that we needed the help if we wanted a place large enough for two kids. At least until he passed The Bar and started practicing. Pa bought a place with cash that Thomas agreed wasn't too much and we arranged a monthly rent. It was a compromise.

It was a modest home, closer to the university. A single level three bedroom with two bathrooms. One of the bedrooms was very small, and we put Carol's nursery in that one. The largest bedroom was the master, and Eugene was in the third.

Thomas worked long hours with the clerkship. He had to pay his dues. Any spare time he had was spent studying for The Bar. But he assured me it would all be worth it. Working for Judge Douglass would set the tone for his whole career.

Tonight he came home later than usual. I'd fed Eugene and sent him to bed. Carol was up for a feeding and I was mixing up some formula—turns out they did have something besides cow's milk for babies. She was eating more baby food now, but liked the formula to help her sleep at night.

It was about nine-thirty when Thomas came through the front door.

"Hungry?" I called from the kitchen.

"No, Mason bought supper." Mason was another clerk.

Thomas came into the kitchen. I was standing in my house coat, holding Carol in one arm, shaking up the baby bottle with the other.

"One of these days he's gonna expect you to buy."

"Naw, he doesn't have a wife. Or kids. He's real understandin', always says it's no inconvenience. Here, let me." Thomas reached out and took Carol with the bottle. He sat down at the kitchen table to feed her. I sat next to him, the exhaust from the day hanging over me like a fog.

"Long day?" he asked.

"About as long as yours."

"I'm sorry, Rose. There's a big case starting this week. But if things go as planned I'll be home at five tomorrow."

I shrugged, "It's fine. Just get those dues paid."

We sat for a moment in silence. The kitchen clock grew loud without conversation. I wanted to climb into bed, but I hadn't seen Thomas all day.

Thomas broke the silence. "I took The Bar."

I looked at him in shock. "What'd you say?"

"Two months ago. I took it."

I tried to process what he was saying. "You've kept this quiet for two months? I thought you were takin' it this summer."

"I felt ready. And I wanted to surprise you."

I stared at his idiotic, grinning face. He was thrilled like a schoolboy playing pranks.

"How—"

"I pretended it was a regular couple of workdays. Well, an important regular couple of workdays. To explain the stress. Remember the Conny case?"

I nodded.

"I made it up."

I shook my head and sighed, accepting the antics I had signed up for by marrying him. "When do you find out if you passed?"

"That's why I'm tellin' ya now. I found out today."

I stood up abruptly, bumping into the table.

"Shh," Thomas laughed, glancing down at Carol, who was now asleep.

"One minute," he whispered, standing up and carrying Carol to the nursery.

While he was gone, I went to the kitchen sink and got a glass of water. Out the window above the counter it was pitch black, and every so often a lightning bug would drift in and out of view.

He wouldn't have made this big thing of it if he didn't pass, right? Then again, maybe he was putting Carol down because he had bad news. Maybe he was trying to keep things light-hearted for me.

Thomas's hand rested on my shoulder, startling me. I whipped around to look at him. His face was serious now, and my heart started to sink.

He took me in his arms and pulled me against him, leaning in. Our cheeks brushed as he whispered in my ear, "I passed." He kissed my neck. The world became small, like we were the only ones in it. I turned in his arms and kissed him back, my cheeks wet with tears of pride and relief. Then we made our way to the bedroom.

My heart felt as warm as Thomas's body against mine. We were finally getting back on track. Soon we'd be out from Pa's thumb. Soon life would look a lot more like we'd imagined it. We could add Eugene and Carol into that picture. It would be easier to do once we were more in control again.

The only thing we still needed to complete that picture was a baby of our own. If I could carry my own child—birth a baby that was really mine—I was certain I would finally feel like a real mother. Then I could be what Eugene and Carol needed—no longer a fraud.

We laid in bed, side by side. Thomas turned towards me, wrapping me up in his arms. The sheets were tangled up around us, leaving me half exposed so the skin of my back pressed against the skin of his chest. My heart glowed, and I longed for this moment to be frozen in time.

"Do you think we made a baby?" Thomas whispered into my hair.

I touched my abdomen, saying a silent prayer. "Maybe."

Her hair was thrown up in a frizzy bun. Not the kind of frizz you avoid, but the tight curly kind, thrown up hastily instead of smoothed out with hot rollers. The messy pile was wild, with a few strands breaking free here and there, hanging in crimped twirls down the sides of her face.

Her spine was straighter than a rod. She stepped gracefully, as if she wore a ballerina's slippers. In fact, she was to me like a ballerina, liberated of her expectations of perfection. Free and wild.

She danced in front of me, her smile filled my soul with light, and I longed to wrap my arms around her delicate waist in a warm embrace.

When she spoke, it was music. She never once stumbled on her words or hesitated in her thoughts. She was eloquent in the strictest sense, but at the same time relaxed. And I relaxed with her.

Confidence. She had confidence. It swirled around her in clouds of contagious security.

I called out to her. *Lily, I miss you. We all miss you.* I'd forgotten how sweet her name was to say. *Lily.*

Then I woke.

I stared at the ceiling. It had been a long time since I had dreamed of my sister. I turned over. Thomas was sleeping soundly beside me. The light of dusk was barely peeking through the curtains. I guessed it was about five. Thomas's alarm would be going off soon.

It had been a few months since Thomas passed The Bar, and his clerkship was almost over. I was looking forward to a more regular schedule, but Thomas was still getting offers and he wasn't sure yet which one he wanted to accept.

I sat up, letting the comforter fall down my torso. The dream lingered, and I ached with that feeling of missing someone you never knew you'd have to miss—someone you took for granted while they were around, their smiles given freely and their embraces unlimited. I wish I had known. I wish I had hugged her longer. And more often. I swung my legs out over the edge of the bed, slipping out from under the sheets. Books cluttered up my night table, and I reached for the reading glasses sitting precariously on top. I breathed the morning in deeply, trying to channel Lily's confidence from beyond the grave.

She'd been so natural with the kids; a nurturer by nature, endlessly patient and easy to trust. My ability to nurture was...lacking to say the least. I'd never been very maternal. When other girls were playing dress up with their dolls, I was content with my nose stuck in a book. Thomas told me I was a great mom, but he didn't have anyone to compare me to. His mom passed away when he was a small child and his father never remarried.

I picked up my Bible and opened to where I'd left off the day before—in *The Acts*. I tried to read, but it was taking too much effort to concentrate.

Carol began to stir in the next room, cooing quietly. She was an early riser. I stood up, moving my glasses to the top of my head. I would get dressed, then try reading again. My legs wobbled for a moment, the muscles still warming up. Tiptoeing to the dresser, I opened a dark, mahogany drawer by its cool brass handle and began to pull out a sensible outfit, something practical for doing the daily chores and cleaning sticky hands. I used to wear silks and chiffon in rich, saturated colors that complimented my warm hair. Now I wore sturdy linens and jersey knits in earthy tones that could hide a strawberry jam stain.

I paused for a moment, considering, then opened the bottom drawer—the drawer of delicate, pretty blouses from my university days. Things I'd worn to impress Thomas during our courtship. All very bookish, but they were me. I removed a blouse to feel the fabric in my hands. It was an ivory silk with mother-of-pearl buttons and lavender floral embroidery on the scalloped sleeve hems. As I lifted the folds of fabric a small book appeared from beneath. Lily's journal. I'd set it aside to give Carol someday and forgotten about it.

I put the blouse back down and lifted the journal in my hands. The front was a paper bound floral pattern, cheaply made, but well kept. The pages were smooth and crisp, filled with blue ink pressed into the fibers, neat and tidy, but in cursive that was gracefully wild. It was like her personal portrait contained in an object.

The sight of her handwriting sent a pang through my stomach. I closed my eyes and breathed, feeling strangely nauseated.

I put my glasses back on and opened the journal to a random page, finding the middle of a passage:

He is so peaceful when he sleeps. My heart aches for him. I never knew I could feel so much joy and so much sorrow at once. I'm proud of him, but I miss when he depended on me for every little thing. He smiled at me today in a way he never has before, a smile that said he really knew he was a separate being from me. It was beautiful! But it also made me want another baby so badly. Maybe this will be the month.

I closed the journal and put it down. My eyes stung and my nose tickled. This was written five years before Lily got pregnant with Carol. I didn't know she had been trying all that time. I'd assumed she and Lenny had planned it that way—that they wanted kids farther apart in age, like she and I were. Did Ma have a hard time getting pregnant the second time, too? Ma and Pa did not approve of birth control, so they had to have either planned it very well for four years or... Did that kind of thing run in families?

I shook off the thought.

I recited Lily's words in my head. *So much joy and sorrow at once.* I was feeling the sorrow. Eugene and Carol, just starting to stir in their beds, my niece and nephew whom I loved with all my heart—I was failing them. Where was the joy in that? They deserved better. But they only had me.

The last few weeks had been chaotic. But really, it'd all started back when Lenny disappeared shortly after the adoption. The original plan had been that Lenny would live with Ma and Pa, on the condition that he stayed sober. Pa wasn't so cruel that he wanted Lenny out of Eugene and Carol's lives. He just didn't trust him to raise his grandchildren. Or manage to keep them alive for that matter.

When Lenny left in the night it broke all our hearts. Especially Eugene's. Ma had held Eugene while he sobbed the next morning, and for the first time I could remember, she became so angry that the look in her eyes frightened me. Thomas had gone looking for Lenny, but Pa called him off the search when Thomas checked in from a payphone.

He's a grown man. We can't force him to do the right thing. Pa had muttered over and over, like he was trying to convince himself, too.

Thomas and I didn't blame Lenny. We blamed Pa. He'd manipulated Lenny into giving up his kids, then made it unbearable for him to stay around. But if Thomas had continued looking for Lenny and by some miracle brought him home, Ma and Pa would've taken it as a deep betrayal. After Lenny left, they wanted nothing to do with him.

But a few weeks ago, at Sunday dinner with my parents, I'd overheard Thomas and Pa in the study, talking about Lenny. The door had been left open a little, so I'd listened in, standing just outside in the hallway, my nose to the heavy wood of the door frame.

"I should pick him up."

"No."

"Rose would want me to."

"This stays between us, Tom."

Pa was the only one who ever called Thomas, Tom. Thomas hated it.

"Lily would've wanted us to."

A painful silence followed.

After what felt like a full minute, Thomas spoke again. "Did they say what the charges were?"

"Yes."

Charges?

More silence. I smelled one of Pa's cigars.

"Leave him overnight."

"And tomorrow?"

"I'm sure they'll provide him with an adequate public defender."

I heard Thomas's feet shuffle across the room. I leaned forward until I saw a sliver of his arm through the crack in the door. He was staring out the window, his back to his father-in-law, who was likely sitting behind his desk like he was Thomas's boss and not his family. Thomas's shoulders were hunched over, his fist clenched. I leaned back again and pressed my spine against the old wallpaper. The plastic clip holding back my hair dug into my skull.

"This isn't the first phone call I've had, Thomas," Pa sighed. I could picture him leaning back in his leather chair. "He's beyond our help. If I couldn't scare him sober while Lily was alive—well, there's certainly no hope for him now."

Thomas exhaled like he'd set down a heavy load. "Fine, I won't interfere—not directly. But I'm gonna ask 'round 'bout gettin' him a probation deal."

I'd left after that. I wanted that moment to be how I remembered this conversation forever. It was the first time I'd heard anyone challenge Pa like that. I fantasized that Thomas had left the study door ajar on purpose, anticipating Pa's demand to keep me out of the loop, hoping I would walk past and overhear. A sort of loophole of rebellion. Something had changed in Thomas after he passed The Bar. He had found confidence.

I was clutching Lily's journal to my chest. I missed Lenny. I wondered where he was now, and if he was ok. I put down the journal and stood. My head swam with the movement. Spinning around, I lurched towards the wastebasket, catching just in time the contents of my stomach.

I placed a hand on my abdomen as if that would ease the nausea. I could not afford to be sick today—it was Eugene's class play.

Thomas stirred. "You ok, honey?" he mumbled.

"I'm fine, just a little dizzy."

I looked down at my fingers, placed gently, but firmly on my stomach. And then it came rushing to me. I hurried to my bedside table, pushing aside my

Bible and an old novel to reach my daybook. Inside I counted the days from one circled in red pencil. Seventeen days. I was seventeen days late.

Thomas came home late from work that night. The kids were already in bed. It had been a good day. Carol had started to pull herself forward with her arms, like an army crawl. Eugene helped me encourage her forward, reaching out to her and cheering her on. Watching him with her was one of the few joys I experienced these days. I treasured it above most everything else. He adored her, and she him. They at least had each other.

I prepared a special dinner for Thomas and me, keeping it warm in the oven. When I heard his car in the driveway, I served the meal on our nice settings. He closed the front door with a thud and sat down on the creaky front bench to remove his coat and shoes.

"Supper's ready," I called to him from the kitchen.

"Be right in."

I took the bottle of wine I'd had chilling in ice water in the sink and opened it. I set it on the table next to Thomas's plate, then sat down. The meal was stuffed duck wrapped in pastry—produced with help from Julia Child. I'd taken notes on the recipe a couple weeks ago and had been waiting for the right occasion to execute it. I also had a custard tart decorated with berries and whipped cream waiting in the fridge. Without schoolwork to occupy my brain, I'd dove deep into French cuisine, testing new recipes all the time. Thomas joked that I was trying to turn domestication into a scholarly pursuit. We would laugh at that, but we both knew it was a joke rooted in truth.

When Thomas came to the table, he looked at my plate, then back at me.

"I thought I'd wait up today." I explained—which was only a half truth. I'd eaten kraft dinner with the kids, too. The nausea had prevented me from eating breakfast or lunch, and once it subsided, I was ravenous. But it didn't hurt not to mention this would be my second dinner.

Thomas smiled. "What a lovely surprise." He leaned down and kissed my forehead before sitting down. "This looks classy. Julia again?"

I nodded. "Stuffed duck."

He picked up the wine and checked the label. It was the '47 Pa had given us on our wedding day.

"Have I forgotten an important occasion?"

I took the bottle and poured him a glass.

"I read something real interestin' awhile back," I began. "Apparently doctors are sayin' women shouldn't drink while they're pregnant." I put the bottle down, then I lifted my own glass of sweet tea in a toast.

Thomas looked at his glass of wine, then at my sweet tea.

"Rose—"

I nodded.

He got out of his chair and knelt on the ground in front of me, reaching up to hold my face and bend it down to his. We kissed, slow and firm. Our tears mixed on our cheeks where they pressed together.

He pulled away, putting his hands on my abdomen. He kept his eyes down while he asked the question that needed to be asked. "How far?"

"Seventeen days."

He lifted his head, surprised. "How long have you known?"

"Since this mornin'," I replied, knowing it would be hard to believe. "I wasn't keepin' track of the days very well. I'd been so discouraged."

He nodded in understanding, and we sat for a moment in silence, an unspoken cautious hope between us.

8

True Colors

Lillian, 1993

Grace picked Niles and I up and took us to her place. Between Thursday and Saturday Grace had furnished one of her guest rooms with a crib and changing table. There was also a highchair in the kitchen.

"Did you buy all this?"

"It's all stuff from Chris's garage," she shrugged. Chris was her brother; his daughter Olive was the one babysitting Niles tonight. She was seventeen and an only child.

"He kept all this around?"

"Yeah. He's a sentimental dork. Plus, I think he's convinced I'll use them someday." She paused, then erupted in laughter. "Well look at that, I guess he was right."

I didn't ask why she didn't want to get married or have kids. Not because I was afraid to—she was an open book and easy to talk to. I didn't ask because I was pretty sure I'd already figured it out, and it wasn't because she was an anti-marriage feminist. Although, I was beginning to think I was becoming one.

I showed Olive how to warm up the bags of breastmilk I'd put in Grace's fridge, then walked her through the bedtime routine. She was a sweet girl, probably the kind of teenager my parents wished I'd been. I thought how strange it was that she and I were closer in age than I was with Grace.

She held Niles and waved me off as we left the house. "Don't worry, we'll be fine. Have fun!"

Grace had ordered a cab to come pick us up. We climbed in the back on opposite sides. Grace was wearing a burgundy slip dress that I'd never seen her wear before. I usually only saw her in her work clothes: pencil skirts, nylons, and cardigans. Tonight, her dress had a low, lacey v-neck with spaghetti straps that showed off her collarbone. She had on five or six necklaces in various lengths all layered up. I was momentarily jealous she was perky enough to go out with no bra—and no leaky breasts to worry about. I'd never stuffed my bra in grade school, but now that I didn't even need stuffing I had three layers of cotton pads in there to ensure I didn't leak through my shirt. Her hair was up in a straightened ponytail with strands hanging down in the front. The whole ensemble gave off a completely different vibe than her usual one. I felt underdressed in my Levi's and Eagles t-shirt. I hadn't been doing myself up much since having Niles.

"39th and Branson," Grace said as she slid into the back of the cab. I got in after her.

The house grew smaller in the back window. Was Niles crying for me right now? Do babies trust their parents to come back for them, or do they believe they've been abandoned every time we go out? I checked my watch. It was just after eight. I hoped he'd go down ok.

Grace was chatting about another professor she worked with who had quit suddenly a couple days ago to pursue his dream of starting a restaurant.

"It finally came out that he'd *already* bought the food truck. Can you believe it?"

"That's crazy."

"Don't say crazy. But yeah, he could've given notice weeks ago. I dunno if he wanted the drama or what."

"Wait, why?"

"Well, he's never been the dramatic type, but who knows."

"No, why not say crazy?"

"Oh," Grace looked at me like she'd just realized I wasn't on her level. "It's just not a nice word."

I raised my eyebrows. "It isn't?"

"It's kinda like dumb or stupid. It's an antiquated term and more offensive now than anything. Mentally ill, clinically disordered...use either one but don't say crazy."

"I wasn't saying I actually think he's crazy."

"It's not offensive to him, it's offensive to people with mental illnesses."

Grace picked at her fingernails. I'd unwittingly pushed a button.

"Sorry," I replied, though I heard the disingenuity in my own voice.

Her face softened anyway. "It's ok. You had no way of knowing." She continued her story like there'd been no interruption.

The cab dropped us off at the corner. We walked past a cafe and an ice-cream place, then stopped in front of a bar called *Branson*, after the street it was on. It was one of those hole-in-the-wall places.

Inside the lights were low. The bar seating was already full, and even more customers sat in the booths lining the outer walls. There was a juke box by the door playing a slow 80's ballad. The song made me think of my teenage bedroom lined with posters of Duran Duran, Wham!, and Whitney Houston. The smell of alcohol was inviting. My mouth watered.

"What do you drink?" Grace asked as we set our purses down at a booth.

"Tequila."

"Straight up?"

Yes, I thought. But I didn't want Grace to see certain sides of me. "A paloma."

Grace went to the bar to get the drinks. She'd offered to buy tonight, and I was glad I wouldn't have to use my fake ID. Grace knew I was young, but I don't think she realized I was only 20.

Grace returned with two Palomas.

"You drink tequila, too?" I asked, raising my eyebrows. I couldn't imagine Grace being a tequila person.

Grace sat down across from me and picked the grapefruit segment off her glass. "Well, I'm usually an old-fashioned kind of gal."

Her wordplay got a chuckle out of me, and the chill that had developed from our confrontation in the cab melted away. Feeling more at ease, I started to sip on my drink.

"I ordered some fries and a pitcher of water. Don't want pain tomorrow." She smiled, her eyes wild like a college girl at her first frat party. Her eyes always gave her away. Maybe she chose to be as open as she was.

"You know the best cure for a morning hangover?" I asked.

"Aspirin?"

"A bloody Mary—without the blood."

She looked at me like she wasn't sure if I was serious or joking.

"I'm kidding," I laughed. She relaxed, laughing with me. I didn't tell her that it wasn't entirely a joke, and that I usually used wine instead of vodka. But I wasn't worried about tomorrow, anyway. I could handle my alcohol. That's something I'd picked up from living with Don. He'd always kept a good supply of liquor in the house, and I used to use it to dull the pain.

Don was an alcoholic. That was part of why I had to leave. But honestly, I could've lived with it if he weren't completely awful when he was sober. Most men started hitting their girls around when they were wasted. Don was a perfect gentleman when he was drunk. He was almost childlike. He showed the most affection after some bourbon and cried like a baby with a good scotch.

When Don was sober, though, he was an ass. Constantly irritable thinking about his next drink. That side hadn't come out very often at first—he was pretty much always drunk whenever we went out during our short courtship. After Niles was born and we couldn't go out as much, things got really bad. He never touched Niles, but I wasn't going to wait for the day he did. The truth was, I'd tried to leave a dozen times before last winter. But the house, the full cupboards, the comfortable furniture—it all belonged to him. And I'd signed a prenup that gave me zero protection, like an idiot. That's what you get for marrying a lawyer. Never again.

We sipped our drinks and sat in silence. I looked around the bar to avoid Grace's eyes. She absently hummed to a song I'd heard on the radio but didn't know the words to. I was getting out of touch. I chewed a bit on my straw.

The newer song ended, and *The Rhythm of My Heart* started playing, and Grace swayed in her seat. "Let's dance."

"I'll need a couple more drinks before that," I laughed and sipped the last bit of my Paloma. The grapefruit wedge brushed against my nose. It smelled crisp and bright. I plucked it off my glass and ate it.

She laughed too, and her voice sounded like a child's on Christmas morning. I was mesmerized.

"I can help with that," she giggled, sliding out of the booth.

While she was at the bar, the waitress came by with our water and fries. I munched on a few until she returned with shots between her fingers and a bowl of lime slices in the crook of her arm. Her Paloma wasn't even half gone, but she pushed it aside to make room.

"Tequila!" She held a glass up. I raised one with her. We both tossed them back. Grace's lips puckered over her lime wedge, sliding over the rind as she bit into the pulp. I tossed back another shot before eating mine.

Grace scrunched up her face and shook off the burn and sour. "Ok, let's go."

I took her hand, the familiar warmth of intoxication tingled in my fingers. My head felt pleasantly heavy, and my thoughts were already starting to relax. Grace led me to the jukebox and chose Cyndi Lauper.

Lying in my bed, I hear the clock tick and think of you.

Grace took my hands and pulled me to the empty dance floor. We stood across from each other, and she started to move her hips and arms slowly to the beat. Her ponytail swayed behind her, and lavender shampoo somehow cut through all the alcohol in the bar. The scent made my heart skip. Her shoulders were petite and narrow, like the rest of her, and they popped up when she moved them. She was a terrible dancer—yet somehow, she still looked good.

You're calling to me, I can't hear what you said.

I joined her. This song came out when I was twelve. *She's So Unusual* was the album that defined my pre-teen identity and remained a kind of anthem of mine over the years. Grace beamed when I started moving. My muscles had memorized the solace of dancing alone in my bedroom as a teenager—singing, standing on my bed. It felt like so long ago, though it had only been a couple years. The girl in my memory was not the single mom who now danced in a bar. But my body didn't know that, and it moved like it'd had never stopped.

The second hand unwinds.

Grace started singing with the chorus. She pointed at me when she sang: *if you're lost you can look and you will find me.* Several other patrons had turned their heads our way, watching. But having an audience didn't faze me—it fueled me. Years of dance training made it effortless. I was in my element. For the first time in a long time, I felt like me. A couple joined us on the dance floor, arms wrapped around each other. Grace took my forearms and danced with me, swaying like the couple. Her fingers on my arms made my heart race. She slid them down to my writs and turned me in a circle.

Time after time...

The song ended and we sat back down at our booth.

"Ok, where'd you learn those moves?"

I laughed, feeling my face flush with the combination of alcohol, movement, and flattery. "I've been dancing since I was three."

Her eyes widened in mock offense at having just heard this.

"Ballroom and contemporary, mostly. I did ballet for a bit when I was younger but grew out of it. Literally." I moved my hand down in front of my chest in a curve, like drawing even bigger boobs over my real ones. I smiled so she'd know it was a joke, and not self-deprecation. Going through puberty had been rough on my ballet career, but I was past all that.

"You'll have to show me more sometime," she smiled back. Her face was pleasantly soft and framed by fuzzy light. I relaxed as the alcohol made its way through my body.

Grace ordered two Old Fashioneds and we finished the night exploring my dance history. When we left there were two empty glasses and two empty shots on my side of the booth. On Grace's side only one shot was empty, her other drinks still half full. *I'm a light-weight*, she'd joked. *I get tired after a couple glasses of wine*. But I was a little self-conscious by how much more I'd had, and how much I wanted to finish hers.

Grace fell asleep on the way home. Her head fell onto my shoulder, and I stayed as still as I could even as my arm ached, not wanting to wake her and cut the moment short. The cab took us to her place and the driver waited for me to collect Niles. Olive was watching TV in the living room when we arrived. She said he'd gone down perfectly, waking up once for a bottle, then sleeping soundly.

I crept up the stairs to the room where Grace had set up the baby things. Niles was in the crib in this big room with nothing else in it but him. It seemed comical—a baby having this much space. Back in Alabama we'd had a nursery, of course. But I'd gotten so used to our little studio apartment. Alabama felt like a place from a different lifetime.

I gathered up his little body, holding him against my shoulder and chest. He was growing so fast. Maybe it was the drinks, but my eyes welled up standing there in the dark, holding him. This room—Grace's house, it felt like a second home. I could just be there with him, safe, and at peace.

By the time I'd come downstairs, Olive had left. Grace helped me bring Nile's car seat and diaper bag to the taxi. Grace paid the driver for his wait and my ride home. I didn't protest her taking care of it. I was in too good a mood. And I honestly enjoyed her taking care of me like that.

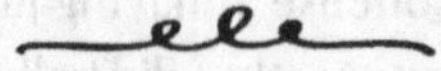

At home I put Niles down for bed and stood over his crib a minute, watching his chest slowly rise and fall. He was a little fussy in the cab, but he went right back to sleep while I carried him up to the second floor of our building. He'd done alright for his first time with a sitter. I was grateful my first time away from him had happened like this, and not for a date with a creepy middle-aged man. I couldn't believe I'd ever considered that. I was certain the weight off my heart, of no longer being beholden to him, would be worth the loss of income. Every penny.

After I was sure Niles was still out cold, I stripped down to my underwear. I pulled wads of cotton out of my bra. They were soaked through. I reached back and unhooked my bra. It was a relief as the pressure around my ribcage released, and the cups unattached themselves from my breasts. I left it on the floor and put on an over-sized t-shirt that had been left crumpled at the foot of the bed, then opened the small coat closet that functioned as my only storage space. I didn't have time to take much when I left Don, but I did make sure to grab my CDs and tapes. I had an expansive collection, and they were my most valuable possessions. An old, second-hand CD/tape combo player was the first thing I'd bought when I had a little extra money around. I pulled a small suitcase out of the closet and flipped through until I found what I was looking for. I went to the player, which took up almost the entirety of the kitchenette counter, and popped a tape in. While it rewound, I got a bottle of tequila off the top of the fridge and took a long pull straight from the bottle. Thankfully this player could skip, and I didn't have to look at the track list to know which one to skip to—track four. I turned the volume down low so I wouldn't wake Niles, though he was a deep sleeper at night.

You with the sad eyes, don't be discouraged.

I let the music control my body, moving through the air like I was pushed by an invisible wind. My body wasn't as toned as it used to be, before having Niles, but it was still strong and flexible.

So don't be afraid to let them show—

I went to the floor, and I was reaching for something. The weight of it would pin me to the ground, but I didn't care. I wanted it. I needed it. I stood up and leapt for it.

Your true colors are beautiful.

Cyndi sang her final *rainbow*. I stood in the middle of that little apartment, milk dripping from my nipples, and wept. I wept because I danced again. Because I felt for the first time since leaving my marriage, that I was truly free.

9

Six Minutes

Eleanor, 2019

One. Two. Three. Four. Five. Six. Six minutes. That's all I had to do. Six minutes without the baby.

Six minutes was how long Danny said it should take me to take a real shower, one where I shampooed my hair and washed my skin. I paced back and forth in the bathroom. I resisted turning on the water. *What if he cried? The rushing pipes would drown him out.* I imagined him alone, screaming, Danny passed out on the floor for some horrible reason. And me in the shower, unaware of everything happening on the other side of the bathroom door.

"Everything ok?" I called out.

"We're fine," Danny responded, exasperated. "We're both fine. Take a shower. You stink."

This was true.

I checked my phone. 6:43. One. Two. Three. Four. Five.

Five more minutes.

I stared at the tub and listened carefully for sounds of a fussing baby. It was silent. Somehow that was worse.

I wanted to turn the faucet, I really did, but I was paralyzed. My head spun with images of that tiny body, breathless on the floor. Danny was gone—*where did he go?*

"Danny!" I threw open the door and bolted into the living room. Danny was on the couch, a sleeping yellow bundle in his arms.

"Eleanor," Danny admonished me with his eyes. "He's fine. You've been apart longer than this before."

I knew that. I knew this made absolutely no sense. I felt foolish. Danny was more than capable. Marc was fine. I returned to the bathroom.

6:45. One. Two. Thr—

"I'm resetting the timer," Danny called. "And I'm not going to start it again until I hear the shower running."

One. Two. Three. Four. Five. Six.

I tried to picture Danny and Marc on the couch: safe, awake, asleep, content. My mind fought against the earthquakes of calamity that appeared in my imagination, an irrational battle of fears and reality. Illogical. But logic didn't stop anxiety.

I turned the faucet knob slowly, letting a small trickle of water free.

I listened.

One. Two. Three. Four. Five. Six.

I turned the knob again.

Two. Three. Four. Five. Six.

A little more.

Four.

More.

Five.

Once more.

Six.

I lifted the shower plug and water rained from above. I tip-toed to the door, opening it a crack and pressing my ear towards the hallway outside. Danny cooed and shushed softly, and maybe I heard a tiny baby sigh? I wasn't sure if it was in my head, but it was enough comfort for me to start getting undressed. I stayed close to the door as I peeled off the clothes I'd been wearing day and night for almost a week, feeling the cool air from the open door cut through the steam that was building up behind me. It was nice on my naked skin. Like a gentle caress. I moved the shower curtain over with the back of my hand, watching the water falling to the porcelain floor. I hesitated a moment longer to listen.

But the water drowned my senses, and when I finally stepped inside, my soul warmed from the outside. I let the water run through my hair, over my face. The droplets gathered on the white tiles on the wall and dripped into the divots of yellowed grout. The steam encased me, shielding me from the outside world. I sat down in the tub, letting the water drum along my spine and drip down my head and off my hair. There were pools and rivers in front of me, sparkling with miniature splashes, and I fell into a trance watching the dancing beads of bonded hydrogen and oxygen molecules, picturing the atomic world within each wonderful drop of mist.

PPOCD. The diagnosis was official now, as of my most recent session with Aliza. *How was I going to survive this? Is my only hope in single moments on the bathtub floor? Would I ever feel normal again?* What did normal feel like, anyway? I'd always been anxious—as far back as I could remember. And my first episode of depression was in the sixth grade. I wasn't sure I'd ever even experienced normal. Many a therapist had told me normal didn't exist. Did normal feel like dancing drops of mist? Did it feel like bonded molecules, perfectly organized into what you're meant to be? A dancer on a clean stage, moving easily through the air, molecules of carbon and oxygen parting the way for a body of bonded structures.

I longed to have the energy to dance like drops of water, bouncing off the rivers by my feet. I opened my hand and let them fall into my palm then spill off like sand. I wanted to be one with them, the molecules of water. So clear in purpose, so easily fulfilled.

A light tap on the partially open door brought me out of my head.

"You did it!" Danny spoke softly, but loud enough to hear over the cascade around me.

"I...I think I can do a little longer." I don't know what force released me to speak those words, but I longed to hold on to this moment—to not think about what lay beyond that door. To keep the battle at bay a little longer. I would pretend for this moment there was nothing beyond me.

"That's wonderful." Danny sounded relieved. "Just come out whenever you're ready."

Does normal feel like being ready?

10

Paint

Rose, 1972

Blood. My heart slowed and stopped, as if too ashamed to beat. Blood. Again.

Small feet pattered past the bathroom door; Eugene's deliberate pace underlined Carol's still uncertain footing. My mind fabricated ideas of what mischief they were getting into, but the distraction didn't last long.

I hunched over and rested my forehead in my hands, mapping the threads in the baby pink underwear that hung around my ankles. *Thomas.* I didn't know how to tell him. The small tinkling plop of a clot hitting toilet water echoed through the bathroom. There was a slight cramping in my abdomen, but not any worse than the last time. Or the time before that. But it was different this time. I was further along—fourteen weeks.

I pressed my hands tight against my eyes in an effort to control my emotion. I had a bachelor's degree. A successful husband. A prize-winning Clafoutis I'd made for the church dessert showcase a few weeks ago. But what is a woman if she can't bear children? I had almost told Ma the news. Now she would continue her not so subtle hints of hope that we'd have a baby of our own.

The ladies in church would whisper whenever I wore an oversized sweater or refused a mimosa at the missionary brunch—the new recommendation for pregnant women to avoid alcohol had become a popular conversation topic among the childbearing ladies. They would loudly announce their refusal of the mimosas saying they were *hopin' for a miracle this month*. The truth was I didn't like drinking in the mornings—it gave me a headache. But finally, I'd had a real secret to keep from them. One that would reveal itself in the most dramatic of ways, protecting me from their poorly veiled gossip and righteous concern. And now it was gone.

"Aunt Rose?" Eugene was outside the bathroom door. "We're hungry."

I checked my watch; two thin gold hands pointed upwards. It was just after noon.

I cleaned myself up while calling back, "I'll just be a minute, hon." His patters receded down the hallway.

I flushed the toilet; red clots and blood smeared bath tissue swirled around until the water pulled them down. Gone forever. This was the funeral my unborn babies got.

Washing my hands, I tried to avoid looking up into the mirror. The water was scalding, and I let it run over my fingers long after the soap was gone. A small glass bowl of seashells sat on the vanity, and I reached over and let water drip from my reddened hands onto their dry, ridged surfaces. They drank up the water thirstily, turning glossy in the moisture. The drips moved slowly down, creating little wobbly stripes. I faced the mirror to check my appearance, turning on the cold water. I took a face cloth from the stack on the vanity and wet it. Pressed against my face, the cold was like a cleansing breath.

That's three.

I left the bathroom and found an empty hallway. I made my way to the kitchen where Eugene and Carol sat patiently at the table. Eugene was helping Carol with a coloring book.

"What are you turkeys hungry for?" I asked them.

"Grilled cheese and tomato soup," Eugene responded, not looking up from the picture.

"Cheese!" Carol shouted.

"Yes, cheese," I answered her enthusiastically. "That's some great talkin', little one." Momentary relief came over me with the new word. Carol knew about six words—well 'cheese' made seven. The pediatrician said she should know 10-20 by now. We'd been working on it, but I didn't really know what I should be doing. It had never occurred to me how babies learn to talk.

Carol called me *mama* and Thomas *dada*. Eugene called us *Aunt Rose* and *Uncle Tom*—he'd picked that up from Pa, but Thomas never corrected him. I think he didn't mind the nickname when it came from Eugene. Probably because Pa used it condescendingly which Eugene obviously did not. As for me, I didn't know how I felt about either name. Mama. Aunt. Neither was right.

The anniversary was last month. Not our wedding anniversary, that was coming up. Last month was *her* anniversary. One year since my sister died. We'd celebrated Carol's first birthday the week before. Ma put together a whole affair. All the relatives within 200 miles were in attendance. It was the most lavish party for a one-year-old, probably ever. Macarons in pastel rainbow shades, salmon puffs, caviar, and escargot were delivered to guests on platters. A birthday cake that looked like it belonged as the top tier of a wedding cake sat on a table spread with soft pink linens. Real silver had been polished up for the occasion, and likely more than a hundred gold balloons adorned every corner and doorway. Giant cubic zirconia diamonds studded an ornate centerpiece in the middle of the gift table, a photo of Carol sitting atop it like a throne. Lily would've hated all this fuss; I'd had the sense that we were all overcompensating.

Despite the unspoken rule not to mention the looming anniversary, its discussion became inevitable when Lenny showed up—his first appearance since he'd run off.

"Ten days," he'd shouted, after bursting in the front door. Ma had wrung her hands nervously. "Ten days. We din' see it comin'," he slurred. "And ya'll standin' here like we got somethin' to celebrate."

Pa didn't seem surprised when he showed up. He must have been getting updates about Lenny's case. I don't know if he did time or not, but if he was on parole, he'd certainly broken it. He was barely conscious and reeked of whiskey.

After a few moments of awkward silence, the guests opted to pretend they hadn't heard Lenny—or that he even existed—and continued in their conversating and pleasantries. The women doted on little Carol, who captivated her audience with her big eyes and lyrical babbles, dancing precariously to the gentle music of the live pianist.

"She," Lenny pointed to Carol, who paid him no mind. "She killed 'er."

The room went quiet.

"Don't say somethin' you'll regret," Thomas warned.

Pa grabbed Lenny by the collar and shoved him into the hallway out of sight.

"Do you know what's goin' on?" I'd asked Thomas.

He'd only shaken his head.

A few minutes later I'd glimpsed Pa shooing Lenny through the kitchen. A police car had discretely parked down the street, and an officer was waiting at the kitchen door for Lenny. When Pa returned to the party, I'd heard him mutter to Ma and Thomas, *he won't be showin' up here again.*

I gathered what I needed for the grilled cheese sandwiches from the fridge, pausing for a moment to look at the postcard of the New York skyline stuck with a magnet to the door. It had arrived last month from Celiah. She'd gotten a job at a legal aid office there—secretary work, I think. Next to it was her college graduation announcement. I smiled at her smooth cursive writing. *I should really call her.*

The pan sizzled when I threw a slab of butter on it. I opened a can of Campbells soup and dumped it into a saucepan then added some milk. I sliced the sourdough I'd made last night and began assembling the sandwiches with some cheddar, deli ham, and pesto.

A sticky warmth dripped between my thighs. The napkin I'd put on felt like it'd already soaked through. A sudden heat flooded over my body and everything went blurry. The butter was browning on the pan, the sandwiches sitting on the counter, waiting to be put on. The smell made my stomach lurch and my abdomen throb. My sister's face filled my mind—the day Eugene was born, and the tears of relief on her face.

"Aunt Rose, why are you crying?" Eugene's voice brought me back. I reached up and touched my cheeks—my face was wet, like it had been lightly painted with salty brush strokes.

"I just burned my finger, nothin' to worry your pretty head about."

It was a good lie. And I had burned something—the butter.

But from his seat at the kitchen table, Eugene's eyes gave away that he was too old—or too wise, to fall for my little fib.

My heart melted like the new slab of butter I added to the pan. He had noticed my pain. I had to do better at hiding it. There had to be some hope for us. When he was a baby, barely alive in the world, I was there. I'd been there from the very beginning.

"Hey, Eugene," I ventured, looking back at him. "If you'd like, you could call me...mama Rose?" A decent compromise, I thought.

He turned his wise eyes back to Carol and her crayons.

"You'll never be my mama," he muttered.

Children painted paper, and I painted my face.

11

A Girl Like You

Lillian, 1993

Something about being around Grace made me feel myself again. Months passed, and we went out every Friday, and soon I was calling her my best friend. But in the back of my mind there was a question. A question about something deeper.

We were going to a more popular bar tonight instead of our usual spot at *Branson* due to a private event there. Here the dance floor was crowded and the music only recent hits. We were sitting at the bar tonight. Grace was drinking a club soda but told me to get whatever I wanted. She had been working late all week with her book agent re-writing a chapter or something. She said she was too exhausted to dance or drink, so instead we talked. I made fun of some of my more distasteful and rude clients, and she talked about a grad student whose mannerisms reminded her of me.

When I was four drinks in, she gestured with her fingers across the bar. "That guy over there is looking at you."

I looked up. He was older—about Don's age. He was wearing a collared shirt, unbuttoned at the top, and a loosened tie like he'd just come from an office. His hair had some salt and pepper, and his five-o-clock shadow was dark. Our eyes met. I smiled politely, then returned my attention back to my tequila on the rocks. He was definitely my type. But I was trying to avoid my type right now. I felt Grace watching me.

"How do you know he's looking at me and not you?"

Grace raised one eyebrow. "Really?" Her eyes flitted over my outfit. I'd upped my game for our nights out. I was wearing my best, hip-hugging mini skirt with a black, fitted, boat-neck top that may have been a touch too small for my milk-heavy breasts. What was a young mom to do?

"Did you just give me a once-over?" I laughed.

The man left his seat at the bar and made his way over to us.

Grace looked away.

"Can I buy you ladies another round?" There wasn't an empty stool next to us, but he leaned on the bar between me and the girl to my right.

"I'm all set," Grace answered. "But Lillian here was just saying she wanted to dance."

I shot her a look.

The man smiled. "Lillian?" He reached out his hand. I took it and nodded.

"I'm Sam."

"Rad." I tried to sound disinterested, but his hand was rough and calloused, and I was a bit buzzed.

"Shall we?"

I looked questioningly at Grace. Her eyes were daring, like she'd placed a bet and was waiting to find out if she'd won. What was this game she was playing? I had made assumptions about her, about her feelings, and now she was challenging them.

"Come on, I know you love dancing. Don't miss out on my account." Her tone seemed genuine now.

Sam waited, his dark eyes looking to me to make the next move.

Fine, I'll play her game. I threw back the rest of my drink then slid from the stool, struggling to tear my eyes away from Grace. Sam placed a hand on my back and led me to the dance floor. His fingers brushed the bare skin where my shirt dipped in the back.

My hair was down, and the dark curls bounced as Sam and I danced. I'd been told my bio dad had a Latina grandmother, and that I looked a lot like her. It was the hair they were talking about, I think. And perhaps my hips.

I was a little intoxicated, and my muscles only increased in agility with the lubrication. It warmed me from within, the tingle in my fingers intensifying the feel of Sam's muscled arms beneath them. The music was loud, so we didn't talk much. But he had moves. We danced as partners, and I was surprised when I wasn't bored. His hands moved from my back to my hips. He held my body firmly and moved with confidence. I loved a self-possessed man.

"You know what you're doing," I said.

The music changed to something slower, and he pulled me in closer. Our breath mingled together, and the precariousness of our position was baited in our combined exhales. One slight bump and our lips would brush each other's skin.

"So do you," he replied.

I struggled to control my breath, knowing it could give me away at this proximity.

Sam moved so his back was to the bar. I leaned forward so we were cheek to cheek. His warm breath swept against my ear. I looked over his shoulder at Grace. She'd put her purse down on my stool to save my seat. She was sitting with her back to the counter, watching us. She chewed on the straw of a fresh Old Fashioned. I was surprised she was drinking. Her features were drawn. My stomach did a somersault. But this had been her doing. I decided to ignore her. I was having a good time with Sam, anyway.

Sam and I danced for four or five songs before we came back to the bar to breathe. I could've gone all night. He was the best partner I'd had since Johnny Sanders in high school ballroom. And we had undeniable chemistry. I knew nothing of substance about the guy, but he set me on fire.

"I need to go to the bathroom," I told Grace, taking her cocktail out of her hand and taking a large gulp. "Mm, order another of those," I giggled.

The restrooms were single, private stalls. There was a men's and a women's, which I thought was silly since only one person at a time could use them anyway. The women's had a small line, so I slipped into the men's stall.

I finished up and changed out my breast pads before washing my hands. Someone knocked softly at the door.

"Occupied." I called.

"It's Sam. Can I come in?" My heart jolted like it'd been electrocuted.

I quickly fluffed my hair then turned around and unlocked the door, opening it a crack. Sam pushed in and closed the door behind him. His hair was disheveled from our exercise on the dance floor. His eyes were so dark, they were almost black. My heart raced.

The bathroom barely fit the two of us. We stood facing each other, almost touching. Sam put one hand on my hip, then reached up with the other and brushed my cheek with the back of his hand. He traced down to my chin, then lifted it up towards him. He was tall, even taller than me, and he had to lean down a little to reach me. He smelled like tobacco leaf and musk. His heat teased my lips, until he closed the gap between us. He kissed me slowly, and I longed for him like I had once longed for Don—back when things were good.

My heart pounded, and I was certain he could feel it as I pressed up against him, pushing him against the bathroom door. My hands reached into his hair, our kisses becoming more desperate. He moved his lips to my jaw and down my neck.

I reached around his body to re-lock the door. He pulled away, panting, searching my face with softness in his eyes, His hand remained on the back of my neck.

"I want you." His voice was low and rough.

"I want you, too," I breathed. Our pelvises were pressed tight against each other.

"Would you rather come to my place?" He offered me an out. But he was dangerous for anything more than casual bathroom sex.

"No. It's now or never."

When we came back to the bar, Grace was standing up with her coat on.

"I paid the tab."

"My offer still stands." He brushed a frizzy curl out of my face, his fingers lightly touching my cheek as he did. "If you're up for round two." His smile was dashing, but God if it didn't remind me a little too much of Don.

"I'm tired, but thanks."

He kissed my jaw and pressed a card into my hand. It was his business card.

"In case you change your mind."

I put the card under my bra strap, but I already knew I wouldn't call. Tonight was perfect and men like him were unpredictable. I didn't want to give him enough time to turn on me.

Grace turned without a word and strode to the exit. I grabbed my coat and my purse and followed her out.

"Hey, are you mad?" I called out as I caught up to her.

"Nope." She didn't look at me.

Had I been misreading her all this time? "You practically threw me at him."

"I'm sorry, did you not have a good time?"

"I did."

"So why are you complaining?"

I stopped walking, startled by the uncharacteristic rudeness. "You are mad. Come on, Grace, what'd I do?"

"I didn't think you were that type of girl, that's all."

"*That* type of girl?" I raised my voice.

Grace stopped and faced me. It was late and the streets were quiet. A few people filtered in and out of another bar up the street. Our cab was supposed to meet us at midnight, but it wasn't at the corner yet. We must've left early.

"You started it." The words made me feel like I was a child arguing with my older brother, and I regretted them as soon as they left my mouth.

"I didn't know you were going to fuck him. In the fucking bathroom." We stood about ten paces apart and her voice carried down the street. Her volume didn't bother me—I'd done far worse things than fuck a man in the bathroom. So I spoke even louder.

"You got me, I'm a slut. Now you know. Welcome to the true me. So why do you care so much?" I was challenging her. I'd make her say it. I'd make her answer that question that was always hanging over me.

Grace stared like there was something she wanted to shout in my face, but she was fighting to keep it in. Voices approached. We stood in silence on the street as a couple walked past us.

When their voices faded, Grace closed her eyes. "You drink a lot, Lillian." Her voice was low now, barely audible.

"*What?*" I was blindsided, like she'd shaken me up in a snow globe then expected me to walk straight.

"Everyone makes bad decisions when they're drunk." She stepped towards me, her voice and manner gentle again, like the Grace I knew. But I felt like a child despite looming almost a head above her. Was she shrinking me?

"Stop." Unable to look at her, I stared at the ground. An ant crawled across the sidewalk to the safety of a crack in the pavement. I wished I could do the same.

"I'm your friend, Lillian. I just want you to be safe." She shifted her feet.

"*Stop.*"

She took a few more steps, closing the gap between us. "I've been enabling you. I realize that—"

"Stop!" I shouted. Grace fell silent when she saw the angry tears rolling down my cheeks. "My dad was an alcoholic. He left us. My husband was an alcoholic. I left him."

Grace stood stunned as our cab rolled up next to us. She went to the passenger window and waved at the driver. He rolled down the window. "Just a second," she said. She straightened and turned to me.

"I am *not* an alcoholic." I measured each word with a resolve that could have silenced my old power tripping preschool ballet teacher.

"Ok," she said, her voice submissive. She slowly took my arm, like she was afraid I was a bomb that could go off. When I didn't pull away, she led me to our cab.

The cab ride was silent. Maybe I had drunk too much tonight. I couldn't hold to the present very well, but I was aware enough to see my despondence was worrying Grace. When we got back to her house, she paid the driver and sent him away instead of asking him to wait for Niles and me. She thanked and paid Olive and walked her out to her car. Olive had reported that Niles was soundly asleep in the guest room upstairs, so I picked up the crackling baby monitor and sat on the living room sofa until Grace came back inside.

She sat next to me. The questions hung in the air between us.

"I'm sorry," she whispered.

I nodded in response.

"Do you want to talk about it?"

I shook my head.

"Ok."

I don't know how long we sat there, but it was long enough for me to fall asleep.

I woke up the next morning still on the couch, with a pillow and blanket. I had a slight headache—not the worst hangover, but the first one I'd had in a while. The sun was rising through the large picture window in the living room. It shone through trees, leaving patterns of leaves on the opposite wall. The world was bathed in yellow and pink. There was a chair with an ottoman across from the couch. Some bedding left crumpled on them indicated Grace had slept there. A pang of guilt punctured my chest like a needle. It felt early. She must've gotten sore sleeping there and moved to her bedroom.

I got up and went upstairs to check on Niles. He was still asleep. *What time was it?* Niles was usually an early riser. I went back downstairs, past the living room, and to the kitchen to check the oven clock. It was about a quarter-to-six. The coffee maker was on the counter next to the stove. I started a pot and then sat down at the kitchen table to wait.

The kitchen was large, a dream kitchen for someone who enjoyed cooking—which was not Grace, who lived on take-out and frozens. There was ample counter space, two sinks, and solid wood countertops. It definitely wasn't the original kitchen the house was built with. It and all the bathrooms had been remodeled at some point. My mom would love this kitchen. I imagined her coming to visit, maybe at Christmas, making peach tarts and blueberry scones for Grace and me.

Before the coffee finished, the front door opened and closed, making me jump. Grace came down the hallway, carrying coffee and a brown sack.

"Morning." She sat down next to me and pulled out two egg sandwiches and three muffins from the brown bag. "You're up early. I wanted to make sure you had something as soon as you woke up." She noticed the coffee maker. "This will taste way better." She handed me one of the coffee cups. It smelled earthy and spiced.

"This one's for Niles." She set aside a chocolate chip muffin.

We opened our sandwiches and started to eat. I sipped my coffee, letting it clear the fog in my head. There was cinnamon in it.

"So," Grace ventured, "you were married, huh?"

I swallowed a bite of egg, sausage, and brioche.

"Yep."

"Was he why you left Alabama?"

I nodded. For a few moments we both ate and sipped our coffees without speaking. Grace finished her sandwich and crumpled the paper wrapping into a ball, throwing it into the now empty take out bag.

"You've filed for divorce?"

I nodded, chewing a bite of sandwich.

She mirrored my nod and wrapped both her hands around her coffee cup. "You have an attorney?"

"A family friend is handling it."

Her eyes fixated on me as I took another sip of the coffee. It was good coffee. It cleared my mind and eased my headache.

"What about Niles? Not to assume he's the father," she quickly added. "Sorry, I—"

"He's the father. He doesn't want custody. As long as I don't come for his money, he doesn't care."

Grace took a sip of her coffee then leaned forward, resting her arms on the table, never taking her eyes off me. It's no wonder she was a successful psychologist. Everything about her body indicated that I was the only important thing in the world right now. I felt safe.

"We met when I was seventeen," I continued, finally ready to confide in someone about all this. "I was still in high school. He was forty-three." I looked at Grace. Her expression didn't change. "We met at one of my dad's work parties."

Grace raised an eyebrow at that, but not in a judgmental way. "Your dad's coworker?"

"Yeah. At first I was only doing it to drive my parents cra—" I corrected myself, "to defy them. They worried over me a lot. I think they're afraid I have too much of my birth dad in me. I guess I'm afraid of that, too. So maybe I became it on purpose so I wouldn't become it because of him. It would be in my control, instead. So I pushed boundaries. My parents' and society's. I wanted to show them I was going to go my own way. And yet I chose a lawyer—so I guess not so rebellious as I thought it was." I laughed, ironically.

"As soon as I turned eighteen, I dropped out of school and we eloped. Thing is my parents didn't react the way I expected them to. They tried to be supportive, even though I'd hurt them. Now I can see they were always doing that—being supportive despite my antics. But then Don moved us out of town, and after a while he started making it harder for me to see them. Then I had Niles, and it was terrifying. I almost died having him. And all I thought about was how much I wished my mom was there with me. They'd been right about everything, and maybe Don noticed my change of heart—maybe that's why...why it started." I choked.

Grace took my hand.

"I haven't spoken to them since I ran away," I continued. "They're like, super religious. Divorce isn't exactly considered an option. You get it." She had told me her family was Irish Catholic. I looked at her significantly, and the slightest tell cast a shadow on her features. "I think my mom would understand, but I just know my dad would freak out. I told my brother I was here, just so they'd know I wasn't dead, so they know. But they don't know why I left or what my number or address is or anything. I'm scared that if I give them any clues, they'll tell Don where to find me. That they'll make me come back and honor my vows."

Grace paused before answering, maybe to make sure I'd finished. "I'm glad you left." She squeezed my hand once, then released it and pinched her temples. "I'm sorry—I behaved horribly last night."

I said nothing, waiting for her to say more.

"I should've just asked you, instead of playing those games," she continued. "I didn't mean for it to get so out of hand. And I didn't realize it would hurt the way it did. But now I know." She removed her hand. Her eyes were sad. "You're clearly not gay."

Despite my suspicions and assumptions, my heart still thrilled with the confirmation. I took her hand back.

"I'm sorry, I do like men." I answered.

Her cheeks flushed with embarrassment, but she didn't pull her hand away. "Are you freaked out?"

Again, she surprised me. "Why would I be freaked out?"

"I like women. I mean, romantically." She emphasized *romantically* like I didn't know what gay meant.

"I know. I've known for a while, Grace. Don't worry, I'm not like those people—the ones who hate what they don't understand."

She sighed with relief, her shoulders relaxing. "It's no excuse for my actions, though. I was jealous. And possessive. Clearly, I need more therapy. I've been changing my meds but maybe they're not—"

"Stop. You don't need to apologize any more. And you definitely don't need to beat yourself up. I didn't behave great either." I put my hand on her arm. She looked at me, her eyes filled with remorse. "I forgive you," I said.

She smiled gratefully. My soul lifted with that smile, and I realized the question that'd been haunting me hadn't been about her at all.

"Grace...just because I do like men that way doesn't necessarily mean I don't like women the same way. Right?"

At home the voicemail machine blinked. I knew who it was. But I risked playing it for the vague hope that it was Grace with some answers about what I was feeling. Mr. Davis's voice roared through the speaker. I yanked the machine from its cords and threw it against the wall. I picked up Amanda's pink rock and chucked it at the machine for good measure. Niles wailed.

12

Ms. Maudie

Eleanor, 2019

She waved to me from across the street. I was sitting on our porch swing, drinking iced tea. Danny had found the swing on a social media marketplace and surprised me with it after we closed on the house. The swing, and the tea, and the elderly Ms. Maudie waving as she knelt in her garden made me feel like I was back in Alabama—back home.

Her name wasn't really Ms. Maudie. I didn't know her real name, but she reminded me of Scout and Jem's kind, plant loving neighbor in *To Kill a Mockingbird*.

We'd found the house while I was still pregnant with Marc. Danny got this new, fancy job at an actuarial consulting firm, so we upgraded from our small, one bedroom condo. We'd moved in a couple months after Marc was born. The rent was tight on our single income, but my maternity leave would be over soon. I'd picked up some online freelance jobs filming ASL videos—translations for instructional content mostly. But I missed my day job at the retirement home and was anxious to return. I missed the residents. It was the ideal position for me. I enjoyed being around people but had always struggled connecting with anyone my own age. The only reason Danny and I ever got so close was because he'd always been so open yet at the same time patient with my reservations—it made it easier when I wasn't left anxiously guessing his feelings or feeling pressured to reveal mine when I wasn't ready to. His extroversion complimented my introversion, instead of intimidating it.

The house was small and modest with a little garden bed out front of the porch. I didn't have much of a green thumb, but I liked flowers, so Danny planted poppies and Russian sage. He talked about starting a vegetable garden in the back but could never find the time to do it.

In the evenings, after Marc went down for bed, Danny would catch up on some work from home while I sat on the porch, watching the fireflies drift through the flowers and the front lawn.

Mostly our neighbors kept to themselves, but not Ms. Maudie. She always waved from her garden when Danny or I were out. She complimented our flowers and remarked on the nice weather when she went on walks and strolled past on the sidewalk. When she gardened, she wore a big, straw sunhat and red gloves that went almost all the way to her elbows. That Spring she'd been out nearly every day, digging in the soil, pruning her apricot and cherry trees, and clipping fresh flowers to bring inside. All her work paid off. She had the most splendid garden in the neighborhood, maybe in all of Colorado. It was reminiscent of the gardens I grew up with in Alabama. In the late summer it was a colorful scene with different types of flowers in bloom.

I awoke at three am, my mind sharp and alert. The psychiatric nurse practitioner had changed my meds to better treat the PPOCD. They were starting to help, but they also gave me insomnia. The nurse said that should go away with time, but what wouldn't go away was my new inability to breastfeed. The new medication could be passed through milk, so I had to wean Marc and start him on formula. My milk was taking a long time to dry up though, and I'd been engorged and leaky for about a week now, which didn't help the sleeping issue. I rubbed my sore breasts and checked the baby monitor. Marc was fast asleep. We had recently moved him to his own bedroom. Danny had insisted on it because of how poorly I'd been sleeping, waking to Marc's every sigh or stretch. But ironically, I slept even lighter with Marc in the other room. His heart monitor showed a steady rhythm, but I still got up to tiptoe across the hall and peek in at him. When I saw the distinct rise and fall of his chest enough times to satisfy myself, I went back to bed.

Danny was snoring, so I kicked him under the covers. He snorted before rolling over, resuming his snoring again. He'd been fighting a head cold. That was probably why he'd lost his patience earlier in the night. We'd fought before bed and again the first time Marc woke. About something stupid. I couldn't even remember, really. Danny had been feeling underappreciated. So had I. Neither of us had much left in us after these long days to support the other with.

I rearranged my pillows and the blanket. It was too hot. I kicked the covers off so they bunched up next to Danny. There was light from a single streetlamp streaming in through the slats in the blinds. I turned away from the window, twisting the sheets between my legs. *Why couldn't I be this awake during the day?*

An hour trickled by, followed by another, and the impending morning crept into our room. A warm glow filled the air outside, replacing the light of the streetlamp with the clear and invigorating beams of the sun. My thighs were sticky with sweat, but I pulled the blanket back over me, covering my head.

I must have finally fallen back asleep because I woke with a start to the sound of Marc's fussing through the baby monitor. Danny was gone, already at work. I'd slept through his alarm and everything. He must've given Marc his morning bottle—a kind gesture was Danny's signature move after an argument.

My eyes were heavy and protested wakefulness. I wasn't sure how much sleep I'd got, but before I'd woken at three, Marc had been particularly fussy. He was still getting used to formula. I guessed the longest stretch I'd gotten wasn't more than a couple hours.

I sat on the edge of the bed, dreading the day. My limbs were stiff and heavy. I checked the time on my phone—seven-twenty. I would give anything for even one hour more sleep. I opened my bedside table and took a pill from the bottle inside, swallowing it without water. I coughed on it a minute before it got all the way down. I scanned the room. Dirty laundry scattered the floor. The bed sheet was half off the mattress; I'd been sleeping on mostly bare mattress all night. The air smelled like sour breastmilk and old spit up. It wasn't only this room that was a disaster. Our whole house looked like a tornado had run through it.

As much as I loved my son, he probably wouldn't be here if my first baby had lived, and that fact destroyed me. Every moment I had with him felt like I was betraying her memory. And every moment I pined for her, I neglected him. I did not know how to exist this way, my heart so divided. I did not feel like a fit mother.

Marc's fussing escalated into cries, and he thrashed his arms and legs in the monitor's video-feed. I couldn't postpone any longer. I stepped to the ground, my foot landing in a pile of soaked breast pads.

"Dammit." My dry throat constricted. I wiped my foot off on the carpet.

I grabbed a stained top and some sweatpants from off the floor. The same clothes I'd worn yesterday. And the day before. When was the last time I changed my underwear? I switched out the breast pads currently in my sports bra, disposing of the soaked ones with some wilted cabbage leaves, adding them to the pile on the floor. I made a mental note to get a garbage bag during Marc's afternoon nap and collect all the trash from around the bedroom.

After I dressed, I turned to the mirror hanging on the back of the door to tie my hair up in a bun. I didn't recognize the figure in the reflection. I paused to look her up and down: inches wider than she used to be, hair greasy from days without washing, old mascara smeared under her eyes, and dressed like she should be climbing back under the covers.

Marc's crying became hysterical. I tore myself from the mirror and left the bedroom.

"Coming." I crossed the hall and opened the door to Marc's room.

He flailed, his chubby arms and legs freed from his swaddle. When he saw me come through the door he started to scream. His face was beet red, and fat tears rolled down his cheeks.

"Well, what do you want?" I spoke and signed. I was hoping that by signing he'd learn how to communicate sooner. Having a baby was a constant guessing game, and I wished so badly he could communicate what he needed when he was upset. I approached the crib and he quieted, looking at me with furrowed brows as if to say, *how could you abandon me?*

I reached out and his arms wiggled around like he was trying to figure out how to reach back. I picked him up and let his head rest against my shoulder. He rooted around. "I'm sorry, I wish I could. You'll have to wait for a bottle."

I started peeling the swaddle off. As I moved my hand down to support his bum, something wet and sticky greeted it.

"Shit." My hand lifted away covered in a thin sheen of yellow-brown liquid. It was soaked through the back of his sleeper. "Literally. Shit." The stench was obvious now. I don't know how I missed it before.

I held him under his arms, lifting him away from me so the swaddle dropped to the floor. He was leaking in the front too, and there were two lines of the yellow-brown sheen painted up my shirt where I'd held him against me. I stared at the wall behind the crib and my breathing got faster and faster and my mind detached itself, leaving behind a numbness, then Marc started screaming again, and a vibration surged through me like I was going to explode and each breath shook my chest and hot tears fell over my cheeks. Which crisis do I address first? His hunger or his mess? I wanted to crawl back in bed.

The doorbell rang, and I jumped at the noise. I pulled Marc back against my chest, wiping my face with the back of my forearm. I carried him with me to the door, both of us still crying. I checked the peephole. Ms. Maudie was standing on the front porch, wearing yellow from head to toe—yellow flip flops, yellow cut offs, yellow t-shirt, and a yellow headband with her graying bangs sticking out the front.

I opened the door, trying to stifle my own tears.

"Hello de–" her eyes fell on the soaked back of Marc's sleeper. "Oh, I'm sorry if this is a bad time, I—" she trailed off, surveying my tear-stained and puffy face. Marc was still crying. "Oh honey, can I help?" She put a hand on my shoulder, and that small human touch undid me. I hung my head and let the sobs take over.

She squeezed my shoulder with her hand. "Oh, it'll be alright. Come on, show me to a bathroom."

We made our way to the bathroom and she immediately got busy filling up the baby tub. She took a towel off the rack on the wall and laid it down on the floor, then reached out for Marc. "May I?"

I nodded and handed him carefully over. My tears had slowed, but I was somehow incapable of using my voice. She laid him down on the towel and started to remove his soiled clothes.

"Do you have a plastic grocery bag?" she asked. I nodded silently and left to retrieve one. When I came back Marc was in the tub and the sleeper was soaking in the sink. I gave her the bag and she put the diaper inside, tying it up tight.

I noticed an envelope next to her on the floor.

"The mail boy misdelivered it," she said, catching my gaze. "It says *time sensitive* on the front."

She passed it to me and I pinched it with my clean fingers. It was addressed to Danny. I didn't recognize the return address, so I put it on the vanity for the time being. It was probably a credit card ad.

Marc's cries escalated.

"Hungry?" Ms. Maudie asked. But she answered her own question when I hesitated. "Silly me, how could he not be after emptying all that out?" She laughed. "It's overwhelming, isn't it," she smiled at me empathetically. "I re-member those days."

Her yellow clothes matched the bathmat.

"I'm Daisy," she said, and held out her hand.

"Eleanor." I stepped forward and leaned over to shake it, but then remembered my hand was covered in poop and turned instead to the sink.

"Ah, thanks for catching that," she chuckled, softly. "It's lovely to officially meet you, Eleanor."

"Your garden is beautiful." My voice sounded small and far away.

"Thank you. It was my husband's. Now I tend it for his memory."

"Oh, I'm sorry for your loss."

"It's alright dear, it's been almost ten years now."

She looked at my shirt. "You can go change if you'd like. I'll watch him."

I went back to the bedroom to put on a new shirt. Then I detoured to the kitchen to make up a bottle. Marc's fussing filled the house, so I hurried. When I returned, I added my soiled shirt to the sink and handed Daisy the bottle.

"You have children?" I asked. The tears were finally drying on my cheeks. My skin felt tight from all the salt.

"All grown now. I have twins about your age. And a son a couple years older." She took the bottle and fed Marc while he sat in the bath water.

"Any grandchildren?"

"Not yet."

We sat in silence for a moment as Marc splashed around, suckling and grabbing at his toes. Daisy used the hand that wasn't holding the bottle to clean his legs with a washcloth.

"How old is this little one?"

"Four months."

She smiled at him warmly. "So little. So overwhelmed by the world. It's all so new and surprising, isn't it?"

Daisy helped me dry and dress Marc and then offered to make breakfast. My heart felt the smallest bit lighter with her sincere kindness. And my soul was relieved by the much-needed interruption from my daily grind and inner turmoil.

She sat with me as we had coffee. I had decaf; my new medication didn't mix well with caffeine. It made the insomnia worse. She asked for decaf too, I think out of solidarity because she didn't know I wasn't breastfeeding.

We chatted about sleepless nights and life before kids. She told stories about her kids' worst blowouts and times when she'd also spent days overwhelmed and crying alone at home.

"Ben's longest business trip was around the holidays." Daisy's eyes glazed over as she recounted the memory. Ben was her late husband. "Four weeks. Those were the loneliest four weeks of my life. There was one day, I don't remember what happened, but the kids had me on the end of my rope. I fell apart in front of them."

A shadow moved across her face—possibly the slightest of winces. "The poor kids were dumbfounded. They all stood there watching until Sara finally came up and hugged me. Oh, she must've been six or seven at the time. Her little arms wrapped around my thighs." Daisy smiled, her eyes filled with nostalgia. My face mirrored hers, like I was remembering with her.

"I put on a Christmas album and we all laid down under the tree. It must've been a sight," she chuckled. "Four bodies sticking out, heads hidden by the bottom boughs. We looked up through the branches at the lights. It became our new tradition. Every year we played music and crawled under the tree." Daisy's eyes crinkled in the corners as they fell back onto me. Her brown skin was pleasantly worn, like she'd lived a happy life so far. There was something about the lines and wrinkles of a face that could reveal the kind of life a person had lived. There were stories there.

The hours slipped away until it was lunchtime. We felt like friends already, and I trusted her, so I confided in her about my diagnosis.

"I'm so glad you're getting help," she said after I mentioned therapy. "I most definitely had post-partum depression with my first baby, and then probably again with the twins. But back then it wasn't well recognized. I never had any help with it. Or even knew what to call it."

"How did you get out of it?" I asked.

Daisy's lips flattened, and I guessed the answer before she spoke. "I didn't." My heart dropped like a stone.

"But things are better, now." Her eyes brightened as they met mine. "About ten years ago I finally saw a doctor who recognized what was going on."

"When your husband died?"

She nodded. "My kids helped me find a grief counselor. It helped."

Though her eyes were smiling, there was pain hidden behind them—pain I knew well. They were the eyes of a woman who has lost something precious.

We paused our conversation to put Marc down for his nap, and I invited her to stay for lunch. She insisted on buying us takeout. "The break in routine will do you good." We ordered from a Peruvian place she said her father had loved because it reminded him of homecooked meals growing up in Peru, before he immigrated to the states.

We talked about ourselves outside of motherhood and depression. She was thrilled to find out I was an ASL interpreter. We laughed, and the years between us shrunk into inconsequential, arbitrary numbers. It was as though we lived parallel lives, she was just ahead of me on the timeline. My mom would've said our souls knew each other from another life.

Shortly after lunch, Marc woke up and I left the kitchen to get him. When I returned, Daisy had wandered to the living room. She stood by the fireplace holding a small picture taken from the mantle. I froze in the hallway. She heard me and looked up.

"Who is this little one?" she asked, holding up the photo.

The photo was of me. Me in a hospital bed holding a tiny body. A hand-quilted baby blanket with flowers and butterflies in pinks, purples, and yellow almost swallowed the tiny form.

Daisy saw my face and put the picture down, quickly changing the subject.

We made more small talk, but I was now guarded. My mind spiraled into its dark hole, and not even Daisy's pure compassion could coax me out. The was sun hanging low by now anyway, casting angles of light into the living room that reflected off dust particles in the air. Daisy made the polite pleasantries of leaving, along with a promise to do this again sometime. I responded appropriately, but she knew I had closed off. She hugged me tenderly, telling me to knock on her door if I ever needed anything. Her arms were surprisingly strong, and she smelled like green leaves and roses. I chastised myself inwardly for shutting down, shutting out.

"It's ok, Eleanor." She spoke as if she could hear my inner thoughts. "I understand."

A familiar kind of comfort filled my chest, like when you're a kid and your mom held you after a nightmare.

Danny came home a few minutes later. I sat on the couch, holding Marc as he cried for some unknown reason. Danny saw my face, and I knew he could read me immediately. He always could tell when I was thinking of her. He joined me on the couch wordlessly and pulled me into him. The three of us sat there huddled together. Against Danny's chest I felt that same warm comfort. It was safety. Home.

13

Red

Rose, 1972

Blood. That's how he found me. I'd drawn a bath after the kids went to bed. The cramps that started earlier that afternoon had become unbearable. The bleeding was so heavy, I had to stuff a hand towel in my underwear. I hoped a soak in hot water and Epsom salts would do me some good. Thomas was still at work, and I needed a distraction from worrying about the inevitable conversation we would have when he got home.

I poured a glass of wine and brought it with me to the bath, letting the alcohol dull my senses. I stared at the rings on my hand, holding the wine glass. The family ring didn't fit with the wedding band Thomas had chosen for me. I turned the ring around, so the stone was hidden under my fingers, and looked away. Shadows danced on the rosy, pink walls, made by flickering candlelight, and my eye lids relinquished their fight against exhaustion.

Then I was in a lake, like the one we used to stay at every summer with grandma and grandpa Dillard. I was young again, and so was Lily. She was in a black two piece that Pa would not have approved of. She stood up in grandpa's canoe, waving at me as I tread water by the dock. The boat bobbed up and down like a lullaby. I dove into the water and swam towards her. My bathing suit was bright red, and as I swam, the water turned red around me in swirls, like the suit was leaking color. I got to the boat and lifted myself up, but Lily was gone. Instead, there was a baby lying on the floor of the canoe. Water was filling it up fast. I picked the infant up and began to swim back to shore, holding her above the water in one arm and propelling us forward with the other. My bathing suit dyed the white linens she was wrapped in. They looked like spots of blood.

I made it to shore and laid her down on the muddy bank while I caught my breath. When I looked back at the water, the whole lake had turned red. My bathing suit dripped red water down my legs. I knelt by the baby and moved the blanket away from her face. I gasped. The baby was Carol.

"Rose!" Thomas yelled, waking me with a start.

The bathwater was pink.

He found me, stained and helpless, swimming in my own evidence of failure. My own female contradiction. Shameful and barren.

He drained the bath and helped me out, but my legs were weak. He asked me if I knew how much blood I'd lost. I understood what his words meant, but I couldn't sort them out in my head. Everything was blurry—in my eyes and in my mind. My consciousness was locked away behind a wall of numbing passivity. He called Ma to come stay with the kids then carried me out to our car.

The next moment I was aware, I was lying in a bed in a small room. Bulky layers of incontinence pads were stuffed under and between my legs. White cotton, white walls, white sheets, white gown—and I am red.

I am always red.

An IV tube coming out of my arm was attached to a bag filled with clear fluid. I felt nauseated and dizzy. My sight blurred every time I turned my head.

The doctor came in. White coat, white hair, red lips.

He called it an ultrasound machine. Strange shapes grew and shrank across a tiny screen. When he pulled out the wand it was dripping red.

Words drifted to my ears, understanding but not listening.

Incomplete spontaneous abortion.

Septate Uterus.

Inviable.

Barren.

The doctor left to give us a moment, and we each had ours in our own way. We were two people in different worlds, trapped in the same nightmare—the same Shakespearean tragedy. And we all know how the tragedies end.

Thomas sat silently by as they pumped new blood into my veins and performed a procedure to dilate my cervix and remove the fetus. *Fetus*. I hated the cold, clinical feel of the word, but in this moment it was the more bearable word to use.

The next morning, the nurses prepared me for discharge. "Doctor says she needs to go on the pill," she said, handing Thomas a prescription. "If she gets pregnant 'gain, it's likely it'll end up jus' like this. And she lost a dangerous amount of blood. We don' want that again."

Thomas nodded, taking the prescription and folding it neatly.

We drove in silence. Thomas stopped by the pharmacy to pick up the pills.

Barren.

The word floated in the stale air of my mind, filling it like cotton, pressing on the boundaries of my skull.

"We don't have to tell your mom about these," Thomas said, when he returned to the car. It didn't matter, anyhow. Even without the pills, I would still be unable to... I would always be red.

We pulled up the driveway and Thomas killed the engine. We each sat in that same silence, unmoving, feeling the unspoken wave of pain connecting us in a horrifying way.

"Rose," Thomas spoke, low and quiet.

I stared out the windshield at small specks of dirty rain stains.

"Rose," he repeated, shifting in the driver's seat to look at me straight on.

I didn't look at him, begging him in my mind to leave me be. I couldn't do it; I couldn't take the disappointment. I wasn't enough—not for him or anyone. I was unable to do what a woman was supposed to be able to do. The very thing my body was supposed to be constructed for.

He sighed, then got out of the car. He walked around to my door and opened it, reaching around me to unbuckle the seatbelt. It was humiliating.

"Can you walk?"

I nodded, but he grabbed me around my waist anyway, propping me up as we shuffled up the walk to the front door. The distance was dizzying. We paused by the door so Thomas could free a hand to open it. I closed my eyes to steady myself. But when they closed, instead of black, I saw red.

14

Sociology 101

Lillian, 1993

Grace didn't bring up my drinking again. And she never set me up again. She made up for that night's blunder with a steady re-earning of trust, keeping boundaries and letting me instigate our nights out for a while. She also didn't push me to share where I was at in regards to my sexuality, and I was grateful for that. The revelation was new to me, and I wasn't sure what it meant or what I wanted. As far as I knew, I'd never met anyone who was attracted to both men and women. While I couldn't deny that I cared for Grace as more than just a friend, this all could be a rebellion against society that would get us hurt for real. I'd done a lot of things that would upset my family, but always knowing exactly how they'd react. Dating a woman—I had no idea what they'd do or say. I had self-inflicted my estrangement, and I liked knowing that I was in control of that. I liked the idea that once the divorce was finalized there'd be nothing they could do, and with that security I could go back home anytime I wanted. It was like having training wheels. I wasn't so sure I'd be able to keep the training wheels if I came out as bisexual. Mom would never disown me, but I didn't know about Dad. He was difficult to read. My grandfather would've shunned me without hesitation.

I learned that while Grace still attended Catholic mass on Christmas and Easter with her brother and his family, the rest of the year she went to a small, non-denominational congregation that was gay-friendly. Her continued devotion to religion was strange to me. I had explored the idea of spirituality, after my encounter with Amanda over a year ago, but I was still wary of organized worship. Missouri wasn't quite so bad as Alabama, especially in St. Louis, but prejudice and self-righteous zealots existed everywhere. I was already a single mom and newly divorced. So, I stayed on the outside of church doors. I think Grace understood all of this, innately.

Niles took his first steps at Grace's house. We sat on the ground across from each other passing him back and forth, arms outstretched and ready to steady him or help him back up when he fell. Grace excused herself in the middle of it, and when she returned it looked like she'd been crying. She was there for his first words, too. She celebrated the milestones with me like she was part of the family. For all her talk about never having kids, she sure loved Niles. I wasn't sure if she was against kids in general, or simply against herself getting impregnated.

She had been lonely before we came along. While she had a fairly close relationship with her brother, she wasn't out to him. That made it different. With me, she let her guard down. I cherished that. And it filled me with a measure of pride. I liked that she was closer to me than anyone else. I liked that I was her safe person. I found myself blushing with the tinges of green envy whenever she showed familiarity with anyone else.

"You're like Niles's second mom," I'd told her once, late at night as we watched some soap opera.

She'd looked at me, the light from the TV screen casting highlights and shadows across her face. Her eyes had glowed, literally like a deer's in headlights. But they weren't fearful. They held an affection I'd never quite experienced from anyone else before.

"I love him," had been her whispered response, barely audible above the TV. Later, I wondered if she hadn't said, *I love* you. I couldn't decide which it had been.

The symposium was the first thing Grace had invited me to in a long time. She was there to read an excerpt from her upcoming book in preparation for its release. It took place in a large lecture hall at the university. There were at least a hundred people in her audience. The seats were in a sort of semicircle around the podium and blackboard, each row ascending like it was an intellectual stadium.

I felt out of place there. I was sure I stuck out like a sore thumb. I was the same age as the college students in the audience, but I was convinced they could all see right through me—that I was a fraud being there. The single mom, high school dropout.

I sat in the front row on the very end, offering smiles whenever Grace glanced in my direction. She was an excellent public speaker. If I didn't know her mannerisms as well as I did I wouldn't have been able to tell she was nervous. But I did know her, and I saw what no one else saw: the twitch of her eyebrow, her eyes growing infinitesimally wider whenever someone raised their hand to ask a question, and the way she caught my eyes in hers when she scanned the crowd.

But my smiles caught his attention, too.

He was on the other side of the semicircle, almost directly across from me. In the second row. He had his dark hair gelled perfectly and wore a suit and tie, his long legs stretching out from under the desk. His body language said he owned the space he was in. He looked too mature, too well dressed to be a student. I caught him staring when my eyes wandered across the rows of desks. Instead of quickly looking away as most people do when they accidentally lock eyes with someone, he kept his gaze steady and grinned when I found him, holding his eyes on mine.

The kind of men you meet at an intellectual event are the kind of men you picture a future with. They're the ones who you want to call you the next day. Who sleep over and make you breakfast. They're stable. I'd always been attracted to a well-educated man—perhaps it was that southern conditioning. It was hypocritical, considering my own history. But underneath my fearless rebellion there was the all too human need for security. That hadn't changed even after how poorly things ended up with Don.

"A mixed episode is not the same as rapid cycling, where the mania and depressed mood are still separate and distinct—" Grace looked quickly at me as she answered a student's question, and I smiled at her encouragingly. She reciprocated with the tiniest lift in the corners of her mouth as she spoke, then continued to scan the audience.

My eyes drifted back in his direction. He was still staring. His eyes were dark, and damn, but they could pierce a heart from across the room. I brought my hand up and rested my chin in it, pointedly turning my attention away from him and towards Grace. I feigned disinterest. *I'm not here to flirt with you, Mr. Man.* But the rest of my body stayed hyper-alert to his attention.

After Grace finished her presentation, the audience filtered out to make their way to other classrooms for other panels. I waited at the chalkboard behind her, leaning back against it. Some lingering students lined up to shake her hand or ask more questions.

He approached.

"You a friend of Dr. Bird?" Now that he was closer, I could guess he was probably in his mid or late-thirties—around Grace's age—still in physical prime, but also experienced.

"Yes," I extended my hand. "I'm Lillian." I put on a façade of academic professionalism. But I felt like those eyes could see into my soul.

He took my hand and shook it. "Dr. Harry Allman."

"Pleasure, Dr. Allman."

"Call me Harry."

"Alright, Harry." My eyes narrowed playfully. "You're obviously not a student. What brings you here?"

"I teach here, in the sociology department."

"Sociology?"

He nodded.

"What's a sociology professor doing at a psychology symposium?"

"What do you know about sociology?"

My façade melted away. "Absolutely nothing," I admitted, laughing. He laughed with me.

"We both study people," he gestured at Grace, who was still conversing with students. "The difference is that Dr. Bird studies the mind of the individual. I study groups of people and their interactions."

I raised my eyebrows, "So today you were studying the group of people that comes to a talk about mood disorders?"

Harry chuckled. "Today my interest was interdisciplinary." I couldn't deny my attraction to a man using intelligent words like *interdisciplinary*.

Grace finished up with the last couple of students and started collecting her things. I started edging her direction. Harry's stance turned with me.

"And is your interest here academic or pleasure?" He emphasized *pleasure*, filling it with double meaning. I didn't know if she was out at work, but he spoke like he knew.

"I'm the moral support." I feigned a brag, flipping my hair from my shoulder flirtatiously. Okay, he'd intrigued me a little. For a millisecond, so subtle I wasn't sure if I imagined it, he looked disappointed. Like I wasn't going to be the challenge he wanted me to be. But he said, "in that case, I have to get your number."

Nice try. "Sorry, I'm afraid my moral support services are proprietary."

He smiled at my joke, then leaned in like he was going to hug me or kiss my cheek, stopping just short. "I'll let you get back to it, then."

I half waved as he turned to leave. "Banks." I'd tried to say bye and thanks at once. My cheeks flushed.

But he was already walking away, so I prayed to whatever power existed that he hadn't heard me.

Grace approached, the last of the students and professors trickling out. "Sorry about the wait," she said, linking her arm in mine before leading us out of the classroom.

"It wasn't long." Our feet moved in sync, without effort from either one of us. She took two steps for every one of mine. The sound of our shoes on the hard floors made a *clop, click click*, *clop, click click*, with every step.

We grabbed our things from a chair by the lecture hall's door—Grace's satchel and my purse.

"What'd you think?"

"It was really great. You're the smartest person I've ever known, Grace. Like, wow."

She smiled wide, her eyes sparkling from the praise. I forgot all about Harry Allman in that moment.

"Thanks, I think it really did go well."

Grace drove us back to her house where we picked up Niles. Grace's sister-in-law had babysat for me this afternoon since Olive was in school. I hugged Grace goodbye with a final *congratulations*, then drove home.

I carried Niles up the single flight of stairs to our apartment door. The stairs creaked with every step. The sound had become familiar and welcoming over the last couple years. At the top, I reached into my purse for my keys. A corner of something brushed up against my fingers. I pulled it out. It was a business card.

Harry Allman, PhD
Professor of Sociology
Washington University

I turned it over. Written on the back in scrolling letters he had written: *Dinner at Liverne's, 8:00 Sunday*

My heart fluttered. Apparently my rejection had enticed him. But damn, he was smooth.

15

Act Your Age

Eleanor, 2019

Aliza said it was a good idea to be around other moms. But God, I hated mommy group. Everyone bragged about their kids hitting milestones early—some of the babies Marc's age were already walking along furniture. There were a couple other moms like me, showing up in sweatpants and old baggy t-shirts, no makeup and hair in knots. But all the other moms came in expensive yoga pants and smoothed out ponytails at best, and at worst high heels and freshly curled beach waves.

One week, some of the moms started talking about careers they left, and after that there were two distinct cliques in mommy group—the moms returning to work, and the moms staying home. But even among my fellow working moms I felt like an outsider. They consistently complained about how much they wished they could stay home, and how they were only working because they couldn't afford to live on one income. There must've been something wrong with me, not feeling the same way. Even if Danny and I could afford for me to stay home indefinitely, I wouldn't want to. I didn't say that, though. I worried it would look like I didn't love my kid as much. My anxiety over leaving Marc had subsided with the medication and was replaced by a need to be alone. Right now, I was only working on the weekends and a couple evenings a week, but I loved the break from the house. And the break from Marc, honestly. Aliza said that was normal and even healthy, but I didn't dare reveal my true feelings to the other moms. I wanted to feel like a real human being—outside of being a mom. And so many of the other moms there had already had a chance to have a career. Most were ten years or so older than me, with years of life experiences already lived. I had decided so young that what I wanted more than anything in the world was to have kids. I worried now that I'd jumped the gun. What experiences might I have had if we'd waited before getting pregnant the first time—when my world shattered, and I became so much older than my age?

I used to feel my age. I remember high school, coasting along the drive that went past our house, my best friend at the wheel while I sat in the passenger seat holding a long neon tube of bubbles. The windows had been rolled all the way down and the radio turned all the way up. I dipped the bubble wand, pumping it up and down before sticking it out the window. The wind around the car blew through the wand, bubbles streaming next to us. Most of them popped almost immediately, but some floated in the reflection of the side mirror, drifting away up towards the treetops.

We sang at the tops of our lungs but were still drowned out by the radio. Wind stung my eyes and made them water.

If I could escape and recreate a place that's my own world, and I could be your favorite girl...

My phone rang, I didn't recognize the number, so I ignored it.

I didn't mean for you to get hurt...

Voicemail.

I turned the radio down and listened. One hand held my blackberry phone and the other the neon tube, bubble solution dripping onto my fingers.

"Who is it?"

She glanced at me, and when she saw my eyes she rolled up the windows and silenced the radio, mid *sweet escape*.

"I need to go to the hospital," I said.

I remember that day clearer than any other. In the hospital I'd found my grandparents waiting for me. They didn't want me to see her like that, but I'd insisted. She was lying in a hospital bed, asleep. A police officer stood nearby, writing on a clipboard. Grandpa stood next to him and watched what he wrote. She was hooked up to an IV, her arm bandaged from wrist to elbow, and the doctor explained that she would need a blood transfusion.

"I don't understand," I'd said to grandpa. "What happened?"

Grandma had answered before he could. "She had an accident in the kitchen."

Her tone warned me not to push the matter further.

The doctors ignored me after that, speaking only to my grandparents. Their eyes shifted in my direction as they lowered their voices to whispers. Grandpa remained silent. Grandma would nod and utter *thank you*s.

I slipped past the curtain that gave the ER pod some semblance of privacy and wandered down a dead-end hallway with vending machines and a family bathroom. I waited until the voices of some nurses in the adjoining hallway faded away, then pulled out my blackberry, hitting speed dial 3 for my brother. He'd been across the country in California for college.

"Grandma's not telling me what happened," I told him in hushed tones.

"Of course, she isn't. But it's obvious, anyway."

"Right," I said, drawing out the vowel. I shuffled my feet.

"Wait." There was surprise in his voice. "They still haven't told you?"

I froze in place, my heart falling into my stomach. A million thoughts ran through my head, like a list of catastrophic headlines on a news site. Was she sick? Dying?

"It's so not my job to tell you this," he continued, uneasily. "But...she did this to herself, El. She cut herself."

It wasn't until he'd said it aloud that I realized I'd always known, deep down; my mom was depressed. Not just depressed, suicidal.

"She told you she's depressed but not me?"

He sighed, and his breath crackled in the phone. "No, grandpa told me. A few years ago. They're probably just trying to protect you, El."

When I was little, my mom had been infallible in my eyes. She was the kickass single mom like in the movies. Even when it stared me in the face, I refused to admit to her having any kind of weakness. But that day changed everything. I started to think of my childhood differently. The weeks she'd spent in bed all day every day, the nights she'd come home drunk, the looks exchanged between my grandparents...she'd been lying to me, all this time. She was always telling me my mental illnesses were nothing to be ashamed of and yet she had kept her own from me. What had angered me the most was that hypocrisy.

A couple years before that hospital trip, she had coaxed my secret darkness out of me. I was sitting on my bed after school, instant messaging my best friend on my laptop. She had stood in the doorway holding a book against her chest.

"What?"

She stepped cautiously into the room. "Hey."

"You're being weird, Mom."

"Sorry." She sat down on the bed, placing the book on the comforter in front of me. It was my copy of *The Bell Jar*. I set my laptop aside.

"It's beautiful." She searched my eyes.

My breathing sounded too loud.

"Sad, too." Her eyes continued to search. I knew she wasn't talking about Sylvia Plath's words. Like so many of my other books, I had written in the margins of *The Bell Jar*'s pages. The words I wrote in Plath's only novel were in a similar tone as her story contained in its pages. I had written poems. Melancholy poems.

"It's okay to feel overwhelming sadness, sometimes. To be lonely. You can talk to me about it."

I shrugged.

She breathed in deep. "It's ok if you can't talk to me. We can get someone else for you to talk to."

"What, a shrink?" I gawked.

Her lips bent in a sort of grimace. "A therapist, yes. There's no shame in getting help, baby."

I turned away and stared at my knees, tucked up against my chest.

"I'll let you think about it." She kissed my head, then left the room.

She'd found me my first therapist. She drove me to all my sessions. Grandfather paid for them—he had insisted. I later found out he'd told her it's what he wished he'd done for her when she was my age.

What my mom didn't realize was the lesson she had taught me inadvertently. She taught me that moms do everything for their children, and nothing for themselves. That moms aren't allowed to struggle. They have to keep it hidden.

Now that I was a mom myself, I was even more upset with her. Not for the self-harm or even the essential ending of my childhood. I was upset with her because to this day she'd never admitted to me that she was ever sick. She pretended that day in the hospital had never happened.

Before becoming a mom, I'd taken her advice; I hadn't been ashamed of my struggles. The world was growing more accepting of my neurology, more open about anxiety and depression. But post-partum OCD? No one talked about that. And ingrained deep in my psyche was the image of a mother who did not allow weakness in herself, who tried to hide her darkness away so that it never touched her children. I hated myself for being weak. I would stare in my baby's face and loathe the darkness inside of me that threatened his perfect light.

I'm twenty-five now, but I don't feel it. I feel much older, my youth slipping between my fingers like fine sand. My peers were always posting online posing in rave outfits, in sequined dresses holding elaborate cocktails at nightclubs, or on beaches in Mexico in bikini bottoms cut high above their hips with waif-like waists and pleasantly round asses featured in the most flattering angles. My Friday nights involved poopy diapers, reruns of *Gossip Girl*, and crashing in bed by nine.

The days were lonely when Daisy, my Ms. Maudie, was too tired to stop by. On those days I was left alone with Marc. And with my thoughts. Aliza had taught me to visualize my intrusive thoughts, to play them out and determine what I would do in the worst-case scenario. It was a way to turn the intrusions around into something empowering. *It's like practice. If you practice the worst-case scenario, you'll feel more in control.*

I imagined that my mental illness would make Marc resent me. That he'd grow up waiting for the day he could leave home. But I wasn't even sure what I wished my own mom had done differently. What I wanted was my childhood back, and that was impossible. How would I make sure I didn't rob Marc of his childhood? The visualization didn't work so well on this one.

I was lying in bed, Marc next to me watching cartoons on my phone. It was a routine we'd picked up when I was too tired to do anything. I watched him, watching the screen. This wasn't what I had imagined when I pictured myself as a mom.

In college, my roommates used to joke about how I'd be the first to have kids. How I'd make my own organic baby food, do all the mommy-and-me classes, and keep an immaculate house. They were right about me being the first to become a mom, but the rest was bullshit. I couldn't blame them for the expectations—I was always an over-achiever and a perfectionist. I was one of those kids who did the extra credit even though I already had an A. I never would have imagined myself like this. In mommy group I felt like the at-risk dropout. The one just trying to get a passing grade.

I reached over and pulled Marc to me. His eyelids were fluttering. I turned off the nursery rhyme show playing on my phone and wrapped him against me in his blanket. I felt his breathing, the rise and fall of his little body, pressed against my chest. His eyes closed and his breathing slowed. The gush of warm air from his nose against my cheek calmed me. I relaxed, knowing that in my arms he was safe. Maybe I wasn't making him baby food from scratch or killing it at mommy group, but here he was, breathing in my arms. He was alive. And I of all people knew not to take that for granted.

16

Blind as a Mother

Rose, 1972

You girls can be anythin' you wanna be. Ma used to say that when Lily and I were young. We used to always watch her paint. She'd take her easel out to the garden and immortalize the flowers in watercolors or oils.

"What did you wanna be when you were a kid, Ma?" Lily had asked her one day.

She'd paused mid-stroke on a Juliet Rose petal. "I wanted to paint."

"So, you got what you wanted," I said. Lily glared at me, and I knew there was something she understood because she was older. I was annoyed that she seemed to be on the inside while I stayed ignorant and too young to understand. When she became a teenager, I'd felt I'd been left behind. She was beautiful and popular, and developed an interest in things like makeup and dating while I still wanted to have campouts in the backyard and sleep under the stars while she read me *The Secret Garden* or *Pippi Longstocking*. I still wanted to pretend we were orphans, fighting to survive in a grownup's world by keeping the magic in our imaginations alive.

But Ma answered my unspoken question, in a way that I never fully understood until now. And perhaps Lily hadn't fully understood back then either. "Sometimes what we want changes with the changing of seasons, like a hound wants outdoors until it starts to rain. You girls are what I never knew I wanted."

Lily rolled her eyes.

"But you still paint," I said.

"I do." She looked at me thoughtfully. "I have more than many wives 'round here could hope for. But that don't mean I don't want more for you girls."

"More than being a painter?"

She chuckled. "You could be a painter if you wanted, honey. You can do anythin' you want. Just do it bigger. And louder. And don't let any fool get in your way. 'Specially a man."

"Not another pep talk 'bout college, Ma." Lily said.

Ma fixed on Lily sternly. "You best thank your lucky stars you have that option, Lily." She looked at both of us. "But no, I wasn't gonna bring it up just now. What I'm doin' is askin' you girls a favor."

This time Lily appeared as much in the dark as I was.

Ma looked in each of our eyes with an earnestness I'd never seen in her before or since. "Do what I couldn't."

I sat in the empty bathtub, wet from a shower. The water had gone cold, but I wasn't ready to leave, so I'd shut it off and sat while the water dripped off my skin. That cotton headache hadn't gone away. The doctor said it could be a side effect of the blood loss. But I attributed it to that word: *barren*. A side effect of crushed dreams, broken marriages, and worthless women. That wasn't true though—I didn't believe other childless women would be worthless. Just me. I couldn't explain why the rules were different for me. They just were.

Outside the bathroom door, Thomas redirected Carol's wobbling steps back down the hall to the kitchen. A chill went through me, and an aching feeling grew up from my bones. I lifted my head and stared at the bathroom wall. My mind planned. Plotted. I needed to free Thomas of this bond my father had forced upon us. Free him from me. He had always wanted kids—little versions of himself wandering about. He should find someone new, someone able to give him what he wanted. Pa certainly wouldn't blame him. When Lily had announced her pregnancy with Eugene, he'd said: *At least she's givin' us grandchildren. She ain't a total loss.*

In college I wrote a 25-page analysis of the Bronte sisters' tragic romances—the ones they wrote about and the ones they lived. Women have so much more now than they had back then, and yet I, a modern woman, still found myself a dependent housewife, defining my honor by what my uterus could or couldn't do.

I got out of the tub and put on a clean pair of underwear, stuffing in one of the huge pads from the hospital. I slipped into my lavender housecoat. I was still damp, but I didn't have the energy or the motivation to dry off with a towel. I peeked out the bathroom door. One of Ma's records was playing in the living room. Thomas had filled her in on everything. She stayed to help us get settled in for my recovery. I was grateful she did; the doctor instructed I should rest for at least two days. Thomas had called the firm as soon as we got home, arranging to take the rest of the week off, which was approved easily—one of the perks of being a big shot lawyer now instead of just a clerk. But even with him home it was comforting to have Ma there to take care of the things Thomas had no inkling of how to do, like laundry and cooking. She had spent the morning and part of the afternoon making casseroles and other meals to stock up our freezer with.

The hallway felt long as I moved down it to the master bedroom, wishing not for the first time that we had an ensuite bathroom. Opening the bedroom door, I slipped in, shutting it gently behind me.

"How are you feelin', sweetheart?"

I jumped and whipped around. Ma was hanging clean laundry up in the closet.

"You gave me a fright, Ma. I didn't know you were in here."

"I'll be out your way in a minute." She smoothed out a freshly ironed dress shirt and hung it on Thomas's side of the closet. The bed had been made with fresh sheets. The floral comforter was spread neatly and turned down with the top sheet. She'd also put down an incontinence pad. The corner of it poked out from under the covers. I wrinkled my nose but sat on it anyway. It crinkled under me.

Ma paused, holding my long, navy-blue skirt that she'd picked out from the basket, and turned to inspect me. The bottom of the skirt draped down from her hands, dipped in gold and orange embroidery.

"I don't know what to say, Rosie."

A flush of heat crashed over me, and I was suddenly very aware of my naked body beneath the bathrobe. My head started spinning. I brought my legs up onto the bed and sat back against the pillow, relaxing my head back against the wall. The pad crunched between my legs, and under my bum, and I shifted my hips uncomfortably. I didn't want to talk right now. I didn't want to see her disappointment—not only for this loss, but because now she knew I'd kept all the pregnancies from her.

"I 'spose first, I oughtta say I'm sorry. For what you've been goin' through."

I braced myself for what came second.

"I just…" she trailed off, then put the skirt back in the basket and came to sit next to me on the bed. I scooted over a little to make room between me and the edge for her. "I just wish you'd told me. Thinkin' 'bout you losin' all those babies, alone—"

"I wasn't alone, Ma."

Her eyebrows furrowed.

"I had Thomas."

She smiled sympathetically. "Ah, well sweetheart, men don't experience it the way we do. They're losin' somethin' they never really had in the first place. Which is still tragic of course, don't misunderstand. But mothers…we held those babies. We carried 'em for however long. It's a different kinda loss."

We sat in silence for a moment as her words sunk in. "You've lost a baby, Ma."

"Yes, sweetie. At least five."

I inhaled in a quiet gasp.

She reached out and took my hand. "After all those years I'd lost hope. You were my little miracle, Rosebud."

My body was heavy, so I let it fall against her. My head rested against her shoulder, like it had so many times when I was a girl at a loss for answers. She wrapped her arms around my shoulders, hugging me to her almost desperately.

"They want me to take the pill." I waited for the shock—the judgement.

She sighed deeply and squeezed me tighter. "And you best take it. I'm not 'bout to lose both my girls."

I looked up at her, eyes wide.

"Oh, don't act so surprised, Rosie. Where do you think you got all your feminism from? But you better not tell your Pa 'bout it. Come to think of it, let me handle him. I'll tell him the doctor said you can't get pregnant. No need for him to know why or how."

I realized I'd been putting her in a box, the same box as Pa. Her complete understanding gave me the courage to confide in her the fears I'd been harboring. "I don't know how to be their mother. I barely knew how to be an aunt 'fore all this." My voice was barely audible above the serenades that filtered in from down the hall.

"No woman on God's green earth knows how. Not at first. Even those of us that carried an' birthed our children."

Her words should have been comforting, but instead a cold darkness settled over me. If all women ventured into motherhood blind, how much more blind was I—a woman who wasn't a real mother.

"I'm truly sorry it's all happened this way, hun."

"You don't have anythin' to be sorry for. You didn't choose for me to have a broken womb."

Ma inhaled deeply. "I mean the whole damn cake, Rose. The wedding. The adoption."

I almost laughed hearing her curse. "Don't be silly, that was all Pa."

She started to stroke my hair. "And I was as complicit as the getaway driver."

I didn't correct her. I agreed with her. But I didn't want her to know I did, so I said nothing.

"Now, it don't excuse my responsibility, but I was overwhelmed with grief. Your pa...well, he's trickier to reason with than a stubborn mule at my best. In my sorrow, I'm ashamed to say, I was powerless against him. You have a taste of that grief now—of losin' a child."

I sat up. It was like I was seeing her for the very first time.

She continued, "I told myself it was fine. You and Thomas were in love. You were headed for the chapel anyway. And those babies, my grandbabies—there was no one better for them than you, honey. I believe that still. With all my heart."

Tears started to fall from her eyes, and like a contagious yawn, my eyes welled up, too.

"But that all shoulda been your choice. All I could do was entreat your father to put the wedding off so you could finish university."

"You did that?" my voice croaked.

Ma looked into my eyes and reached out to rub a tear off my cheek. "It wasn't enough, baby. I shoulda protected you, like the mama bear I'm s'posed to be."

I wrapped my arms around her and cried into her chest. She held and rocked me slowly, the same way she used to when I was a child and woke from a nightmare. I pretended it was the same, now. That everything was a scary dream, and soon I'd wake up.

"I'm sorry, too," I choked. "I've been isolatin' myself from the family. From you."

She stroked my hair. "We all grieve in our own way, sugar."

She held me in silence until I tired myself out. As my sobs slowed, she spoke again. "I've started paintin' again, you know."

I sat up to look at her. Tears had dried on her cheeks, but in her eyes I saw a glimmer of hope and life that had been absent since the day she'd held Lily's hand as her life left her body.

"You'll be ok," she continued, smiling as she wiped another tear from my cheek with her thumb. "Trust me, baby. I've been on this path where you walk now."

She tucked me in bed and kissed my cheek, then left me to sleep.

17

How it Happens

I decided to meet Harry at Liverne's. I dressed up in a tight, little black dress with a scoop neck and spaghetti straps. I put my hair up in a giant claw clip with some of the front curls loose and framing my face. I put on some eyeliner and a light pink gloss. I finished the look with hoops and chunky Mary Janes.

I had Olive watch Niles at my own apartment for the first time. There was a sort of unspoken agreement to leave Grace out of the loop. I know Grace and I weren't dating but it still felt like it would be better for her not to know—besides, this probably wasn't going to go anywhere. Olive didn't much care about the secrecy. She loved Niles and needed the cash. She was in college now and saving up for next term's tuition. She wasn't particularly attached to her aunt in a way that would compel her to divulge my new social life, anyway.

It had been a long time since I'd eaten somewhere this nice. I parked in a side lot instead of using the valet; I really couldn't spare the tip money. Two years ago, I wouldn't have cared about skipping a tip, but now I knew what it was like to survive on those crumpled up ones and fives people dug out of the bottom of their purses. I wasn't going to use the valet then snub them. The public lot was only a block away, and I didn't mind walking. Besides, the valet service reminded me a little too much of the uptight society life I'd tried my whole adolescence to get away from.

Inside, a chandelier hung from the vaulted ceiling in the lobby. I gave Harry's name to the host and they brought me to a table in the back, near the kitchens. It wasn't quite eight, and Harry hadn't arrived yet. The table was covered with a cream, linen tablecloth and set with three forks, two spoons, two plates of different sizes stacked on each other, and two different wine glasses. *Damn, Harry. This place is the real deal.* The host asked if I wanted something to drink while I waited, so I ordered a pinot noir. It felt like the appropriate thing to do in a place like this, rather than sit at an empty table. I imagined how happy my dad would be if he knew I was on a date with a university professor at a place like this. Well, if I hadn't already been married and had a kid, he would've. I was a lost cause now.

Harry arrived wearing a different suit and tie than the one he'd worn at the symposium. As he approached, I was unsure if I should stand up. At society functions growing up, the men always stood up when the women entered a room, but I couldn't remember if it went the other way round. It was an odd thing to forget. But my memory hadn't been its sharpest since being pregnant and having Niles. I stayed seated.

"Hello Lillian. I hope I haven't kept you waiting long." Harry approached, hesitating a moment before bending over to hug me.

"No, I just got here." I half rose from my chair to meet him, squatting somewhere between standing and sitting while he wrapped his arms around my shoulders in a partial embrace. My cheeks flushed while I flashed back to my grandmother's cotillion lesson about graceful greetings. She was probably turning in her grave right now. I'd never mastered the delicate intricacies of high-society behavior, but I'd never been awkward before either. Especially on a date. I was out of practice.

Harry sat down and answered the waiter's inquiry about a drink, ordering the whole bottle of the pinot I was drinking. He was the perfect gentleman. He could give the society men in Alabama a run for their money—the men I'd poked fun at with my friends as teenagers. But the ease of our introduction last week had not continued into this evening. While we made small talk, I shifted uncomfortably in my chair.

After a few minutes of silence with our food, Harry spoke. "I'm sorry, I'm not sure why this has been so awkward."

I was relieved he felt it too. "I'm having a lovely time," I said, politely. God, who was I, defaulting to the polite tactfulness I'd been raised with? This place was doing things to me.

He raised his eyebrows incredulously. "You're having fun?"

I stared at him, knowing my face was probably giving everything away.

"You can be honest with me," he said. "Polite is boring."

I tightened my lips into an uncomfortable smile, glancing around. "It's a nice place, really, I appreciate you planning all this. It all kinda reminds me of my grandparents, though. And debutante balls. Antiquated shi—uh, I mean stuff. Sorry."

He laughed. "Don't apologize on my account."

I returned his smile and snickered.

He raised his hand for the check. "Let's go somewhere else for dessert." I liked how he took charge.

We went to a gelato place across the street. Harry got a bowl of chocolate sesame seed and I ordered a cone with a scoop of chocolate and a scoop of strawberry. We sat down at a booth to eat. The seats were a slightly sticky vinyl, and yet I found myself feeling much more comfortable than I had been in the ornately upholstered chairs at the restaurant. The air was cooler and breathing came easier. I slouched in my side of the booth, licking at both flavors at once.

"Nice choice." Harry commented on my cone.

"It's like a chocolate covered strawberry."

We sat talking, long after the frozen desserts were gone. Every so often he'd reach over to touch my arm, or brush against my hand. I began to return the gestures, the movements coming gracefully again, like an intricate ballet with a partner I'd danced with many times. Flirting was second nature once I was out of my head. I laughed at his jokes, even the lamer ones. He told me about places he'd traveled to. He tried to describe the layout of a street, a detail which would become important to the joke in his story. He took napkin and then pulled a pen from his suit coat that he'd laid out next to him on the bench, then he moved to my side of the booth, sliding in close to me. His tie was loosened now, and the top button of his shirt undone. He rolled up his sleeves to draw on the napkin.

His bare forearm lightly grazed against mine, sending a shiver of excitement through my chest. I hoped he didn't notice the subtle goosebumps. Every small movement made as he wrote shifted the muscles in his arm, pressing against my skin. I moved a little closer, so our legs pressed together. He finished his drawing and lifted his hand, brushing the back of his fingers against my bicep, moving up to my shoulder, then brushing my curls away from my neck. He said something funny, and I laughed the appropriate amount. He looked into my eyes and held them captive. I could only listen as he went on, knowing speaking would give my shallow breaths away.

He brought his hand down to my mid-thigh in a comfortable, familiar way, his thumb stroking the inside. I wished he'd bring it higher, to the hem of my short dress.

The staff began wiping down tables and getting ready to close as Harry recounted how he'd ended up teaching sociology in St. Louis.

"I still don't understand why you'd pass up New York." I finally interjected.

He grinned, leaning back in the booth and removing his hand from my body. "St. Louis is more my speed."

I could still feel where his hand had been, burning on my legs. He weaved his hands together and rested them across his chest. It was so careless and cool, and it made me want him even more.

"I'd love to see New York, just once."

"Once is plenty. Though if I were with you, it'd be worth seeing again."

I blushed.

His eyes were a deep, golden brown, like dark caramel, and aloof like a movie star's.

The girl who had been taking orders earlier approached us shyly. "I'm sorry, but we're about to close." Her brow was scrunched together in worry.

"Ah, so you are." Harry started to get up. "We'll get out of your hair."

She smiled and relaxed, clearly relieved we took being kicked out so well. Harry got his suit jacket then held out a hand to help me out of the booth. My legs had stuck to the vinyl and made a ripping sound when I peeled them off. He kept my hand in his as we left.

The sun had set hours ago, and a couple stars glittered through the light pollution of the city. The air was warm. Summer was going out with a bang. The sounds of cars and people going to and from various night-life locations filled the silence between us as we walked side by side down the street. A group of laughing men and women waited with us at the traffic light, the smell of alcohol on the light breeze.

As we crossed the street to the lot where I'd parked my car, Harry asked if I wanted to go home with him for a nightcap. If I still hadn't seen this going anywhere, I probably would've said yes. But this man was relationship material. I didn't want to look easy—I had a hunch he liked a chase. Plus, I'd told Olive I'd be home by midnight.

"What, you think you can buy me dinner once and get in my pants?" I joked. He put his hand at the small of my back as we as we approached my car. When we reached the driver's door, he turned me by my waist so we faced each other. He leaned in, pressing me gently against the car door.

"No, but maybe your dress," he teased. His fingers wandered to the hemline, tucking under it just enough to touch bare skin at the back of my upper thigh. I breathed in sharply as he brought his lips close to mine. Our noses brushed against each other, and I smelled his cologne. It was sharp and spiced, with an underlying musk and subtle tobacco. His lips almost reached mine, close enough I could feel the heat radiating from them, then he leaned away again, stepping back. I was about to protest for the way he'd teased me, but he spoke first.

"You're one hell of a woman, Lillian."

The compliment silenced me, and I closed the distance between our lips. It was gentle, as most first kisses are. But long, too, with a certain intensity I was sure we both felt.

I played his words on repeat all the way home. *You're one hell of a woman.* My heart fluttered every time I thought of his scent. I could still feel the warmth of his hands on my leg, my arm, my neck.

I couldn't sleep. Maybe it was the good wine. Or the gelato. No, it wasn't either of those. It was the man who had somehow taken me from cautious reservation to deep pining in a single night. I thought of his lips fitting effortlessly against mine, like cushions against soft curves of a woman's body.

I got out of bed and took a glass from the cupboard. I went for the boxed wine in the fridge, but then thought of the expensive pinot from dinner that lingered in the back of my throat. I couldn't follow that up with my bargain stuff. I reached up on top of the fridge and brought down a half-empty bottle of El Toro. I ignored the glass I'd taken out and drunk straight from the bottle.

When the bottle was empty, I finally fell asleep.

He called the next morning, under the pretense of ensuring I got home ok the night before. We talked until I had to get ready for work, while I sipped on a small glass of the boxed wine to ease my hangover.

"Can I call you tomorrow?" he asked.

"You're a lot more attentive than most guys I've dated," I teased.

"I'm not most guys."

Before our second date, I told Olive I'd be out late and took a cab. This time when Harry invited me over after our dinner at a Thai joint near his place, I said yes.

His apartment was pleasant but had the personality of a hotel room. There was little there to give me insight into who he was. A couple academic journals sat on the coffee table, the living room was immaculately tidy, and the whole flat devoid of photographs.

We sat on his couch, a stiff, gray thing, and he opened up a bottle of Moscato. He leaned back, resting his feet on the coffee table. I sat on the other side of the loveseat with my legs crossed, still trying to get a bearing on my surroundings. The room had a TV and a gas fireplace, but not much else. Not even a decorative lamp or a bookshelf. I sipped my wine. It was sweeter than I typically went for, but a good vintage.

"So, something's been on my mind since our date last week. I have to know more."

I froze, wondering if I'd said something that gave away that I'd been married, or that I had a kid. Or was technically still married. Or literally anything from my past.

He grinned like a teenage boy. "Debutante balls?"

I laughed, my body relaxing. "Yeah, Alabama is pretty entrenched in the past."

"It doesn't sound like the worst thing." His voice was still teasing, though. "Your folks took care of you, clearly."

I sensed weight behind the comment and waited for him to continue, turning my back to the arm rest so I was facing him better. We had talked on the phone almost every day that week, and it was like we'd known each other far longer than we had, and I could tell there was something he wanted to say.

He moved his feet off the coffee table and sat up, leaning forward and looking down into his wine glass. He swirled it gently. I reached out and put my hand on his knee, hoping he would understand that I was inviting him to open up.

He noticed my hand resting on his knee and shot a smile of gratitude sideways at me.

"I grew up in Chicago," he began. "We were poor. My dad was never in the picture. My mom..." he paused and rubbed his fingers against his temples before draining his glass. "My mom worked *nights*." His voice darkened with contempt. It took a moment before I understood what he meant. My mouth parted slightly with the realization. My stomach lurched. I set my glass down on the coffee table and stared at the floor.

"I was only seven when I figured out what she did. In high school," his face scrunched up in disgust, "one of my classmates recognized her when she chaperoned a school dance. His dad was apparently one of her...regulars." The words hissed from tight lips, controlled but dripping with scorn.

My head pulsed with panic, hot and flushed.

Harry continued. "He'd caught his dad with her a couple weeks before. It ruined his parents' marriage. The kid was pissed, and I became an outcast for three years. Not just disliked—despised. A second-class citizen raised by a whore." He said the word like it burned him. I flinched, but thankfully Harry was paying me no attention, engrossed in his recollection of the past.

"That's what I was known as—the homewrecker's bastard kid."

He let his words hang in the air a moment. I was paralyzed. Niles had been called a bastard before. I was sure that any moment he'd turn to me and say, *I know what you've done*. I measured my breath, it seemed much too loud. He would know. He would see shame across my face like a brand.

But when he turned to me, his eyes soft and pleading and pain etched into his forehead, he reached out and took my hand. My shock must've seemed an appropriate reaction to him.

"I've never told anyone that before. Thank you." He brushed a clump of curls from my cheek. It was a vulnerable affection. He suddenly seemed to me like he was still that boy, humiliated and betrayed by the woman who'd been most important.

The tension eased with my next exhale, and I smiled at him sympathetically.

He sought my comfort. I rubbed his back between his shoulder blades with the tips of my fingers. It was something my mom had always done, and it was instinctive now.

"I'm sorry you were treated that way," I broke the silence.

"One time when I went to chess club, I found the other boys all gathered around a chalkboard placing bets about which stuck up kid's dad was my father."

My mouth was dry, but I didn't know what to say, anyway. He read my expression. I didn't know what was there, but I was never good at poker. I tried to relax my jaw.

"I know what you're thinking. No, my dad wasn't a client. He was her boyfriend. I always knew who he was, he just wasn't around. She started her," he winced, "*business* after that good-for-nothing man left. She said she didn't have any options, but..." he trailed off again, without any indication he planned to say aloud what came next. He scoffed, shaking his head.

I tried to shake off the parts about his mom, focusing on his dad.

"I can't understand exactly what you went through—are going through." I took a deep breath. "But my bio dad also lef—"

"—can we talk about something else?"

It was abrupt, and I took my hand off his back, worried I'd done or said something wrong. "Sorry, of course." I was on edge now. An anxious energy pulled me away from him, and I retreated into myself.

He sat up straighter, turning on the couch to face me. "A distraction would be nice." He moved his hand up my thigh, leaning in.

I hesitated. His disgust for his mother hadn't exactly put me in the mood for intimacy. But his eyes were longing, and I jumped at the chance to flee from the subject of selling sex.

"Yeah?" I moved in closer, letting his hand move up my waist. He rested his face into my shoulder, breathing into my collarbone. His hands moved to my breasts, and he started kissing my neck. My jaw. Up to my lips. His were hungry and urgent. His hands continued to travel over me, down my back, lifting the back of my shirt.

Mr. Davis popped into my head, the way his hands had also traveled over my body and his lips had also hungered. I pulled away. "Sorry, I think I'm a little shaken."

I couldn't tell if he was upset. His eyes were calculating. His head cocked curiously to one side like he was fascinated by what had occurred.

"Can I use your phone to call a cab?"

He nodded, his breath still heavy.

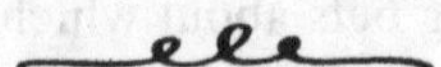

The next day was Sunday. I always took Sundays off. A habit, I guess. I took Niles to the park at the apartment complex next door. While technically our building wasn't part of that complex, it was generally understood that we could use the playground and picnic area. It was a friendly neighborhood. The day was sunny and warmer than it'd been in a long while. Winter was melting away, and I smelled the approach of Spring. Some mounds of packed snow remained on street corners and in large piles in parking lots, leftover from where the plows had gathered them up. There was a small one on the edge of the sidewalk next to the playground, and some older kids were using it to make a fort. I recalled the winter storm near the border of Alabama and Tennessee on that fateful journey two years ago. I was like a different person now.

I put Niles down when we reached the lawn, letting him run the rest of the way. He screamed with delight as his little legs waddled beneath him, like a duckling trying to keep up with its mama. He fell twice, rolling to his knees to push himself back up. He was so flexible, bending himself in half with his bum up in the air and legs straight up as his hands pushed against the ground. His tiny shoes were muddy, and there was a big wet spot on the back of his jeans and the hem of his little red fleece hoodie. The grass was still brown and the trees bare. But the ground was damp, ready to embrace the green season. I imagined how beautiful the little courtyard would be in a couple months. I recalled the cherry-blossom trees next to the playground, and I pictured their pink and white blooms floating in the wind across the benches and slides.

We finally got to the park, and I helped Niles go down the slide a few times before we moved to the swings. I pushed him for a long time, my thoughts on Grace. We hadn't seen each other outside of cleaning her house since the symposium. I felt guilty for keeping Harry a secret. It felt like I was betraying her somehow, for finding someone else before I could figure out my feelings for her. So I'd been avoiding it. I missed her, which hurt. But I couldn't do complicated right now, so I tried to think of Harry instead. I pictured what it would be like if he came to the park with us on Sunday afternoons. I imagined him pushing the swing, both of us laughing at Niles's hysterical giggles. But the fantasy was intruded on by thoughts of his mom. If he ever found out about Mr. Davis...I shook the thought, instead rehearsing in my head how I would tell Harry I was a divorced, single mom. As frightening as that was, I had hope that he would accept it. He was a distinguished, intelligent, stable man. Those are the kind of men that are ok with things like kids. Right?

Niles fell asleep to the rhythmic sway of the swing. I kept pushing. I watched his face as he swung away from me, then fell back down to my waiting hands. Would he resent me someday, like Harry resented his mother?

ele

"I need you to promise me something, Lillian." It was a Friday, and our fourth date. We lounged on the sofa, Harry's head in my lap. I stroked his dark hair as the credits of *Joe Versus the Volcano* scrolled up his TV screen. His face was relaxed, angelic-like in that vulnerable position. His neck pressed against the skin of my thigh, my short skirt riding up.

"Hm?" I coaxed him to continue.

"If I ever hurt you, will you tell me what I did?" He rubbed my calf with his hand.

I studied the profile of his mouth.

"What do you mean?" I asked, cautiously.

"It's just that things have ended less than amicably with other women. And I honestly have no idea what I did wrong. I just wish, if I screwed up, they would tell me what it was I did."

I looked at him, curiously. "Do you want to talk about it?"

He sighed. "It's not exactly a fourth date topic."

"You won't scare me," I laughed. Maybe it was selfish, but I was hoping whatever baggage this was was worse than my own.

He sat up and picked up the remote, turning off the TV set and ejecting the rental tape without rewinding it.

"It was a long time ago." He stood to retrieve the tape and put it back in its case. "But I almost got married. She left me at the altar." He returned to the couch and sat back down, picking up a handful of popcorn from the bowl on the coffee table.

"And she never told you why?"

He shook his head. "Never heard from her again. Her family got her stuff and told me not to contact her. So, do you promise to tell me what I did wrong?"

"If things go south, I'll tell you why." I studied his eyes. I wanted to show him I could be trusted. I wanted to protect him from the hurt—my hurt. From the dark side of being a woman trying to survive in this twisted world. His mom should've never let him find out what she did to survive. I wouldn't let him find out about me.

He smiled, staring into my eyes. "Thank you, Lillian." He reached towards my face. "Just know, I wouldn't hurt you on purpose."

We kissed, and I felt this man could love me. I let him take it all.

That night when I got home, a letter was waiting from my lawyer. After paying Olive and sending her home, I opened it with shaking hands. The divorce was official. It was over. Don would never be a part of my life again. I cried with relief, then when I could cry no longer, I took the letter and pinned it to the wall with a thumb tack. I kissed Niles's forehead as he slept, then got a new bottle of tequila down from on top of the fridge, celebrating until the bottle was dry.

I arranged with Harry to meet up again the next day. I told Olive I'd pay her double for the short notice. I had to tell him about Niles. And Don. I rode the high from last night and let it give me courage.

We met in the late afternoon at a botanical park close to his place. He bought ice-cream and we walked along a boardwalk surrounding a big pond filled with koi fish and ducks. When we sat on a bench overlooking the water, I finally spoke. "Harry, there's something I need to tell you."

"I know," he said.

I turned to him in surprise, my heart racing.

"I can tell something's on your mind."

I breathed in, then exhaled through puckered lips. "I have a son. A two-year-old. His name is Niles. Like Miles but with an N." *Because I want to seem unconventional on the outside but am secretly afraid of straying too far from the societal standard,* I added in my head. My anxieties about Harry's reaction came with a stream of self-effacing thoughts.

Harry stared at a couple of ducks on the water, silent.

"I had him with my ex-husband." *Ex* tasted so good in my mouth.

His shoulders relaxed. He nodded. "Ok."

"You don't mind?"

He looked at me with that now familiar cock of his head. "I suppose most men would, wouldn't they?"

I smiled. "And you're not most men?"

He grinned and winked at me, then turned his attention back to his ice-cream and the ducks.

His smile filled me with relief. It meant acceptance. This was the start of something big, I could feel it. I was the luckiest woman in St. Louis; of all of them, Harry picked me.

"I met someone."

"Lillian?"

There was a pause over the receiver, then a deep sigh. "God, Lillian. Do you know how long it's been?"

My brother had his own wife and kids, and I didn't want to bother him by calling much. I'd called once about a year ago, using a payphone so he wouldn't get my home number with his caller ID. This time I used *69. He knew I was in St. Louis, but that was it.

"Don and I are officially divorced. Don't tell Mom and Dad."

He didn't respond.

"How are they?" I asked.

"They've been worried sick about you since the day you disappeared, if that's what you're wondering."

"I wasn't."

"You know Dad interrogated Don for weeks trying to find out where you went. Now he's trying to get him fired."

"Fired? Why?"

He hesitated.

"What have you told them?" I pressed.

"Just that you called once to say you and Niles were safe." He said *once* like it was a dirty word. "They at least deserved to know you were alive, Lillian."

"That doesn't explain why Dad's trying to get Don fired." I spoke through my teeth.

"Lillian, please," his voice softened. "I had to tell them why you up and left without warning."

I hung up.

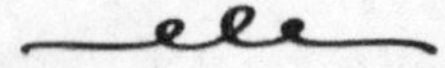

Five weeks after our first date at Liverne's, we went to another fancy restaurant. We'd made fancy places a bit of an inside joke—snickering behind the waiter's back, getting ice cream at a sticky parlor after. This place was the nicest yet, though. We arrived together, since I'd met at his place first for a pre-dinner rendezvous. The host led us to the table. Harry kept a hand on my back, and I enjoyed the public display of affection. Of commitment, even. The gesture was tender.

We turned a corner, and I saw him. He was sitting at a table with a young, small woman I didn't recognize. And we were walking right towards them. I was sweaty, flushed. I tried to make myself smaller, somehow. But I was so damn tall and wearing a bright red dress and it was already too late. Harry narrowed his eyes at me, probably sensing my unease. Or maybe my face matched my dress.

"Lillian?"

Harry stopped abruptly and turned to look at the man who'd called my name.

"Lillian, it is you!" Mr. Davis stood and grabbed my shoulders, leaning in to kiss my cheek. I could smell the cigar smoke on him, and it made me woozy. When he leaned back out, his eyes bore into mine. They were angry, and dangerous.

"Mr. Davis." I hoped he couldn't hear the tremor in my voice.

Harry reached out a hand. "Dr. Harry Allman."

Mr. Davis turned to Harry as if just seeing him. "Ah." He shook Harry's hand. "Howard Davis, of the Davis Group. Perhaps you've heard of us?"

"Can't say I have." Harry replied, coldly.

I stood in silence, my eyes fixed on Harry's face, trying to read him. I felt my pulse in my ears.

"Doctor, you said? Of...?"

"Philosophy." Harry didn't elaborate. I was glad he was keeping this conversation brief.

"Ah." Mr. Davis turned back to me. "Lillian my dear, I was so worried about you after our little spat. You never even called to say if you were dead or alive. I've been wondering how you're getting along without your benefactor." He laid thick meaning in his words. "But it appears you've done well for yourself after all. Not as wealthy a replacement though, I'm sure." He looked Harry up and down as if daring him to engage in this pissing contest. "But I'm sure you compensate her well for her services."

Harry stiffened next to me, his arm dropping from my back immediately.

Mr. Davis grinned. "Goodbye, Lillian." He winked then sat back down. The woman with him looked at me, her eyes wide. I wondered if she was shocked by my revealed impropriety or frightened by Mr. Davis.

Harry and I ate our dinner in silence. When we left the restaurant, he hailed a cab for me, put me in, then left wordlessly to see the valet for his own car.

Harry didn't call for days. I was crushed. I wanted nothing more than to show up at his place to make some excuse—to beg him to take me back. But I was terrified he hated me now. I replayed that night when he'd told me about his mom, fixating on my memory of the contempt in his voice and on his face.

After one week of no communication, Harry finally called. He asked me to meet him at his apartment. I hoped this meant he was ready to hear my side of the story. I didn't know if I would tell the truth or lie. I called Olive right away. She hesitated to drop her plans so last minute but offered to pay her $100 and she was on her way. I'd been sure I'd already blown it with Harry, but this could be my shot at redemption.

When I knocked on Harry's door it opened immediately, like he'd been waiting with his hand on the knob. He pulled me in roughly, slamming the door shut then pushing me up against it. He sucked my neck, grabbing my breasts hard enough to hurt.

"Not even going to buy me dinner first?"

He ignored me. His hands slid up the skirt of my dress, fingering the hem of my underwear.

I pulled his hand away. "Come on Harry." I tried to keep my tone light-heart-ed, but my breath caught on his name. *Why isn't he asking about Mr. Davis?*

He finally looked into my eyes. His were glazed over like a predator ready to make his kill. My hands shook. I pushed him off my chest and escaped into the kitchen.

"Can we have a drink and talk?" I opened the fridge but didn't find any beer.

He reluctantly followed me, then sat at the small, square kitchen table that had only one chair. His eyes were still wild, but on his angular, stubbled face he was as gorgeous as ever. His hair had fallen forward on his forehead, and that slight imperfection made him a little less intimidating. My heart dared hope.

Was he taking me back, no questions asked? Forgiving me just like that? It didn't seem likely.

"I'm out of booze," he finally said while I was looking inside the fridge. I closed it.

"Ok, can we just talk then?" I leaned against the counter.

"Fine. I'll start. You don't need to play this charade anymore."

"What charade?"

"Look," his tone was casual, like he was mentioning some inconvenience with the weather. "I don't mean any offense here. You're obviously not my usual type."

I stared at him, my breath catching as the bubble of whatever hope I'd had left violently burst.

"If you're referring to what Mr. Davis said, he's just an asshole. He was a clien—"

"No, I'm over that, now." His voice was tight, like he wasn't really over it. "What I mean is, I usually date intellectuals."

I scoffed. "You don't think I'm smart?" I suspected I was being punished, somehow.

He got up and stepped towards me. I pressed myself tighter against the counter behind me. "Come on Lillian. Don't tell me you really think a normal relationship is in the cards for you. Single, working mom, and barely making ends meet. Or, I suppose at times making ends meet in more inventive ways. But I help you blow off steam." He tugged on a belt loop on my jeans, pulling me to him. "And you're my little experiment. We can keep being those things for each other. Why not?" He said it like it was a game, and I should be so lucky to be a part of it.

"Experiment?" I breathed the word against his lips as he bent closer. I tried to lean away.

"You know, trying something easier. And—" He looked me up and down, then shrugged. "Fuller. You're lucky Lillian, a guy like me is usually out of your league. But of course, you know that."

I stood there while he fondled me, breathing heavily in my ear. I was too shocked to respond or stop him. My deepest insecurities had been proven true. I wasn't good enough for him. But he wanted a part of me anyway. Somehow, he hadn't kicked me out the door. He hadn't completely abandoned me after discovering my secret. I should be relieved, right? He only wanted friends with benefits. Because I was damaged goods.

But a horrible realization occurred to me. It was more devastating than Harry's words, alone. I'd been falling in love with him. How could I have let my guard down? How could I have been so stupid? I was usually the one in control. I'd never gone puppy-eyed following a man around hoping to catch his scraps. But I craved whatever Harry would give me.

I let him push me towards his bedroom. I wasn't remotely in the mood after that blunt assessment of where we stood, but he was doing me a favor, right? Afraid that if I stopped him, he would send me away forever, I let him shove me face down on the bed. He finished and rolled over. I waited for his breathing to slow, then quietly sat up and fixed my clothes. Then I snuck out, leaving him snoring with his pants around his ankles.

18

Saranghae

Eleanor, 2019

Daisy visited as often as she could. At first, she'd come up with excuses: she made too many cookies, found some old baby toys, or got a coupon in the mail she thought I'd use. But after a while she started coming over without pretense. She staved off my loneliness like an old hunger that was finally being nurtured.

After a while, I started going over to her house, too. I'd bring Marc in the stroller and we'd work in her garden, shoulder to shoulder. The rich, mineral soil smelled best after a summer rain. Like a dirt path in the woods. Daisy had one of those foam pads to rest her knees on. I sunk my knees into the moist soil. It gave me a reason to shower when most days I didn't feel much like showering. Planting season was long over so we pulled weeds. I'd despised weeding as a kid but doing it with Daisy was a comfortable routine. Routine I needed.

Marc would crawl around in the grass, pulling at the blades and squealing when he found a leaf or stick. I was grateful for the motivation to take him outside. I would put him on his tummy and lie down in front of him, so we were nose to nose, and I could smell his baby soap mixed with cut grass. One time I snapped a photo of him looking up from behind bright green blades, his dark gray eyes clear as polished stone. The sun shone from behind his wide-brimmed bucket-hat that protected his soft skin. I had Danny get it printed out on a canvas for the living room.

On the hot days in late August, Daisy and I would work only a little, then go inside for some sweet tea. She had found a recipe after learning I was from the South so I could *have a bit of home* in Colorado. It wasn't like my grandmother's, but it was good. And better than the taste was the sentiment behind it.

I felt safe with Daisy, in more ways than one. Like I could wear shorts around her. With her I wasn't self-conscious as much about how different my body had become after having Marc. Daisy was on the plump side as well, and she seemed to care very little about superficial things. It was nice wearing shorts in the summer heat.

One day, after watering the garden, we were sitting in the kitchen at Daisy's small, dining table. It was made of a pale wood, probably oak, inlaid with muted blue and green tiles.

Daisy was holding Marc on her lap, mushing up for him pieces of cooked carrot from her garden. As she mushed, the sweet, bright, caramelized aroma of roasted root flooded my nose.

"How have you been, Eleanor?"

"Hating mommy group."

She laughed. "I don't blame you. I never seemed to fit in with other moms, either. But I think a lot more moms feel that way than we realize."

"Maybe," I sighed. "But no one ever talks about how hard it is. Not really. They talk about being tired, or whatever, but not about the real stuff."

"We can talk about the real stuff, dear."

I smiled at her. "I know." I paused, considering. "I've been thinking about my mom, lately. She was always trying to hide any signs of her own weakness but in the same breath encouraged me not to hide mine."

Daisy nodded then looked down at Marc, who was squishing the mushed carrots between his fingers. She picked up a rag off the table and wiped some up that had gotten on his face.

"My therapist gave me another diagnosis. PTSD."

"Of course."

I floundered between offense and surprise.

"No one who loses a baby comes out unscathed," Daisy said.

"How—"

"I know, Eleanor. I figured it out the very first day we met—when I found that photo on your mantel."

Her hands held Marc around his belly. The skin of her arm where it met her wrist was thin.

"She was born too early," I said. "She didn't even live ten minutes."

Daisy reached out with one hand and took mine. We sat for a moment in silence before she pulled me in and embraced me. The tears flowed as if a dam had been removed.

She held me on one shoulder, and Marc on the other. And in that moment a warm light was ignited in my heart. A warmth that can only come from a mother's embrace.

Marc fell asleep in Daisy's arms, and she told me more stories about her days of motherhood and about her late husband—real stories. Stories of struggle and weakness.

"On our seventh anniversary, Ben and I were having a rough patch. I'd just had the twins. Having a baby really puts a relationship to the test already—and twins? Well, it's not losing a baby together, but it was still a test."

"Of course."

The sun was falling in the sky. The afternoon had disappeared like the fading lights of lazy fireflies. Danny would be home from work soon. The old clock hanging against the wallpaper in the kitchen clicked pleasantly.

"Ben decided he wanted to surprise me by recreating our first date. Get the spark going again. The thing is he remembered a very different version of our first date than I did," she chuckled. "Our first date had been a disaster. But in hindsight he remembered it through rose-colored lenses."

I laughed with her, thinking how that sounded so much like Danny.

"We both learned something. Down the road, the disasters don't matter so much, only the feelings you shared with each other."

The air grew heavier. Daisy's eyes misted. My heart shared in her grief. At the same time Danny was imprinted there. I needed to be with him now like I'd never needed to before. My heart ached, and any doubts I'd had about us fell away. I loved him with everything in my soul. That never changed, even when I'd struggled to feel it—to feel anything.

"We got through that rough patch," Daisy continued, "just like we did everything else. As long as we did it together, we knew we'd be ok."

When Danny's truck drove past Daisy's picture window, headlights cutting into the dusk, I gathered Marc up and left to meet him. He saw me coming from across the street and waited for us in the driveway. The world was bathed in rosy hues from the lowering sun, no tinted lenses required.

"Hey there," Danny said.

I stopped a few feet from him, taking him in. Marc turned his head on my shoulder, still asleep. The world around us shrank, and all I saw was the three of us. Danny's dark hair blew gently in a breeze. It was warm and effortless. When I said nothing, his smile faded.

"Is everything ok?"

"It's us against the world, right?" I asked.

He erased the distance between us in a single, long step, reaching out to wrap his arms around Marc and me. My ear pressed against his chest, his heartbeat thumping against my cheek.

"Always." He choked.

We stood there, the two of us intertwined like the statue in Aliza's office, with Marc between us. Marc was the gold, and Danny and I carried the weight together.

"*Saranghae*," Danny whispered against my forehead, his lips brushing against my clammy skin.

"I love you, too."

19

Mama Rose

Rose, 1972

After another load of laundry and hugs and kisses for the kids, Ma left us to our own devices. Thomas was in the kitchen heating up the meatloaf and potatoes Ma had made earlier. Is this enough for him? I thought of the fear in his eyes when he'd found me in the tub. Then of his smiles each time I'd told him I was pregnant, overshadowed now by the pain etched into every part of him when the doctor gave us the news.

I got out of bed. I went to the closet and parted the curtain of suits and dresses to reveal a small wooden trunk. It had been my grandmother's, left to me after she passed away. The surface was scratched from use. I lifted it carefully. Every little noise I made seemed so loud. I took it to the bed and opened it up. Inside were various keepsakes: a crocheted baby blanket, a cross stitch of a cabin in the woods, and some of my late grandmother's diaries. I removed these items and put them in the bottom drawer of my dresser—with Lily's journal. Then I took off my rings, holding them in my fingers. I considered them both: the heirloom that never belonged to me, and the wedding band Thomas had chosen. I put the engagement ring in the drawer with the other things, but I couldn't bring myself to leave the wedding band with it. Instead, I brought it to the wooden trunk, and placed it inside.

I gathered clothing—only the necessities. Underwear, socks, jeans, and some sweaters. Footsteps in the hallway stopped me abruptly, and I tossed in a fist full of bras and under shirts before quietly closing the lid and shoving the trunk under the bed. I slipped into the covers where Ma had left me, closing my eyes and pretending to be asleep.

The door creaked open. It was quiet outside the bedroom. Carol was probably in bed by now. The mattress shifted as Thomas lay down next to me. I opened my eyes and tilted my head towards him. He was staring up at the ceiling, lying on top of our quilt, fully clothed including his shoes. I wanted to close my eyes again, continue the pretense, but something about his demeanor held me, and I left them open, waiting.

I don't know how much time passed. Animated voices filled the house when Eugene turned on cartoons in the living room. The bathroom door opened and closed. Footsteps pattered in the halls. Carol woke and cried for a glass of water, which Eugene fetched for her.

Thomas reached out and clutched my hand.

"Rose, I hope you see this won't change a thing between us." His low voice was almost a part of the ambient sounds of night.

"Don't it?" I whispered.

He rolled to his side and leaned in, kissing my forehead. I let him pull me into him, and I sobbed. I released the pain I'd been trying to keep away. It came gushing forth in waves so strong I was certain they'd wash him away. But he held me against them, strong and unmoving. He held me until my sobs slowed and my breathing became more even. He reached out and brushed a sweat-dampened strand of hair from my face. His brown eyes were soft and concerned. "We're a family. You, me, Eugene, and Carol."

There was a quiet knock on the bedroom door. We lifted our heads as a piece of notebook paper slid in from underneath the door. Footsteps retreated down the hall, and Eugene's bedroom door closed.

Thomas got up and retrieved the note. He unfolded it and read to himself, then held it out. "It's for you."

The edges were torn from where they had been bound. I took it, my hands shaking. Thomas put his arm around my shoulders.

I'm sorry I said you would never be my mom. I know you miss her too. I think Mama Rose is good. I hope you feel better soon.

Eugene

The next morning, I put my rings back on and unpacked the trunk.

20

When it's too Late

Lillian, 1993

Days went by, and Harry didn't call. He was probably done with me—got one more round in then tossed me aside. But maybe that was for the best.

I sat by the phone Sunday night, but I knew it wasn't going to ring. I stared out the window. The streetlights below were emitting an eerie and depressing glow through the thin curtain I'd made out of cheap bedsheets.

You're not my usual type.

Not-your-type my ass. He'd picked up on what Mr. Davis had implied, and he hadn't liked it. Why didn't he just tell the truth? Then I could've explained myself. Explained that I wasn't a prostitute. That Mr. Davis had been more like a sugar daddy—the first and last. And he'd insisted and pushed while I drug my feet through the whole affair.

I still hadn't told Grace about Harry. I'd told myself it was because there was nothing to tell. I was only dating a guy. But I wished she'd known now. Maybe she'd have advice for me.

I dialed her number. My hands were sweaty and stuck to the buttons a little. The voicemail machine clicked. I hung up, not sure why I'd expected her to answer at one am

On Thursday, I showed up at Grace's an hour early for my regular shift. I was anxious to talk—to spill everything. She answered the door still in her pajamas and a robe. At two in the afternoon.

I stood blinking in the doorway. "Are you sick?"

"You're early." Her voice was tense.

"Not *that* early." I indicated her attire. Niles rushed past me to find the toys Grace kept around. Grace hadn't ever been bothered when I came to work early, before. It had been a while, I supposed.

She moved to the side to let him in, then gestured for me to enter as well. "I took a personal day," she explained, though her eyes shifted nervously.

"What's wrong?"

A voice called from the kitchen. "Who is it, sugar?"

Sugar?

"Just the cleaner," Grace called back.

The words stung more than they should have. It was true, I was the cleaner. I don't know what else I expected her to call me to the stranger in the other room. But *just*? Was that really necessary? It felt like a rejection. Was she ashamed of me? Embarrassed? Did she think of me like Harry did: fat, stupid, and damaged?

"I better get some clothes on," the woman laughed from the other room. My stomach rolled itself into knots.

Grace glanced at me, her cheeks flushing bright red in a blotchy pattern. Like I was a mistress who discovered her lover was married or something. "I'll get them for you," she said, then disappeared up the stairs.

After taking a moment to get over the shock, I started my work in the main level bathroom. The electronic music of a toy started from the guest room upstairs. She still had all the baby things up there. Grace's footsteps came back down the stairs, then through the hall. The bleach burned my eyes. I'd used too much, and I guessed it smelled the way a crime scene probably smelled after getting scrubbed down.

Footsteps and low voices emerged from the kitchen. The bathroom door was open a crack to air out the bleach, and I could see down the hall in the reflection of the mirror. Grace appeared at the front door with a tall, thin woman. She had long, thick, chestnut hair that fell in waves around her shoulders. She was wearing a slip dress with high heels—clearly last night's attire. She leaned down and kissed Grace, Grace's face between both the woman's slender hands, then left. Grace turned towards the bathroom. I quickly put my head down, going back to scrubbing the sink. She came down the hallway then knocked softly on the door, looking through the crack where the mirror reflected me back to her. I moved out of the way and allowed the door to open. Grace leaned against the door frame, her jersey knit robe hanging down below the red satin shorts of her pajama set. The chemise had lace lining the low v-neck. I looked away and focused on the sink.

"Sorry about that." Grace said.

"No, it's my fault. I shouldn't have showed up early without calling." I turned away from the unrinsed sink and started on the toilet.

Grace stood for a moment, watching. When I looked up again, she was gone. I finished the bathroom and prepared to move to the kitchen. She and Niles started singing the ABC's. She was clearly avoiding me.

I finished the cleaning, called Niles down, and left without a word, smiling cordially when she saw me off from her doorway, balancing a basket of folded laundry on her hip—some of the items clearly folded with help from Niles. Her robe blew around her ankles.

I had no right to feel betrayed. She was never obligated to wait around for me. I certainly hadn't waited. But I realized I'd been pretending. Pretending nothing was there. And as hurt as I was right now, I knew I'd hurt her just as much. Maybe even more. She just didn't know it yet.

His words haunted me in my dreams, and I woke each day on fire. I was filled with a vibration. It coursed through me as I went about the mundane parts of my days. Everything was meaningless, inconsequential. And I burned so hot my body was unbearable to exist in. I wanted nothing more in the whole world than to be accepted by him. I was ready to beg. It had been two weeks since we'd seen each other. Or talked at all. Despite the things he'd said and done at our last encounter, I missed him. God, I loved him. I hated myself for it. But it was undeniable. Like the burning of skin under a July sun.

When I thought I might fall apart from not hearing his voice, I finally called.

"Lillian. Good to hear from you."

My heart jumped at the sound of his voice. So casual and cool. I was surprised by the positive reaction.

"You, too."

"I thought you weren't speaking to me."

"What?"

"You seemed upset last time. You left."

"I thought you wouldn't want to see me again. You didn't even call."

"You free tomorrow night?" He ignored the allegation.

"Sure."

"Come to my place."

Maybe I could salvage this after all.

Sometimes he was so impatient, he would be waiting for me in the hallway outside his apartment. He'd grab me roughly and start tearing off my clothes before we even made it inside. I let it feed my ego. If I couldn't entice him romantically or intellectually, at least he desired me sexually. He must've not been as bothered as I thought about Mr. Davis. He just didn't feel as deeply as I did. He was never satiated. And I was an *experiment* that seemed to be working. He claimed a stake on my being and guarded it ferociously, but it wasn't romance. I devoured it—the sex, the lust, the feeling that I was desirable. I pushed down any longing for something more, resigning myself to the emptiness of physical pleasure without intimacy. Life wasn't a fairy tale. It wasn't going to be that passionate teenage love story I'd had with Don. Not ever again. If Don had taught me anything, it was that romance doesn't last.

Christmas came and went. Harry didn't do anything with me for it. We didn't even exchange gifts. And Grace and I were still awkward, so Niles and I spent Christmas Eve and Day alone in our apartment with a small, one-foot tall tree.

But we really were friends, too, Harry and me. In the cooldown of the afterglow he would confide in me. They were the only moments when I saw him vulnerable, like a regular person. One night, he told me about being falsely accused of sexual assault in high school. He'd gone to court and everything. But it didn't even go to trial.

"She was my girlfriend. She was just mad that I'd dumped her. But it ruined me. If I had been an adult, they could've put me on the registry." I didn't ask why he would've gone on the registry if there was never even a trial.

In his vulnerable moments I'd forgive him for everything else. It wasn't his fault he couldn't love me properly. He'd been hurt too deeply. And he turned to me to console him. I loved feeling needed by him in that way. It was the only softness I could get from him. But that girlfriend started to keep me up at night. I hated her for that. And I hated his mom. And the woman who'd left him at their wedding. They'd scarred him, and now I had to pick up the pieces. But most of all I hated myself for not being any better than those other women. I couldn't be another one leaving.

I confided in him sometimes, too. I told him about my family. My name. My origin story. We said things we never spoke to anyone before. It wasn't a normal relationship, but nothing about my life was normal. I'd ruined things with Grace, and now he was the only person I really had in this city. But the no-strings-attached routine we'd created shattered when aunt flow didn't show up.

We were laying on his bed, our breathing slowing. "I'm pregnant," I said.

He hesitated. "Are you sure it's mine?"

The insinuation stung. I turned to look at him, my jaw hard, trying to hold back harsh words.

"It's yours." I said flatly, like we were an unhappy married couple arguing too passionately over whose turn it was to take out the trash.

"Don't get defensive. A man has to ask." His nonchalance was irritating me.

I rolled away from him and sat on the edge of the bed, picking my clothes up off the floor.

He sat up. "So you weren't careful." It was an accusation, not a question.

My face flushed. He's the one who didn't like the feel of a condom. And I couldn't afford birth control or plan B. I put on my bra and didn't dignify his accusation with a response.

"Wipe that sour look off your face. Don't worry, I'll cover the cost to deal with it."

I stopped buttoning my blouse. "What?"

"I'll find you a clinic that's discreet. Afterward we don't have to speak about it again." He spoke like he was my fairy godmother.

I stood up and faced him, blouse half done up and legs bare.

"That's *my* decision."

"You made this my problem, too." His tone darkened as he sat up, and I shoved down the twinge of fear in my chest.

"I don't need your permission." I'd put up with all his antics, but this was too far.

"Have you considered the complications of keeping it?" His tone reminded me of my Sunday school teachers when I was little, listing off the eternal consequences of lying to your parents or touching yourself.

"This isn't my first rodeo." I started buttoning again, not taking my eyes off his face. I would not show him that I was frightened. Even though inside I was trembling.

"And look where you are—a single mom. And..." his eyes lingered a little too long on my naked thighs. "*Used up.*"

The stinging of tears sparked through my nose like an electric shock. "I won't ask you for anything. You don't have to be its father. Or even pay a dime."

He paused, looking at me like he was confused by what I'd said.

He got out of bed, still naked, and approached me. His eyes were dangerous. He drew his brows together like he was hurt. He reached out to me, and I flinched back. But he only put his hands on my arms and rubbed them.

"I'm not saying I won't step up." He ran his fingers through my frizzy curls. "I just want to make sure you're making the right decision—for *you*. With two kids—well you'll be closing off whatever potential you had, forever. Are you sure that's what you really want?" He looked at me questioningly.

I recalled when I had imagined him with Niles at the park. That image had to have come from something real. There had to be something paternal in him.

"I want you to meet my son."

He turned away. "Get dressed. I'll call you a cab."

Grace's eyes glimmered at me from across the bar. I'd suggested we go out. I needed to tell her about the pregnancy. And about Harry. She was the closest thing I had to family here, even when we weren't really speaking. She'd lit up when I suggested going out, and I felt sick knowing the bomb I was about to drop on her.

"You seem sad, Lillian." Her forehead wrinkled in concern.

"No, just thinking."

"What about?"

"Niles, actually."

"Olive's got him, he's fine. I know it's been a while since she babysat." Another thing I'd been keeping from her.

"No, it's not that. It's...I met someone."

"What?" Her voice betrayed her, coming out like a dry squeak. She cleared her throat and took a sip of her drink. Her eyes were wide like perfectly round orbs.

"I met someone," I repeated, my inflection rising like I was uncertain of the fact myself. Sultry jazz played by a live band drifted over our conversation, like our own soundtrack. I saw us sitting there like we were in a movie, and I was in the audience. I kept one hand in my jacket pocket. I'd put the pink stone in there, and fingered it now for courage.

"Oh." There was hurt in her voice, and the guilt weighed on me.

"You did too, didn't you? The woman at your house awhile back?" I didn't know what answer I was hoping for.

"No," Grace said. "That was casual. A one-time thing." I felt guilty and sickly happy at the same time.

"Tell me about your...someone." She brushed off whatever she was feeling and leaned in, propping her elbow on the bar space between us. It amazed me how she could prioritize me over her own feelings. I felt even guiltier.

"I think you know him."

Her mouth parted open the tiniest bit. "Come on." She pushed at my arm, playfully. But I could see that she was shattered. In that moment, I wished I'd never met Harry.

I took a deep breath. "Harry Allman?" I waited for the recognition.

Grace looked like she might faint. "The symposium."

I nodded.

She nodded and gazed downward, her face no longer even trying to hide her disappointment. I could see she wasn't fond of him. A tight silence fell between us, and suddenly I was too aware of the sounds around me. Between syncopated notes, a discord of voices interspersed with laughter, and benches scraping and shifting and sending vibrations through the floor. Billiards clunked and it was as if they were pounding inside my head.

"How long have you been—"

"Pretty much since the symposium."

She breathed in sharply and I studied her face. She quicky wiped away a tear, but I'd already seen.

"I'm sorry I didn't tell you sooner."

"Oh no, that's ok." She smiled, but it didn't hide much. "It's your life, Lillian. You don't have to share anything you don't want to."

After too many more moments in silence she finally spoke again. "And why were you worrying about Niles?"

I bit my lower lip and rubbed my thumb on my glass, wiping away condensation. "Harry doesn't want to meet him."

"Why?" she demanded.

"Oh, I mean," I shrugged and cupped my hands around my glass. "I'm sure he does, eventually. Just not right now."

"You need to end it." Grace's voice was harsh and flat. The tone was unfamiliar, filled with anger.

"Excuse me?"

"I'm not saying that as a jealous admirer." Her candor surprised me. "I'm saying it as your best friend and someone who loves and cares about you. The symposium was months ago, he's had plenty of time to get used to the idea that you have a kid. And you should know, I don't think he's a good guy. He's made passes at me before, and he knew about me when he did. It was like a sick game to him. Turn the lesbian."

I gaped at her. "Come on, Grace. I can't get attention from a guy without you finding some way to cheapen it." I immediately regretted the words. Grace looked like I'd slapped her across the face. And it felt like I had.

"That's...not..." she stammered. "Lillian, is it even serious? Can you see this guy as a—" her voice broke, "a dad?"

"Doesn't matter if I can. It's too late." This was not how I'd wanted this to go. But I was too proud to step away from anger.

"Too late, how?" Her eyes glimmered again, this time with an unplaceable emotion. She glanced down quickly at the soda water in front of me, and back up to my face. "Lillian." The panic behind her words told me she'd already guessed.

"I'm pregnant."

21

They Always Ask About Your Childhood

Eleanor, 2020

"What was your childhood like?" Aliza sat in her swivel chair, her desk behind her. Between us was empty air, and the dull colored rug on the floor. She leaned slightly forward, attentive. Lamplight reflected off her glasses. "I know, that old chestnut," she smiled.

"It was a good childhood."

"And how's your relationship with your parents now?"

"I talk to my mom, sometimes."

"And your father?"

"No."

Aliza let the abruptness of my answer linger between us. I tasted the silence like a bad lemon, sour and bitter all at once.

Finally, I gave in. "I never knew my dad. Don't particularly ever want to."

Aliza nodded.

"My grandparents helped raise me until I was six, when my mom got her own place."

"Did your grandfather take on that fatherly role for you?"

"No." I paused for a second, then the words were released like a deep sigh. "Well, not at first. He wasn't as involved when I was little, so we weren't really close until after my mom got her own place. He was involved, just not a lot. I think he would've liked to be more, but my mom didn't have a great relationship with him for a while. It got way better after we moved out."

"That must've been hard for you, seeing that strain between two people who were important to you."

"I dunno. I was too young to catch onto anything. Maybe because she's kinda anti-men in general, so nothing felt that out-of-the-ordinary." I shrugged. "It's taken her forever to warm up to Danny. And it's still like a full-on interrogation sometimes when she calls. I get that she had some bad experiences, but that doesn't mean Danny's like that." I was getting a little worked up.

"Yeah...Can we talk about something else?" I asked.

"Sure," Aliza smiled reassuringly. "How was your week? Anything new?"

"I was vulnerable this week."

"Good. Tell me about that."

"I told Daisy the truth. Well, actually she kinda already knew."

"The truth about what?"

I chewed at a piece of dried skin on my upper lip.

"That I lost a baby."

"That was brave of you to open up about. Do you want to talk about that now, Eleanor?"

I hesitated. But the comfort and release I'd felt with Daisy lingered in my memory, urging me on. Maybe it was time.

"Every time I look at Marc it's like I can't give him my whole heart, because part of my heart died the day Ru—the day she did." I choked on her name, the familiar sting of tears beginning in my eyes. Aliza passed me the box of tissues she kept on her desk. She leaned forward in her chair, resting her elbows on her knees, and gave me a minute to compose myself.

"I feel like Danny must be disappointed by me. Like I'm letting him down. I changed that day and he never agreed to marry this person I am now. He committed to the girl I was before. He didn't sign up for all this."

I blew my nose. Aliza picked up the white wicker trash bin from under her desk and held it out for me to toss the tissue in. She remained silent, listening.

"The new meds are helping, though. I'm not taking baths with my clothes on anymore. Or sorting my shoes." I half laughed and shrugged. "But I'm still not the same person I was. I don't think I ever will be."

It was my final statement, but Aliza still didn't say anything. It was like a game of chicken—who would crack first under the heavy weight of silence. She watched me, glasses flashing light. Her white hair was pulled back into a ponytail. I looked down at the couch cushions I was sitting on, then started to scratch at a seam. I was suddenly aware of the gentle ticking of the clock on the wall. I'd never noticed it before.

It felt like five minutes passed, but when I peeked at the clock it hadn't even been one.

"That's it." I finished.

"Ok," Aliza nodded in acknowledgment. "Thank you for sharing that with me. I want to point out that Danny did agree to marry the person you are now. He promised to stand by you in all circumstances. No one stays the same as the person they were when they got married. And I'm sure Danny changed, too. He also lost a child. Trying to return to an old version of ourselves is futile. You can only move forward."

I thought of the other moms in mommy group talking about getting their bodies to bounce back to what they were pre-pregnancy. I wrapped my arms across my belly instinctually. But Aliza was right. Danny had changed. I'd barely noticed, being too preoccupied with my own grief to be concerned about his. His change hadn't been as dramatic or as explosive. He went to grief counseling for a few months after it happened, but besides that he had done his healing in the open where I could see it progress. I'd taken it for granted while I harbored my pain internally. Maybe that was the problem. Maybe I'd been closing him off. And now I wasn't sure if he even knew the me I'd become in the process.

"Does this mom thing ever get easier?" It was rhetorical more than anything.

"You could ask your mom."

I leaned back on the couch and smirked. "Ok, I get it. You want me to talk about my mom."

Aliza's expression was unchanging, refusing to reveal anything. She waited for me to continue.

"My mom wouldn't get it. My grandparents were always there to raise us when she couldn't. She was always there, like physically. But she could check out whenever she wanted and not have to worry about my brother and me being taken care of. There were times when she wouldn't leave her room for days. Every time she had one of her episodes—" I stopped. I hadn't realized I was still so upset about this. I couldn't say the words out loud. That I'd always thought her isolation was somehow my fault. I took a deep breath and regrouped. "Point is, she wouldn't open up to me even if I wanted her to."

Aliza sat up and took out her notebook. "What kinds of episodes did your mom have?"

"She was depressed a lot. But I didn't know that until high school. I had no clue what was going on with her when I was little. I just thought she was tired a lot. Or..." I averted my gaze, "that she just needed to be away from me."

"It sounds like she might be the exact right person to talk to about how you've been feeling, lately. Maybe she'd open up now that you're a mother, too."

"No way. She's too ashamed. She's such a hypocrite, always so adamant about me getting therapy and the medication I needed, but I never once saw her go to a therapist."

"Have you ever asked her if she has?"

"No."

"Do you know if she has a diagnosis?"

"No. I'm assuming she doesn't. Since you have to, ya know, actually go see a professional for that."

"What do you think the worst thing is that could happen if you confronted her about her mental health?"

I considered all the possible scenarios before reaching what in my mind would be the most catastrophic. "That she would be so overcome by guilt and shame for destroying my childhood, that she tries to kill herself—and actually succeeds this time."

A shadow crossed over Aliza's eyes. I'd caught her off guard with my uncharacteristic candor.

After therapy I drove to the retirement community for an evening shift. I was grateful to have the time to process the session away from Danny and Marc. The home was a large, single-level building filled with apartments. The hallways made a big 'X' through the building, and at the center of the X was a cafeteria, an entertainment room, and a parlor. Usually, the rooms were open to the residents for various leisure activities of their choice, but on Friday and Saturday evenings they held scheduled events—like poker nights or dancing to a live band. It was these events that they needed extra ASL interpreters for. There were two of us who currently worked part time.

Tonight, they were screening *The Wizard of Oz* in the entertainment room. I sat in a chair on one side of the pull-down projector screen. Julia, the other part time interpreter, sat on the other side. The front row was reserved for the deaf and the second row for the hard of hearing. They needed two interpreters for the films because many of the residents also struggled with their sight. I preferred the day shifts, when my job was to keep the ASL-speaking patients company. But until Danny and I figured out childcare I'd have to wait to go back to work full time.

"Are you coming tomorrow for the children's choir?" Julia asked me as we waited for the residents to arrive.

"No. Niki is going to cover for me. Danny and I are going out tomorrow for our anniversary."

"Oh, happy anniversary."

"Thanks."

Julia was a college student, and despite my own college graduation being less than three years ago, the stark differences in our life situations made the age gap feel as wide as it was between the residents and me. I had no problem relating to the residents, but with her it was like I was a foreigner.

I'd interpreted *The Wizard of Oz* several times before, so it was a laid-back shift. At times I'd glance over at Julia. She was very animated in her signing. My style was more lyrical—almost dance-like. I often skipped some less important lines to spend more time in the emotion of the characters. It's not a choice I would make for every movie, but for a classic rich in symbolism and music, I wanted my interpretation to convey the art.

The movie was wrapping up with the wizard presenting his gifts to Dorothy and her friends. He offered the Tin Woodman the heart shaped pocket watch and recited one of the most famous lines of the movie: *And remember, my sentimental friend, that a heart is not judged by how much you love, but how much you are loved by others.* The words penetrated my own heart. I fixated on them as I clocked out and climbed in my car to go home.

I was struggling to connect with Marc. I was struggling to connect with Danny. But when I looked back on the past several months, time after time Danny had shown unconditional love to me. I thought about how Marc lit up when he saw me and recognized my face. And the times he was inconsolable by all except me. I had spent years cultivating love with Danny, and nine months giving everything to Marc before he was even born. He had listened to my heart's rhythm from the womb, learning it, learning me. We were already connected. Just because I was struggling to feel it, didn't mean it wasn't there.

I wished the change was as easy as a heart shaped pocket watch. But at the very least, recognizing how I was loved by Danny and Marc was an epiphany—and more progress than I had made in months. Figuring out how to open my heart up again was, for the first time since she had died, attainable.

"Ruth," I whispered her name aloud. And I cried. But I could say it.

22

Legacy

Rose, 1972

"Hey, Peavy. Naw, that doesn't sound right. You'll always be Whitfield to me."

"Celiah?" I was surprised to hear her voice through the receiver. Besides the postcard from New York, we hadn't been in touch since the wedding. I set down the pastry bag of Pàte à Choux I'd been piping in little logs on a baking sheet.

"Ah, so you haven't forgotten 'bout me," Celiah teased.

My cheeks flushed, and I was glad we weren't speaking face to face. "Celiah, I really wanna apologize." I considered how to put what I was feeling into words, then gave up. "For basically, my whole weddin' day. I should've re-arranged the seating chart when you showed up. And I should've known the plantation was a slap in the face. And I knew how important that court case was to you, and it should've been just as important to me, 'cause you're my friend. I'm real sorry."

There was silence on the other end. I started twisting the phone cord, waiting for an acknowledgement. "And I'm sorry I never responded to your postcard," I added, needing to break the silence.

Celiah sighed. "I know you got your own stuff, Whitfield. It's just the story of my life, ya know? *If* a white person cares, they only care if we're there to remind them to."

I didn't know what to say. I held the phone up with my shoulder and picked up my pastry bag, desperate for something to fill the emptiness.

"I know you're tryin'," Celiah finally broke the silence. "I do appreciate that. I just wish it wasn't only 'cause you have a Black friend. That's not why I'm callin', though." Celiah resumed her cheerful tone, leaving me jolted. "I'm gonna be in town next weekend and need a place to stay. Can you and Peavy put me up?"

My jaw tightened. I was annoyed she'd say something so serious then move on without giving me a chance to respond. I hadn't kept in touch. But she didn't pick up the phone either; if she had, maybe she'd have known exactly what stuff I'd had going on.

"We'd love to." I tried to relax my voice, like it was no big deal.

Celiah hesitated, the awkwardness felt on both sides. "I wouldn't be puttin' ya'll out?"

"Not at all," I responded, maybe a little too fast.

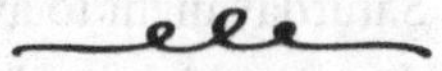

Thomas picked Celiah up from the airport. I was nervous about a long car ride alone with her. The things she'd said had pricked at me since she called. I didn't tell Thomas about the conversation on our wedding day, or the apology I'd given on the phone, but with one casual fib about some cramping, he offered to pick her up immediately. He said he was looking forward to the chance to catch up.

When Thomas and Celiah pulled into the driveway, I waited in the front hall. Dinner was reheating in the oven and the kids were in bed—it was already past nine.

"Rose, guess who's fixin' to be a lawyer." Thomas exclaimed as he opened the front door, Celiah's suitcase in one hand.

Celiah laughed. "Ah, it was gonna be a surprise, Tommy."

"Tommy?" I raised my eyebrows.

Celiah snickered and Thomas rolled his eyes. "She knows how to get my goose, this one."

Celiah bopped his arm. "Have I ever told you, you remind me of my brother, Ray?"

"Frequently," Thomas laughed. She'd said that all the time back in college.

She turned away from Thomas and stood facing me, looking me over. She smiled widely. "You look a picture, Whitfield."

She hadn't changed a bit, except that her afro had gotten bigger. She had an oversized t-shirt on with her bell-bottom jeans, like she used to wear when we studied late together in each other's dorm rooms. My heart warmed in her presence, the familiarity and nostalgia hitting me together. "You too," I smiled.

Celiah jumped forward and wrapped her arms around my neck. She was taller than me, and my head rested into the crook of her shoulder as I hugged around her back. It was like there'd been nothing awkward between us at all.

We stayed up after Thomas went to bed. I changed into jeans and a tank top and made some sweet tea. We sipped it at the kitchen table, sitting with our legs pulled up against our chests. I felt young, like my actual age, for the first time in months.

"So," I began, "fixin' to be a lawyer?"

"That's why I'm here. I'm interviewin' at U of A tomorrow."

"Roll tide!" The words slipped off my tongue like we were back at school, sitting in my dorm room on a Saturday night to avoid the parties. I never liked the crowds, and Celiah loved them—which is why she always said she needed to avoid the distraction like the plague.

She gazed out the window above the sink as if she could see the university in our back yard. A couple fireflies glowed then disappeared in the hot night. "Can't you just see it?" she asked. "Oh, I'd stick it to 'em, wouldn't I? A Black woman, at Alabama Law."

I knew she was talking about her grade-school teachers. Her face was hardened, bearing the burden of her life's obstacles in her cheekbones. But then her warm eyes became dreamy. She was everything she was despite those who had failed her every step of the way.

She had told me stories—what it was like for her growing up Black in Alabama. She got used to some of it, like getting sent home to fix her hair, the clear preference for her white classmates, the anger from white kids on the playground that still lingered a few years after Brown v the Board of Education. She didn't let that stuff get to her, anymore. But what she still harbored anger for were the times her teachers told her she'd never go to college. I was angry for her, though I knew I could never truly understand. I hated that I couldn't. It made me feel distant from her.

"I can see it." I answered her.

She turned to me, as if just remembering I was there.

"Look, Rose—" She hardly ever used my first name. "I've realized I wanna apologize, too. You lost your sister and took on two kids all within a month. I wish I had been there for you, too. I wish we'd been there for each other."

Her vulnerability crumbled my own walls. "I've been feelin' awful since our call last week, Celiah. I'm real sorry that I cared only because you were my friend. I can't change that that was why I cared before, but I promise you that I'll try harder—I've already got a list of reasons to care, outside of you."

"I'd like to hear that list sometime," Celiah laughed. "I appreciate you're tryin'. You've never been content with ignorance, and I admire that about you."

I smiled. "You aren't either."

"I s'pose not. But I wish I'd called and told you how I felt sooner."

"You sent a postcard."

Celiah nodded. "I was hopin' you'd do the hard part and pick up the phone."

I braced myself. "There's more that's gone on that I haven't told you, Celiah." I told her about Lenny leaving, and the mystery charges against him. She fumed as I told her how Pa made Thomas promise not to tell me about it. I shared with her about the miscarriages. She took my hands and held them firmly, then wept when I wept. Then I mustered all the courage inside of me and told her about the doctor's diagnosis. Celiah had never been interested in having kids of her own, at least they weren't in her five-year career plan. But that didn't change the clear grief for me that I saw in her eyes.

"Damn, Whitfield. I wish I'd've known." She shook her head. "The universe's conspirin' 'gainst you."

I let out a single ironic chuckle. "Enough of that, now. Tell me 'bout legal aid."

Celiah nodded, sympathetically, and obliged the change of subject.

"I have a sense of purpose. Purpose in somethin' bigger than me. I'm gonna make the world a better place for my nieces. For all those Black babies bein' born right now. Right now I'm helpin' individuals, but after I'm bonified a lawyer," her eyes glittered with ambition, "I'm gonna change the system. From the inside."

I envied her. I wanted her sense of purpose. Something bigger and outside myself.

It was a quick weekend. Celiah finished her interview Saturday morning, then flew out on a red eye Saturday night. This time, I drove her to the airport.

"Ring me once a week, now, ya hear?" We embraced on the curb by the drop off lane.

"Every Sunday," I confirmed.

She picked up her suitcase and walked towards the big glass doors of the airport. "'Cept not tomorrow, 'cause I'm gonna be beat."

I laughed and waved, watching her walk backwards a minute before turning to enter the building.

I got back in the car, ready to be alone with my thoughts on the drive back from Birmingham to Tuscaloosa. Celiah was going to be an amazing lawyer. The jealousy crept up in me again, and I thought about what Pa would say if I got a job.

But Celiah had been, and would yet go through, so much worse for her career. I suddenly saw my cowardice. Why couldn't I get a job? What could Pa do? He wasn't providing for us. We were looking for a new house now that Thomas was moving up, one we could get our own loan for, that would be in our names. What hold did he have over me now?

My hands held the steering wheel, light reflecting off the diamond on my finger—an heirloom from the era of plantations. It was never supposed to be mine. Lily had worn it for eight years. And it carried a heavy legacy—a legacy of ungodly violence and captivity.

I cranked the window down and wiggled the ring off my finger. It was time to start fresh. To create my own legacy. I tossed the ring out the open window, gone in a moment as I sped down the highway. I hoped someone who needed money would find it. Left on my finger was the simple wedding band Thomas had given me. It was more my style, anyway.

23

Soul Sister

Lillian, 1994

My swelling belly became a constant reminder of my impending dependence on Harry. When the baby came, I'd be out of work for a few weeks. The doctor had given express instructions about that, because of some strain on my heart in the pregnancy. I'll become wholly reliant on Harry's income until I could go back to work. After a few months, I moved into Harry's apartment. We needed to save for the medical bills, and one rent made more sense. I didn't have a lot to take with me from my place, but I was surprised at how sentimental I was about the secondhand furniture I'd collected. Grace let me hold a lawn sale at her house to try and get some cash off some pieces before donating the rest. It was like being erased.

Grace hated that I was moving in with him. She never said, but I saw it on her face every time he came up. She supported me anyway—with frequent reminders that her home was open to me, too. *If you change your mind*, she'd say. And it always sounded like a plea. Deep down I knew I had her to fall back on. Regardless of the issues that had come between us, there was something there that connected us in a way that couldn't dissolve that easily. But my guilt for how I'd treated her kept me distant, and once I was living with Harry, I barely saw her anymore outside of work. Two days a week I would arrive at her door, wielding my caddy of sponges and disinfectants with Niles by my side. I think she added another day just to see me more. She would meet me in a nightgown, hair tied up hastily, and dark circles around her once sparkling eyes. She would mumble what she needed done, and say she had a headache before lumbering up the stairs back to bed. I was concerned that she was missing so much work. Her book release was coming up and her agent kept leaving voicemails on her machine.

Honestly, she intimidated me; her family wealth and professional status were things I'd learned to care little about over the last year, but they always lingered in the back of my mind. People like her—I depended on them for my livelihood. People like her were willing to pay someone to clean their house for them. But beneath the surface of all our interactions was that unbreakable bond, and I clung to it during the times it felt impossible to breathe.

Pregnancy tanked my sex-drive. But Harry's libido remained strong and un-phased by the baby bump. Each night after I put Niles to bed, Harry would be waiting for me. On the nights he got drunk, it was even worse. He didn't used to get drunk like this, but it was becoming more frequent after Niles was introduced into his life. The day Niles spilled milk on his ugly area rug, he drank a six-pack of beer and half a bottle of wine before coming to the bedroom where I was reading. He'd thrown the book from my hands, revealing a new aggression I hadn't seen before. Then he'd forced himself on me. I'd been too shocked to push back, to even move. I thought of his high school girlfriend, the one who had accused him of assault, then pushed her out of my mind again. Like I had so many times before. He apologized the next morning, embarrassed by his drunken state, then asked to pretend it never happened.

After a while he stopped waiting for me every night. Instead, he'd watch TV or go out to get a break from us. I'd go to bed without him but would always wake when he eventually came in and climbed in next to me. I would lie on the very edge of the mattress, muscles tensed, unsure which nights he would decide to take me in his rough arms and turn me on my stomach—which the bigger I got became more and more uncomfortable. When he didn't want sex, I stayed awake listening to his breathing slow until they became light snores. Even then, it would take time for me to relax enough to finally drift to sleep. If he got really drunk, he'd sleep deeply. On those nights, I'd sneak out to the office and curl up with Niles on his little toddler bed. Other nights I snuck booze from his liquor cabinet, which he kept fully stocked lately. Only enough to take the edge off and help me sleep. Or dull the pain when he wouldn't let me sleep. And each morning I woke with a heavy shame for whatever damage I was probably doing to the innocent being growing inside of me. I would resolve to stop. But the hunger consumed me—the thirst. I *needed* it. I didn't know how to get by without it.

I was five months along when Grace called. It was late—or early, and Harry had been sleeping. I stumbled out of bed while he groaned about the ringing.

"Hello?"

"Lillian. I need you. Please, come over."

"Grace?"

"Please Lillian."

"Niles is asleep, Grace do you know what time it is?"

"Please Lillian, please." She started to sob.

"God, Grace. What's going on? No, don't answer that, I'll be right over." I hung up.

Harry mumbled from bed, "What time is it?"

"That was Grace," I said, ignoring his question. "She sounded really upset."

"She's a grown-ass woman, let her deal on her own."

I ignored him.

"Niles." I walked across the hall to Harry's office and gently woke him. "Niles, we're going to go see aunt Grace now, ok?" He sleepily sat up while I found socks and shoes for him.

Harry called from the other room, "what, you don't trust me alone with the kid?"

I slipped my hand under Niles's mattress, pulling out an envelope of cash and Amanda's pink stone. I'd sold my car the week before on Harry's insistence. He said it was a waste for us to have two cars when he could drive me or I could easily take the bus. So I grabbed some change for the payphone outside and rushed Niles out the door.

Outside, I called a cab and we waited in the warm night.

Grace was on the floor in the middle of the kitchen, surrounded by what looked like the contents of every cupboard. The glint of shattered bits of china warned me to set Niles down on the couch in the living room before wading through the wreckage. As I navigated through mixing bowls and frying pans, I observed Grace's demeanor carefully. She sat with her knees drawn up to her chest, hunched over with her chin resting between them. Her hair looked as if it had earlier been neatly drawn up in a tidy updo, but now hung around her face and shoulders, tangled in the back like a child who hates brushing their hair. Her eyes were obscured by some of the loose strands. She didn't look up when I entered, or when I made my way closer. Finally, I kicked away the last casserole dish that stood between us and knelt in front of her, lowering my head to find those emotive eyes behind her shroud of blonde locks.

"Grace," I spoke gently, like I did with Niles when he was afraid of the dark. I looked her over, but thankfully she seemed uninjured.

She stared at nothing, barely blinking. I lifted a clump of hair from her face and pushed it behind her ear. She slowly lifted her head to meet my gaze like she'd only just registered my presence. The charismatic glimmer her eyes often held wasn't there. But there wasn't sorrow there either. No flare of anger or fear—both of which I'd witnessed on rare occasions. Looking into her eyes in that moment was like staring into a void. A bottomless well of nothingness. Of all the stories her eyes had told me, this was the most terrifying of them all. I felt her gaze in my very soul. I held my breath for a minute, then let out a shaky exhale.

"Grace, what happened?"

She didn't say a single word. Not when I helped her through her disheveled kitchen. Not when we passed by Niles, asleep on the couch. Not as I helped her up the stairs. Not as I tucked her into bed.

I went back downstairs to gather up Niles and carry him up to the guest room—the crib and other baby items were still there. He hadn't slept in a crib in a while, but I put him in, afraid he'd roll of the guest bed. Then I went back to Grace's room, climbing in next to her in the queen-sized bed. Although I was worried about Grace, I was relieved not to be in a bed with Harry. I slept peacefully for the first time in months.

The next morning, I called and rescheduled my clients. I was going to call Harry, but I decided not to. He wouldn't be happy, and I didn't want to open that can of worms. He'd never bothered to ask for Grace's home number, and now I was glad he hadn't. I left Niles and Grace asleep as I got to work on the kitchen. Thankfully, not all the china was broken, just a few pieces. As soon as the floor was cleared, I got started on some breakfast.

Niles came downstairs, summoned by the smell of eggs and toast. Being at that age where everything begs a question, I tried to come up with a two-year-old friendly explanation for the events of last night. But he jumped up at the kitchen table like we'd always lived there, chattering away happily in his made up and emerging vocabulary, not a single question on his lips. It was the most animated I'd seen him in weeks. I hadn't even realized until that moment that he'd been so subdued at Harry's.

The events of the rest of the day consisted of Niles making himself at home while I nursed Grace back to health; a strange endeavor as I had no idea what it was that ailed her. But I covered my bases. I kept her warm, drew her baths, made her soup and tea, and brought her all sorts of things to read—from the precious first edition classics on her bookshelf, to her Bible, to a couple of trashy magazines I'd taken from a client's recycling bins. When I knew Harry would be at work, I went back to his apartment to pack some clothes for Niles and me.

For three days I took care of Grace. She left bed only to use the toilet and soak in the baths I drew for her. She only spoke once the whole time to suggest that Niles could use the guest bed instead of the crib. I told her I'd been using the guest bed and he'd been sleeping with me. She didn't even nod in acknowledgement.

On the morning of day four, I came to her room as soon as I heard her start to stir.

"Grace," I ventured, sitting next to her on the edge of the bed, "I'm going to wash the sheets today. Is that alright? I can set you up downstairs on the sofa if you'd like. Maybe you could watch some TV?"

She sat up and started picking at a toenail, avoiding eye contact. I watched her, my heart breaking.

"He told me to stay away."

I gaped for a minute, stunned that she'd spoke. "Who? Stay away from where?"

"Away from you."

I froze, feeling ice creep up into my chest. I asked again, already knowing the answer. "Who?"

She looked into my eyes and I saw everything there, laid out plain as if words had scrolled across her face.

My cheeks burned. A sensation of floating overcame me, and for a moment, my body threatened to collapse. Finally, I calmed myself enough to speak. "Is that why you've been..." I stopped, not knowing what to call whatever was happening.

She shook her head. "I changed my meds, again. It'll get better from here, don't worry. I just—I needed a friend. I needed you. And I finally decided I didn't care what he did. I'm sorry if I crossed a boundary."

"You didn't. I'm glad you called." I paused, not wanting to bother her too much with questions, but craving answers. "Grace?"

"Hm?"

"Did he threaten you?"

She chewed on a thumbnail. "He said he'd out me to my parents. Send them a letter, or something." Tears made her eyes look like moons reflected in water. "You must think I'm such a coward."

The butterflies in my stomach turned to stone. I wanted to throw up.

"No, Grace. Of course, I don't. But why didn't you tell me sooner?" My voice cracked.

Grace slid down the bed next to me. "I was afraid." She looked at me, her eyes pained. "Afraid you'd think I was making it up. You already know I'm a slightly jealous person." She smiled, and it was the first time an expression of hers was that ingenuine. Behind the smile there was shame. "And you didn't believe me before, about how he'd hit on me at work." I felt gutted with guilt but said nothing. She continued. "He told me how you two were talking about getting hitched, and I–"

"He said *what?*"

She cocked her head curiously, and I thought her features lightened a little. A glimmer of hope.

"What a *dick*," I said. I laid back onto the bed, my legs hanging off the edge. Grace followed my lead, turning her head to look at me. Her eyes searched for an explanation.

"He's made it very clear our situation is temporary. Once the baby comes, I'm on my own. He says he'll send monthly checks, nothing more. I don't even want the checks, honestly."

"To be honest I'm relieved to hear you say that, Lillian. But are you sure he's not trying to surprise you or something? In some twisted way, granted."

I laughed, humorlessly. "Trust me, he doesn't even want his family and friends to know I exist, let alone marry me. I bet he only said that to keep you away."

Grace rolled to her side and propped her head up on her elbow. "What are you doing with him, Lillian?"

I turned my head towards her, shifting my shoulders on the comforter. Her eyes looked pained—and safe. So safe. I let the peace of her presence flow through my being. He would never give me peace. He had probably raped me. His high school girlfriend...I never got to hear her side of the story. I now welcomed her presence in my head, convinced that if I had the chance to meet her, I'd hear a very different story. One I personally knew all too well. Shame buried itself deep in my chest for ever thinking so poorly of her.

I couldn't bear to look at her as I answered, "I thought it was love at first." I stared at the ceiling. Tears rolled down the side of my face, dripping into my ear and pooling in the bridge of my nose. "But it never was. It's been some sick game. By time I figured it out, it was too late. I'd fallen. He's been playing me—and I've been letting him because I fall too hard, too fast."

Grace wrapped her arm across my chest and around my shoulders, then rested her head against mine. A warm calm settled through my bones. Our breaths were in unison, and she sighed into my cheek with a relief that penetrated my skin and seeped into my soul. We laid there, her forehead against my temple, until a loud pounding erupted from the front door.

24

Us Against the World

Eleanor, 2020

Classical music played through the restaurant. Danny wore a button down with a tie. I was wearing the long, dark blue dress that I'd worn for my maternity photos. Nothing else nice fit anymore. It was our fifth anniversary. Daisy was babysitting Marc while we had a nice dinner out. Danny had wanted to do an overnight at a hotel, but I wasn't ready to leave Marc overnight. So, to make up for it we went to *La Papillon* to celebrate. We were pretty much perpetually exhausted, and I didn't really feel up to much romancing. But Daisy's story about her and Ben tickled in the back of my mind, and I reminded myself of my Tin Man revelation from the night before. I cycled through the moments of connection Danny and I had had since Marc was born, even if they weren't necessarily romantic ones. I think I was trying to convince myself it wasn't all lost.

The host led us to a booth and my stomach dropped. Danny was already getting in.

"Sorry, I'd prefer not to sit in a booth," I told the host before he had the chance to hand Danny a menu.

The host hesitated in confusion, then adjusted. "Sure." He looked like a college kid.

"Sorry." I rubbed my pointer finger with my other thumb and glanced at Danny. He was as chill as ever about things.

The host took us to a table with chairs, and Danny moved one out for me. It was silly, but sweet.

When the host left us with our menus, he spoke. "What was wrong with the booth?" He was reading his menu, acting casual. I appreciated that.

"I've gained a lot of weight." I stared down at my own menu but sensed Danny putting his down.

"So that means..."

He didn't get it. He was thin and lanky. His family were all thin and lanky. When we were dating, his parents had flown in all the way from South Korea to meet me. His mom's first comment to him when she met me was that I was too chubby. She had said it in Korean, but Danny's little sister translated it for me later. My mother-in-law wasn't a mean person, she just spoke her mind. But after two pregnancies, I was even larger than I'd been back then.

"You can't scoot back in a booth. The table presses against my stomach. It's just not as comfortable."

"Oh." He looked at me, eyebrows scrunched together. I could tell he felt guilty for not realizing.

Danny ordered for me, a habit we'd started while we were dating, because of my social anxiety. I would tell him what I wanted before the waiter came, and he'd do all the talking.

"This is nice," he said after the waiter left with our order.

"Yeah."

He reached across the table, palm up. I put my hand in his and he held it firmly, as if in earnest. My wedding ring glittered in the pendant light that hung above our table.

"I feel like we've leveled up," Danny said, "Eating at a restaurant with three different forks."

This made me chuckle despite my lingering embarrassment. Danny could almost always make me laugh.

"We better watch out or we'll get all bougie," he continued, encouraged by my reaction. "Start buying organic diapers and drinking sparkling water."

"Trade the RAV in for a Range Rover," I played along.

"Pretty soon we'll be indistinguishable from your grandparents."

The waiter came by with the white wine Danny ordered. "Just a little," I instructed the waiter. Danny and I didn't drink very often; we didn't even keep alcohol in the house. Alcoholism ran in my family, so we limited our consumption to special occasions.

The waiter left and Danny lifted his glass. "To five years." We toasted and each took a sip. It was tangy and deliciously dry. Easily the best wine I'd ever had that we'd bought ourselves.

Danny chatted about a project he was working on at work while we waited for our food. I nibbled on some bread and absently scanned the restaurant.

There were landscape paintings on the walls. The texture of the brush strokes made more dramatic by lights that shone on the canvases from the ceiling. These were original works, not prints. One was of a tree darkly silhouetted in pinky sunset. It reminded me of Daisy, and I resisted the urge to take out my phone and snap a photo of it for her. We'd agreed to no phones this evening, leaving the ringer on only in case Daisy called with an emergency.

After the food arrived, we spent a few minutes eating quietly, only speaking to comment on how good the food was. Danny had ordered confit de canard with a side of ratatouille. I was having coq au vin with a side of soupe a l'oignon. It was some of the best food I'd had in a long time. The onion soup was comforting and the chicken in the coq au vin tender. Danny gave me a taste of his duck. As we slowed down, we started to reminisce over the last five years.

"Everyone said the first year would be the hardest," Danny said.

I laughed. "Well, our marriage has hardly been typical." I ate the last bite of chicken.

Danny smiled, a smile that reached up into his dark, teardrop curve eyes. "I wouldn't have it any other way."

I paused, searching Danny's face for anything that would give his inner thoughts away.

"Can I be candid?" I finally asked.

"Of course."

"I haven't exactly been the doting wife lately."

"You've been through more than most. We both have."

"Aren't you ever tired of all of this?"

Danny paused, seriously considering the question. "Physically tired? Of course. But tired of us? Of our life? Never."

"What if I'll never be the same. What if our time of passion and romance are gone forever? What if I can never give you peace?"

Danny propped his elbows on the table and locked into my eyes with intense resolve. "I love you, Eleanor. I don't care how long it takes. I don't care if the romance can't ever be revived or if we never have sex again. I just want you to be happy."

"What if I can't be happy?"

"Do you really believe that?" Creases had started to form around his lips—a precursor to wrinkles—and they deepened with his concern.

"I don't know what I believe anymore."

Danny reached his hand out again, and I reluctantly gave him mine. "Then trust me. I know you can feel happiness again. This won't be forever, I promise."

"How can you promise that? You don't know."

"I do know. I dunno, I just do."

"I feel like you don't even know me anymore. And that's not your fault, it's mine."

"Then I'll get to know you again." He grinned, "that sounds pretty awesome. But I think you need to give me a little more credit. Sure, you've been withdrawn, but I know you inside and out. I've seen you through all of this. I see you, El."

And I did feel seen. In that moment, it felt like we were both completely new people. But somehow we knew each other as deeply, if not more deeply, as we ever had.

The waiter came and took our plates. He asked if we wanted dessert, and Danny ordered crème brulé—my favorite—to split. When the waiter left, Danny leaned towards me, his long torso reaching easily across the small table. One hand supported him on the tabletop, the other reached out to hold my cheek. Then he kissed me, gently and with a tenderness unparalleled.

"It's us against the world," he whispered.

There was a small fluttering in my chest. A spark of romance.

25

How it Ends

"It's him." There was panic in her voice.

I half ran from the doorway of Grace's bedroom to meet her at the top of the stairs. In the front entrance below, through the long, skinny windows that framed the front door, Harry was standing on the porch, pounding on the heavy wood that was the only thing between us and him. Grace looked at me, fear in her eyes, before running to the guest room to check on Niles.

"He's still asleep," she whispered, as if Harry was the Daredevil and would hear her from outside and over his incessant pounding. He was yelling something, but it was slurred and hard to understand.

The lights were off and the day was sunny, but in case he could see inside the windows, I pressed my back against the wall, and slid carefully down the stairs.

At the end of the staircase, I stopped next to the long window. I couldn't see him anymore, unless I were to lean forward, which I didn't do. But now I was close enough to understand what he was saying.

"Bird, you bitch, I know she's there. Open the fucking door!"

Grace disappeared down the hallway upstairs, then returned with the cordless phone from her bedroom.

"Lillian, I know you're in there. Open this damn door—I'll throw your stuff in the street!"

I slumped and let my back slide down the wall until I was sitting on the floor, then drew my legs up against my chest. Grace was speaking into the phone.

"You whore—you don't end this. I do."

There was a sudden crash, and a beer bottle smashed into the glass pane next to me, cracking the outer pane before breaking and splashing beer all over the porch. Grace and I both screamed. Even from the bottom of the stairs I could see terror in Grace's wide eyes. She continued to speak into the phone, her voice rising.

"—cracked a window. He threw a bottle at the window."

Harry quieted at the sound of our screams. I held my hands tight over my mouth, tears pooling onto them and dripping between my fingers.

"Mommy?"

My heart stopped. Everything stopped. Niles drifted from the hallway with groggy steps, fists rubbing at his eyes. Grace turned to him, the phone shaking in her hands. She reached out and pulled him on her lap, holding him tightly with her free arm while she spoke softly to him. Niles looked down at me, scared and confused. Would my son be destined to live out his childhood bouncing from abusive man to abusive man? Would this new baby? I had to protect them. I had to find that lion inside of me and uncage her. She was there. I knew it. She'd come out before. *How did I do it before?*

"Lillian."

I started. It sounded like he was in the room.

I dared to lean forward enough to see him leaning against the door, his mouth pressed against the crack where it would open.

His voiced lowered, still commanding, but not violent. "You need me." He paused, as if considering something. "You need me, *Lily*."

My heart pounded in my head. No one called me Lily except my mom. He knew that. The nickname filled me with fire—with rage. It was clear to me now—the manipulation. He took the most vulnerable thing I'd ever told him and was trying to use it against me. Fear melted on the heat of anger; I understood his game now, and I wouldn't let him play anymore. Not with me. I stood up and walked past the window to the door and leaned in above the doorknob. I pressed my mouth against the crack directly across from him. I hoped he could smell the mint on my breath through the rubber seal.

My voice was calm. Firm. Powerful. "It's over." The words tasted dangerous and sweet. I imagined Don on the other side with him, both standing stupidly. "You're a shit of a man and you'll never be a real father. I don't need you—I never needed you." The words came like a battle cry, and I meant them—it simultaneously shocked me and fueled me. The lioness was free.

He raised his voice again. "I'm not done with you, dammit. Don't you know what she is? She can't give you what I give you."

"I don't want what you're offering."

Sirens blared from up the street. I peeked out the window. Red and blue lights flashed in Grace's driveway.

Harry started pounding on the door again. I jumped back. "You fucking bitches, you think the cops will save you? I'll be back. I'll come for you."

But his words had no power anymore. I overheard the officers speaking to him. He shouted back and they slammed him against the door. I moved to the side window that wasn't cracked. An officer was holding him. Harry was so small next to the uniformed man. The other officer was putting him in cuffs. She was short, but her arms were muscled and her shoulders broad and strong. If she and Harry fought, she'd definitely win. I laughed. It made me feel insane, but I couldn't stop.

When they started to pull him down the porch steps, I unlocked the door and threw it open. The officer who'd cuffed him stopped and turned. "Ma'am?" I stood in the doorway in my plaid pajama pants and Black Sabbath t-shirt, arms folded across my chest. I looked him in the eyes as the male officer pulled him backwards towards the squad car.

"You asked me to tell you—if things went south. I bet my reason is the same as those other girls. You're an asshole, Harry. You're a fucking dick who'll never be happy."

The female officer gave me a nod, and I swore there was recognition in her eyes—like she'd had her own Harry before. The officers shoved him into the backseat.

26

Silence

Eleanor, 2020

I started brushing my hair before mommy group. I still wore sweatpants or leggings and baggy t-shirts, but at least my hair was brushed. I had considered quitting altogether, but Marc loved the singing time. I imagined him older, learning to play the piano, doing musical theater, or playing in the school band. I was filled with this yearning to show him everything the world had to offer, so he could find what he loved and pursue it. And I would be his biggest cheerleader, whatever that was. For now, I indulged my thoughts of all the things he might choose. At mommy group, it was music. His eyes lit up when the group leader turned on the back tracks. He giggled and squealed when I sang. And I swore he tried to sing along—his babbles melodious and lyrical.

One of the newer moms, Thalia, sat next to me on the rug and smiled shyly. She sang along to the songs, sometimes singing in Spanish. I always signed while I sang, and we exchanged looks of mutual respect and understanding. I wished I knew Spanish. I had Hispanic blood somewhere down the line, but I'd never really explored that part of my heritage. Sometimes I felt guilty about that, but I'd never even known the side of my family from Mexico.

I usually booked it out pretty quick after group ended each week, but Thalia caught me before I could leave.

"You seem to really like your job."

I looked at her surprised.

"What I mean is, you light up when you talk about it."

"Yea, I love my job. But I love Marc, too," I answered defensively.

"Oh, of course." Thalia flustered, her cheeks deepening under her tanned skin. "I didn't mean—" she trailed off, glancing towards the three women nearest us. "I only bring it up because I like working, too. It makes me feel like a real human. It's nice to meet another mom who feels the same way."

"Oh." My guard melted away. "Yeah, it is nice. Sometimes I wonder if I'm messed up or something. It's good to know it's not just me."

"Do you want to get coffee, sometime?" Thalia asked.

"Sure." *Did I make my first mom friend?*

Thalia gave me her number and I texted it so she would have mine. We texted throughout the rest of the day about missing pre-mom life, being touched-out, post-partum depression—the real stuff.

Marc's first birthday was tomorrow. It was Saturday, and I sat in Daisy's kitchen while she baked a cake. Danny was home with Marc having some father-son-bonding time. As Marc had approached one year of age, it had become easier to develop our relationship. I focused on how he responded to me and reciprocated. It took time, but one day while I was playing with him, I noticed my heart was light. Like, carefree. I had a bond with my child. It wasn't a big moment; it was small, and subtle. But it brought me a semblance of peace that I had been longing for.

Daisy was wearing a periwinkle blue apron with little yellow flowers that I had made for her. My mother had taught me to sew, and she'd learned from her grandmother. Daisy was an amazing baker. She loved breads and Peruvian street pastries the most, but she also had a knack for cakes. For Marc's birthday, she was making almond cake with raspberry jam filling and decorated with blue Italian meringue buttercream. She also had some set aside in yellow for piping. After filling the pastry bag, she handed me the spatula to lick. She'd used real vanilla beans, and it tasted like nothing I'd ever had before. It was light and perfectly smooth. Not too sweet. Anyone who tasted it would never use *vanilla* as a synonym for boring again.

I was sitting at the kitchen table, keeping Daisy company while she worked. She'd made the cakes the day before and was now assembling them, spooning between layers the bright red jam she'd made from the raspberries in her garden. The kitchen smelled like cooked sugar and butter. It was hard not to eat the cake this second.

The news played on a small television on the kitchen counter. It was mostly background noise while we chatted.

"First, we need a crumb coat. Have you ever tried icing a cake and bits kept coming off into the frosting?"

I laughed. "Have you been talking to Danny about my baking skills?"

She smiled. "A crumb coat locks all the crumbs in. Then you refrigerate it so it all stays in place when you do the pretty layer."

Daisy put the cake with its crumb coat in the fridge. She left the door open and looked around inside.

"Hungry?"

I glanced at my phone. It was almost eleven-thirty. "I could eat."

She retrieved some cheese and lunchmeat from the bottom drawers. Bending seemed to be taking more effort than usual. I stood up.

"Let me." I took the food from her and went to the counter for some bread. "Please, Daisy, sit down. You've been up and about the kitchen all morning." She said nothing, but did as I asked, panting as she eased herself into a chair. I almost asked about how she was feeling, but she had been working in the kitchen all morning. Was it normal for someone her age to be so out of breath after that? She was only sixty.

While we ate, I told her about the time I'd hid Danny's birthday cake in the oven.

"He came home for lunch and I had to think fast. What I didn't anticipate was that he'd decide to *use* the oven on his lunch break." Daisy laughed, anticipating the end of my story. "He preheated it without looking inside." Daisy's laughs intensified. I was losing my breath trying to get the rest of the story out. "He was surprised alright." I took a sip of lemonade, trying to calm the laughter in my belly. "Melted frosting all over the oven. It was a mess."

We laughed and ate, then Daisy got the cake back out of the fridge. She showed me how to turn it while spreading frosting with a long spatula. The cake was still uneven when she fell silent and stopped. The turn table ceased spinning and she rested the spatula against the counter, staring at the TV screen. I shifted my attention to the news reporter.

...in a grove of trees at Liberty Park. The victim says she knew the assailant, who followed her after she left the party of a mutual friend. Officer Morison says the victim sustained minor injuries consistent with a struggle. The victim was transported to a local hospital, and law enforcement has detained the suspect.

Daisy picked up the remote and turned the TV off. "Best case scenario, considering."

I gaped at her in shock. "*What?*"

"That they have the suspect in custody." Daisy started spinning the turn table again, smoothing out the frosting. "Most of us don't get close to justice. If they find his DNA in the hospital's rape kit, that girl has a real chance if she wants to press charges."

"*Us?*"

"Survivors, dear." She spoke with such casualness, but I could tell it was a façade.

I stepped forward and stood next to her. "Daisy, I didn't know."

"And how would you? I never told you. I never told anyone, actually. Except my mother. She called me a slut and a liar, and that was it. I couldn't tell another person."

I examined her face. She kept her features stoic, concentrating on the frosting.

"How old were you? You don't have to say if—"

"I was twelve when it started."

I drew my hand up to my mouth, which had dropped open, then was immediately swept up in guilt for my reaction. I placed my hands flat on the counter and pursed my lips, trying not to be rude with unintended facial expressions.

"Yes, just a girl. He was the oldest son of a family friend. Probably in his early twenties at the time, home from college in the summers. We'd grown up together, practically. The first time, he said if I blabbed to anyone he'd tell my parents I'd come on to him and he didn't do anything. The next summer was the same. Then later that year, we moved away. That's when I finally told my mother about it. I'm sure what she said was out of fear. Who would believe a little brown tween over a young white man with a bright, educated future. It was probably easier for her not to believe me, herself."

I turned around and leaned back on the counter, turning my head away to hide my emotion. "I'm so sorry, Daisy."

"It's ok," she said, continuing her work on the cake. "That was a long time ago."

Her knife slid around the cake, smoothing out the frosting into a perfect, flawlessly smooth surface.

"For what it's worth, I believe you."

Daisy stopped icing the cake and turned to look at me. Her eyes were glossy, and I was afraid I'd said something wrong. Then she put down the spatula and pulled me into her arms, hugging me like I was going to slip away if she loosened her grip even the tiniest bit.

Marc was finally napping. I tiptoed carefully out of his room. I'd returned from Daisy's earlier that afternoon. Danny was building a rocking horse we'd bought for Marc's birthday. I paused for a moment to watch him working. He was so devoted. Devoted to Marc and devoted to me. Things had been better since our heart-to-heart on our anniversary. I could feel a spark of some kind. Different than it had been when we were younger and infatuated, but a spark all the same.

I crept down the hallway and to the master bedroom to catch a short nap myself. I sat on the bed and pulled out my phone, scrolling through social media for a minute. An old acquaintance from high school had her second baby. She'd been pregnant with her first the same time I was. The familiar jolt of being triggered stung in my chest and head. I paused only half a moment before scrolling past. I didn't have the emotional bandwidth to compose a congratulatory comment right now. I scrolled past some memes, selfies, and a couple long posts about politics before I stopped at a linked article from the local news station.

Woman assaulted in local park.

I skimmed the article, picking up the details I had missed when Daisy turned off the TV. Would all of this really bring that girl peace? Daisy didn't talk about it—her trauma. And she had found peace. She had peace with her late husband. With her garden. People tend to say the wrong things, like Daisy's mother had. It wasn't worth the risk. Even a trained therapist could mess up and cause more pain. I put my phone away and laid down, staring up at the ceiling.

Daisy was happy now. She'd somehow pushed through on her own. So why couldn't I do the same? Why couldn't I simply pretend my own traumas never happened?

27

A Real Mother

Rose, 1973

The mille-feuille had taken days to prepare. I'd made the puff pastry by hand, rolling and folding the dough again and again, chilling in between each fold. The process was long and laborious, but the reward great. The tops were swirled with chocolate and vanilla icing. All this labor was in honor of the semi-annual Pilgrims of Peace luncheon. The congregation of ladies was meant to be a sort of brainstorming session about how the women of Prince of Peace Baptist Church would donate their time and means in service to the community. But mostly the event was a way for the women to rank themselves amongst their peers—in both spiritual and temporal attributes. I didn't particularly enjoy these social functions—they were exhausting on both emotional and physical levels. But I enjoyed showing off my skills in the kitchen. I'd been practicing puff for a month and was finally confident with it. After years of academic recognition that came abruptly to a close, it would be nice to get recognition elsewhere. Additionally, Ma was hosting this quarter's meeting. She occasionally enjoyed putting on such events. Much to Pa's chagrin, who didn't take kindly to his backyard being overtaken by a hoard of gossiping women. But it was one of the few simple pleasures Ma asked for, and the excuse of religious zealotry was enough to persuade him to hide in his office for an afternoon.

I arrived early to help Ma prepare. Her approval showed when I arrived in my nicest suit, a powder blue one with white trim details on the jacket and pants. I'd also put on grandma's string of pearls for the occasion.

"I know, it's not a dress but—"

"Rose! Well, don't you just look—"

"Like I haven't been wallowin' so much in bath water and bed sheets?"

She smiled sympathetically. "How are you feeling?"

"Better."

I set the mille-feuille on the table among the other refreshments Ma had picked up from her favorite bakery.

"Don't these look perfection." She leaned over my shoulder and took one off the tray. I raised my eyebrows at her.

"I have to make sure they taste as good as they look," she said, innocently. I laughed and took one too. We continued to laugh while we ate, like two schoolgirls who'd stolen pudding cups from the cafeteria line. Pastry cream stuck to our lips and stuck to our fingers. We licked them, throwing etiquette out the window while we were still alone. It was different than we'd been in a long time. A good different.

When the women started arriving, we assumed our duties greeting the guests and showing them to the refreshments. The gathering wasn't particularly large. There were about fourteen women in attendance. But it was quite a lot to gather round the two tables Ma had borrowed from the church. The ladies were delighted with the pink tablecloths and porcelain settings, the fresh flowers in their crystal vases, and Ma's famous sweet tea.

"Annabel, where did you find these gorgeous things?" Mrs. Simons asked, picking up one of the mille-feuille.

"Rose made 'em," Ma beamed with pride. Even better than recognition from the very queens of homemaking was Ma's pride in me.

A few other ladies overheard and gathered round to sample the pastries.

"Rose, my daughter just adores bakin'. Maybe you could teach her how to do these," Mrs. Carson said.

"Do you do cakes? Delia's birthday's next month," Alice Gardner said. Delia was her baby, about to turn one. "I'd compensate you, of course." She tilted her nose up in a way that told me she wasn't offering out of respect.

"Where'd you learn to make all these fancy things?" Margorie asked. Margorie was the eldest of the Pilgrims of Peace ladies, and the most respected. Her stamp of approval all but guaranteed the others'.

I chatted with them, flattered by the attention but also mildly self-conscious in the spotlight. *No, I don't do birthday cakes, and I'm not for hire. Sure, I can teach Tammy how to make 'em. Oh, I learn from watchin' Julia Child, mostly.*

As the ladies mingled and loaded their plates with fruit and mini quiches. I struck up a conversation with Mrs. Simons. She was a few years younger than Ma and had been my Sunday School teacher since she was a newlywed.

"I was thinkin' we could do a drive for some of the inner-city schools this year," I tried out my idea on her. "Their textbooks are all old and outdated, little better than kindlin'. We could raise funds and get new ones. And other supplies."

Mrs. Simons narrowed her eyes, "Rose, do ya mean the schools that are attended mostly by Black kids?"

I nodded. "Desegregation didn't come with equality, Mrs. Simons."

"Please Rose, you're grown now. Call me Beth." She sighed, "As to your idea, I think it's lovely. But I don't think you understand how prejudiced some of the women are. Many of them were 'gainst desegregation."

"*Mrs. Reynolds*, look at you." Malinda Tollson rushed to the back garden gate.

Mrs. Simons and I turned to the source of the commotion. Synthia Hollstrom—well, now Reynolds, strode fashionably late into the garden with her hands caressing a swollen belly. My stomach dropped. Synthia was two years younger than me and had been my personal bully for a lot of our teen years. She'd married a few months ago and had recently moved back to Tuscaloosa after living with her in-laws in Birmingham. Malinda cooed over her protruding midsection, and each of the ladies turned their attention on the newcomer.

I fell back a couple steps, letting the women forward to offer their congratulations and ask their much-too-personal questions. Ma stayed back too, scrutinizing my face for a reaction. I smiled and nodded, trying to show her I was fine. I could tell she wasn't convinced.

"The first one feels such a blessin'."

"How you been feeling, hun? Any mornin' sickness?"

"What're you hopin' for?"

"Little girls are the most angelic things, isn't that so Margorie?"

"A boy will wear you out," Margorie replied. "Just ask Beth." Some ladies laughed, including Mrs. Simons who had four boys.

"Hey, Rose." My heart jumped at the sound of my name. Alice turned her attention on me, holding a plate with three mille-feuille out in front of her, one half eaten. Alice was Synthia's best friend since birth. "When will you be joinin' us in sacred motherhood?"

Eyes fell on me.

"Oh, you must be expectin' by now. It's been, what? Over a year, hasn't it?"

"Shy in the bedroom perhaps?" Margorie chuckled quietly to the women closest to her, eliciting a spark of stifled giggles.

"Margorie," one of them chastised, endearingly.

Some of the women started shifting their feet uncomfortably, avoiding my eyes. I watched them. And somehow watched myself with them, frozen and staring like a child waiting to make sure the creak in the floorboards didn't wake her parents.

"Oh, she'll get busy soon enough. In God's time." Mrs. Simons attempted to placate the crowd and moved next to Ma. She took her hand and added quietly, "you must be dyin' for more of those grandbabies."

"Perhaps I won't *get busy*." The words escaped my lips before I could assess the impact they would have. It was a mere mumble, and only Mrs. Simons seemed to hear it. Her brow furrowed in confusion. I spoke louder, "I don't remember inviting ya'll into my bedroom when I made my weddin' vows."

They all heard this time. They exchanged glances, eyebrows raised and eyes widening like I'd admitted to cheating on my husband. They whispered—not quiet enough—amongst each other, defending themselves.

"It's a little strange, is all, waitin' a whole year."

"We were only sayin' it with good intentions, Rose."

"You can't be one of those feminists."

"Well." Ma spoke softly. Only Mrs. Simons and I heard her.

"No, she can't be on that unholy pill. No Whitfield would ever—"

"Well." Ma raised her voice sharply, and the women quieted down abruptly. Once every eye was on her, she spoke in a low, soft voice, dripping with a dulcet southern charm sweeter than condensed milk. "Well, I *do* thank you ladies, from the absolute bottom of my heart, *really*, for your righteous concern for my daughter's reproduction. Especially after not a single one of you—" Ma looked pointedly at the younger women who had been fawning over Synthia's midsection, "—*darling ladies* brought as much as a dried-out tuna fish casserole when she adopted Eugene and Carol. We were beginnin' to wonder if ya'll cared 'bout her private family affairs at all. But now I see y'all care very deeply—at least for some theoretical babies you know nothin' about. And of course, for the beautiful pastries Rose has so graciously shared with all you lovely bitches today." Several women gasped at the language. Ma turned her eyes on Alice Gardner, whose cheek was bulging with pastry, with a gaze that could've reduced the young woman to a puddle of cream.

Every mouth was shut tight in stunned silence, except for Alice, who vigorously chewed while hiding her mouth with her free hand. She coughed a little as she swallowed.

Ma continued to glare at Alice, her voice now firm and merciless. "Just in case the old biscuit is a bit doughier in the middle than you pretend it is, let me be perfectly clear: Rose is already a mother. One more word about her reproduction and you'll be banned from my home until the day you beg on your knees for Rose's and God's forgiveness."

Her arms were folded across her chest, staring down every woman who dared lift their noses up at her. She was a tall woman, but until now I'd never noticed. She towered above the others like a storm cloud. I'd never admired her so much.

"Shall we assemble?" Margorie broke the silence and led the women to the table.

I went to Ma's side, taking her hand and squeezing it in gratitude. She squeezed back. It was like our own secret signal.

"I'm truly sorry, Annabel," Mrs. Simons said.

"Don't go apologizin' to me."

Mrs. Simons took my other hand in both of hers. "I do apologize, Rose. I didn't know how sensitive a topic it was."

"It's a sensitive topic for many more women than you think," I replied. The three of us sat down at the table.

Mrs. Simons smiled apologetically, understanding shadowing her face. "Yes, I s'pose that's true."

"Rose is just as much a mother as anyone else here," Ma said.

"I agree," Mrs. Simons said. "Oh, Rose. Go 'head an' pitch your idea for the Black schools. I'll support it. And I believe after this embarrassment we can influence some of the other ladies to throw their support behind you. Margorie is fuming. She'll be desperate to save face." She winked.

"Thank you, Beth." I smiled.

28

Does Normal Feel Like Being Ready?

Eleanor, 2020

It's strange how nothing changes when your world shatters. You wake up in the mornings. The neighbors bring the garbage bins to the curb. Your phone glows with a notification—maybe an email or social media. It's all the same, no matter how different you are inside. And as time goes on, you get used to how the world keeps turning, until it feels normal again. That was how it was after we lost Ruth. The world kept turning, and we got settled into routines.

But sometimes the steady beat of time brings with it reminders that my world was still fragmented. Marc's milestones reminded me of the milestones our daughter never got to have. Daisy and Thalia and Thalia's baby Rosco all joined us for the celebration. We went to the zoo, video called our parents, did presents and cake, and after Thalia went home and Danny put Marc to bed, Daisy sat with me while I cried. The truth was, I'd barely registered Marc's birthday at all. It was like I watched it happen from afar, disconnected and outside of reality. That glimmer from my youth was lost, the one that let me live in the moment, and days like this made it harder to pretend I still knew who I was.

"Can we talk about it?" Danny asked after Daisy left.

I answered him with silence, and after a few minutes sitting on the edge of the couch waiting for me to say something, he left me in the living room and went to bed. I recognized hurt and despair in his slumped shoulders as he walked away.

A few weeks later, Daisy came over in an especially cheerful mood. She arrived out of breath, like she'd run across the street. She had a large box with her, so I took it immediately and urged her to sit down.

"I'm fine dear, really." She sat.

"Do you need some water?"

"No, no. I can't stay long. But I needed to show you something."

She indicated for me to set the box on the coffee table, then she opened it. It was full of keepsakes. There were a couple school art projects her kids had done, letters from her late husband from during their courtship, a crocheted blanket that her mother made, and some heirloom jewelry.

"I'm going to send these to my kids," she explained, "but I wanted to enjoy them with a friend first. Tell their stories."

She gave me the history of each object in the box while Marc coasted along furniture, distracting her every so often with his attempts at talking.

The last item she pulled out was a small, silver spoon. "This was mine as a baby. It's a family heirloom. It's been in my family for five generations. It's not pure silver—mixed metal of some kind I think—but it's value in our family was never monetary."

The spoon was simple and unadorned. The handle was about three inches long, maybe four, with a curved end that created a loop for a finger to hold it with. The ladle was narrow and not much longer than a thumbprint. She handed it to me, and I turned it over in my hands. Etched on the back of the handle was *Carito Sofia Alvarez 1861*.

"Carito was my great-great grandmother."

"It's beautiful," I said. I felt the weight of generations pressed against my fingertips. I considered the families who had each possessed this simple object. After taking in the magic, I held it out for Daisy to take back.

She reached out only to fold my fingers around the thin metal. "I want you to have it."

I stared at her, my voice stuck in my throat.

"Please," she continued, "you are family. You cured the loneliness I'd lived in for many years. And I want my honorary grandbaby to have a piece of me. Think of it as a late birthday present for Marc."

"What about your kids? When they have children?"

"I'm giving them other heirlooms. Ones more sentimental to them than this."

I nodded and brought my hand to my chest, holding the spoon close to my heart. "Thank you," I whispered.

She stood up with her box of treasures, saying something about getting to the post office before it closes. She bent over to kiss Marc where he played on the floor.

"I love you, sweet baby," she said.

He kissed her back, a big open mouth kiss that left glistening saliva on her cheek.

She hugged me, then went for the door.

"Wait." I followed, still clutching the spoon. "I need to tell you something."

I gestured to the photo on the mantel. "Her name was Ruth."

Daisy placed her box on the ground then embraced me again. I rested my head on her shoulder and cried with relief.

"Thank you for telling me," she whispered.

I walked her out to the porch, and she hugged me again before walking across the street to her car. When I closed the door, Marc squeaked a delayed, "buh-bye."

The spoon made its home in our little corner cabinet. I propped it up against the back so it stood up. The cabinet held our most precious items: the polished wooden box that held my engagement ring when Danny proposed, a china tea set that belonged to the grandmother I never knew, the little booties Ruth had worn before she died, and some wedding gifts too nice to keep out with a mobile toddler around.

I sat at the dinner table staring at the cabinet while I refilled Marc's sippy cup. Danny sat on the other side of the highchair, chatting about work. A lot of the jargon went over my head. Normally, I would try to keep up anyway, but tonight I was struggling to focus on anything. Marc threw some green beans on the floor. I made no move to pick them up. Daisy hadn't been by since the day she'd given us the spoon. It had been over a week. I'd stopped by a couple times to find no one home. When I called her cell phone it went straight to voicemail. I tried to remember if she'd mentioned going out of town but could recall nothing. I called the floral shop where she sold some of her flower cuttings and they said she hadn't brought anything in for over two weeks. The whole thing put me on edge.

"Anyway, how was your day? Anything from Daisy?" Danny asked.

My phone rang. I pulled it out of my pocket, hoping it was Daisy. Unknown caller. I clicked ignore.

"Who is it?" Danny asked.

I shrugged.

The voicemail icon popped on my screen. "They left a voicemail."

"It's probably one of those scam calls."

But I listened to the message anyway.

One new message, and four saved messages. New message.

Eleanor Sun? This is Terrance Roads. I hope I have the right number; your voicemail just reads off your number. You should probably change that. Anyway, I believe you know my mom, Daisy. She asked me to call. She uh…I guess she was diagnosed with blood cancer a few months ago. Stage 4. She didn't tell us. Her kids, I mean. Maybe she told you, I dunno. Anyway, she's at the hospital now, in the hospice unit, and—

Terrance paused with a muffled sob, and I pictured him bringing the phone away from his face to cry. Daisy had shown me photos of her kids, so I knew what Terrance looked like.

He cleared his throat. *Sorry. There's nothing they can do. She says she's ready to go. The doctors say she has days. Anyway, she asked me to call. She wants you to come see her. She's at St. Joseph's.*

Beep. End of new message.

We went to the St. Joseph's hospice center the next morning as soon as it was open for visitors. It was in a separate building from the main hospital, but on the same campus. It looked and smelled like a dentist office inside, with neutral tones and pictures of ocean views on all the walls. Beneath each framed piece was a small plaque with different bible verses—supposedly meant to be comforting.

Like Adam all shall die, but in Christ all shall live again.

I did not find them comforting.

Daisy was lying in bed, hooked up to oxygen and various monitors. When I'd called Terrance back, he'd explained that the cancer had started attacking her lungs. I recalled the times I'd noticed her labored breathing and it made me angry. Angry at myself for not trusting that voice of concern and doubt. But honestly, also a little angry at Daisy. How could she keep this a secret? Go through it alone for months? But when I saw her there, frail and small, the anger melted away.

The nurse indicated for us to sit at the chairs next to Daisy's bed. Her brows furrowed slightly as she looked over at Marc, babbling in Danny's arms. She looked impossibly different than she had a couple weeks ago. Frailer, like she'd aged ten years.

"Say hi to Nana Daisy," I said to Marc. I gave the nurse a pointed look. She was clearly annoyed at having a toddler in the room. It wasn't her business what Daisy's relationship with Marc was, but I emphasized *nana* anyway.

"She can't talk much anymore," the nurse admonished. "It tires her out."

Danny nodded. "We'll keep the chit-chat to a minimum." He put a hand on my knee, knowing I was fuming.

The nurse left and Daisy turned her head slightly in our direction, her eyes still closed. "She's..." she breathed raggedly, "an asshole." The corners of her mouth twitched in a smile.

My eyes widened. I raised my eyebrows at Danny. Daisy had never sworn before, at least not in front of me. Or even said one unkind thing about anyone. I let out a single guffaw, despite myself.

Daisy opened her eyes, lifting her hand. I took it in mine.

"Let me..." she paused to breathe. Her breaths were shallow, pumping up and down in her chest. "...see my boy."

Danny passed Marc to me, and I sat him next to her on her pillow, holding him in place to keep him from crawling on top of her. She tilted her head towards him.

"Marc." She stroked his cheek briefly before laying her arm back down across her stomach. She closed her eyes again and relaxed her head.

Marc reached out and patted her face. "Na-na Day," he squeaked.

Daisy's lips settled into not quite a smile, but a contended, peaceful expression. I gave Marc back to Danny and took her hand again. Her fingers felt brittle—not the warm, tireless hands I knew. Hands that were so often covered in dirt or smelled of her rose petal lotion. All I smelled now was hospital smell—sterile and medical. My eyes warmed and my nose stung. I breathed slowly, trying to keep the tears at bay at least until we left the room.

"It's okay," Daisy wheezed. "I'm not scared." She opened her eyes and looked sideways at me. "You'll be okay. Just..." She squeezed my hand gently, it was weak, like a baby's grasp. "Don't make my mistake." She closed her eyes again.

I stared at her, blankly. Danny was looking at me, as confused as I was.

There was a knock at the door, and the nurse poked her head in.

"Her daughter and son-in-law are here now."

I nodded and stood up. Danny gave Daisy's shoulder a squeeze and let Marc down to touch her face one last time. I leaned over and kissed her forehead.

"Thank you," I whispered, "for everything." Unable to hold the tears back any longer, they spilled from my eyes onto her cheek. "I love you."

She reached up and brushed my cheek, wiping a tear away.

"I love you, too."

I wished I'd thought to record her that day she'd showed me all the most important things from her life—all those stories she felt she needed to tell before she was gone.

The next day Terrance called to notify me of the funeral arrangements.

29

Manic-Depression

Lillian, 1994

After filing the police report and speaking with some officers about Grace's options for pressing charges, we put Niles to bed and sat at the kitchen table for a pregnancy-friendly drink. We didn't bother with glasses, each taking turns drinking out of a 2-liter bottle of root beer.

"I only know how to run away," I said.

"Sometimes leaving is the right choice."

My eyes wandered around the kitchen while I thought about how running away and leaving were different. Grace's sour cat jumped off a counter and disappeared down the hall.

She took my hand in hers. "You can stay here as long as you want."

I nodded. Black garbage bags of my personal items were taking up a good portion of her living room floor. The police had escorted me to Harry's apartment to get as many of my things as possible. It wasn't everything—mostly clothes. When I looked for my CD collection, which had been stored in a closet in Harry's office, they were gone. I suspected he'd dumped them somewhere before he even came to Grace's house.

"What are you going to do?" I asked Grace.

"I think I'll press charges. So it'll at least be on his record. If he ever does something to another woman...that will help her."

"What do you think I should do?"

The officers told us if we decided to press charges we had a potential case for emotional distress, especially given my pregnancy. Grace contacted her lawyer shortly after and confirmed I could get a restraining order and sue for enough to take care of myself through the pregnancy.

"I can't decide that for you." She reached out and took my hand, squeezing it. "But I'll support you no matter what."

I sat staring at the garbage bags. "I do want justice. But I also want to forget him."

I held onto her hand as if she could pull me out of this darkness.

Each day, I felt colder until I was numb. I longed for tequila to warm me up and make me forget, but I'd asked Grace to get rid of all the alcohol in the house. Graced had helped me find a therapist, and it didn't take long for them to realize that I was relying on booze to a level that wasn't completely healthy—even if I hadn't been pregnant. The therapist told me I needed to discover some healthier coping mechanisms. I'd asked Grace what that meant, so she started doing yoga tapes with me in the mornings and encouraged me to get back into sewing and quilting. Thankfully, Grace had been keeping my sewing machine for me while I'd been living with Harry.

He didn't try to call, even without a restraining order. He didn't try to come by either. I suspected he was relieved we were gone. And I suspected he hated me as much, if not more than I hated him.

My stomach grew bigger than I thought possible, and then grew again, as if it wanted to make sure I understood that I was about to become a single mom of two.

Grace asked Olive if she wanted to pick up my cleaning jobs—she was always looking for part-time work that could be flexible with her college classes. She went with me for a couple weeks so I could teach her everything, and then I took my maternity leave early. It would not be possible without Grace. She put me up in her room and slept with Niles in the guest bed. Though most nights I asked her to stay with me.

Each day was harder to bear as the shame fell over me. Despite defending myself and Niles at the last moment, I felt like a horrible mother for letting things go as long as they did. And I blamed myself for how Grace had been pushed away. I'd let that happen. I'd never even questioned her distance. Some friend I was.

One week I stayed in bed all day, every day, except to take care of Niles. Grace was only lecturing once a week this term. The rest of the week she worked on publicizing her book, which had been released that summer, doing reading events and speaking at panels. Then she did her usual counseling sessions in the evenings.

On Friday, a summer storm rolled in. I laid in Grace's bed, watching the rain fall for the entirety of Niles's nap. I imagined it flooding the window, consuming me in a flash flood. I thought back to the day Niles and I drove through that ice storm. I wished the snow had consumed me back then, before any of this had happened. But then I never would have met Grace.

Later that night I heard her huffing outside the bedroom door after she got home from her sessions. She knocked on the door with what I was fairly certain was her foot, then struggled at the knob.

I got up and opened the door. She was carrying the television from downstairs. "Thanks," she said, then set it on the dresser. Her tiny, lean frame hefting the large TV was comical. She plugged it in and sat on the bed, patting the space next to her. I joined her as she started flipping through channels.

"Let's find something girly," she said.

We started with *Blossom*, then watched some re-runs of *Full House*, followed by *The David Letterman show*.

By the time we'd flipped to David Letterman I was getting drowsy. Eventually, I fell asleep. When I woke the TV was off and there was a slice of pizza on a paper plate on the nightstand. Veggie. Grace was sitting on the vanity stool reading a book.

"What time is it?" I asked. I didn't used my voice much these days, and the words came out dry and hoarse.

She looked up almost like she'd forgotten I was there, then checked her watch. "Almost eleven."

I got up and retrieved the cold pizza, sitting on the edge of the bed to eat.

"I can heat that up for you."

"No, that's alright. What're you reading?"

She flipped the book around in her hand to look at the cover, like she needed reminding what it was called.

"*An Unquiet Mind: A memoir of moods and madness*."

"Never heard of it."

"It's a psych-nerd book." Grace set the book down and gave me her full attention. "It's by a researcher at John's Hopkins who started this clinic at UCLA. She wrote a book a few years ago on manic-depression, but this one is intended more for the people who have it, rather than the professionals who study and treat it. I've been looking forward to this one."

I laid back down on the pillow and closed my eyes, the pizza balanced on top of my belly. "Aren't the super technical books your usual jam?"

She smiled, "Well, the author is kind of my hero. And I relate to her. I don't just specialize in bipolar, I also have it."

I propped myself up on my elbows, only half comprehending her words. My mind was sluggish from the days of inactivity. And pregnancy brain.

"Wait." I pressed my hand against my forehead and tried to force the sluggish out. "You have what?"

"I have manic-depression—bipolar." She paused, thinking. "Remember when we first started going out for drinks, and I pushed that guy on you, then got upset about it?"

I nodded.

"I was manic when that happened. I had been for a week or so before that incident. Then I was so embarrassed it threw me into a depression. That's why I got kinda distant after that." I stared at her in disbelief. I knew she took meds and saw a psychologist, but I had no idea she had the very thing she'd been studying and writing about.

She continued. "Basically, when I'm manic I do risky things, or spend a lot of money, or binge drink. Which is also why I'm a little hyper aware when others drink a lot." The corners of her mouth lifted apologetically. "Mania is kinda like thinking there's no consequence for what you do. And like, feeling capable of anything with this sort of energy that needs release."

"Is that bad?" I asked. Everything she described sounded normal to me.

"It can be, yeah. People get hurt—like how I hurt you."

I nodded.

"Are you—" I was worried I would come across as offensive. "Are you manic right now?"

"No. I have been depressed. You've seen that."

I nodded.

I was starting to recognize the similarities. Everything she said I related to. I'd always been that way. Invincible for a week or two, then as low as the hemlines in my grandma's church. "Grace?"

"Yeah? Don't worry, you can ask me anything."

"Do I have manic-depression?"

She considered a minute. "It's possible," she finally determined. "But you're not my patient, so my opinion doesn't mean much. Did Dr. Reich say something?"

"No. She said she doesn't like to reveal her diagnosis suspicions until she's had a few months of sessions."

Grace nodded, unsurprised.

"There is another option. You could get a full psych eval." She got up and left the room briefly, returning with a rolodex. She slipped through, scribbling onto a legal pad, then tore off the page and handed it to me. On it were four names and phone numbers.

"They all do evaluations," she explained. "If you decide that's what you want, they're all good."

I called the first one on the list the next morning.

We walked into a musty, old room. It reminded me of my father's old office. The furniture was outdated, and the upholstery faded. My belly bumped into a coat rack, almost knocking it over. Grace reached out to steady it. She offered an arm, and I shook my head. I'd asked her to come with me, grilling her with questions all the way there and in the lobby.

Grace stood in the doorway, holding Niles on her hip. "I'll be just outside," she said, reassuringly.

The psychologist, Dr. Roberts, gestured to a maroon couch with rose embellishments in a shiny thread of the same color. The couch had two off-white throw pillows in the same stiff upholstery as the couch, but with embellishments of leaves.

I sat on the end of the couch, next to one of the pillows. The cushion and fabric were stiff, and my hips immediately protested. Dr. Roberts sat himself in an armchair across from me. Next to the armchair was an end table with a notebook and pen. The room was lit by two lamps, but it was still dim.

Dr. Roberts had round, thin-framed glasses that balanced nicely with a full mustache. His gelled hair was thick and dark with a little bit of grey. He wore a light blue polo tucked in with the collar of a white undershirt peeking out from the undone top button. He had on blue jeans, and his gut ballooned out over the waistband.

"Do you have kids?" I asked, before he'd had a chance to pick up his notebook and pen.

He smiled. "My partner and I just had a baby girl through our surrogate."

I breathed out and relaxed my shoulders, letting my hands reach around my belly to caress it. It was a subconscious habit that I'd had in the third trimester with Niles as well.

"Congratulations."

"Thank you. So, what brings you here today?" He asked, crossing his legs and propping his notepad on his knee.

"Well, most recently it's that I left this baby's father."

He nodded and jotted something down in his notebook.

"But it's my whole life that brings me here, I guess. I started seeing a therapist three months ago—after the shit with the baby daddy went down. Oh, am I allowed to say shit?"

He nodded.

"Ok, cool. Anyway, we've been working on my alcohol problem." I took one of the pillows and propped it up behind my lower back. It didn't help much.

"Alcohol problem?"

"She called it self-medicating."

He made another note. "And have you ever seen a therapist before now?"

"No."

"Ever been diagnosed with anxiety or depression?"

I shook my head.

"How many kids do you have?"

"Almost two." I touched my stomach again.

"Same father?"

"No. My ex-husband is my son's father."

Another note. "How'd your marriage end?"

I looked for my feet, only to realize they were obscured by my belly. I looked at Dr. Robert's feet instead. "For the same reason that I left this time," my voice lowered.

"Abuse?"

I sat silent. He waited. What was the hold up?

"Grace, maybe you already know, she wrote a book about bipolar."

"I did know. Do you think that's what you have?" He didn't seem to mind the change of subject.

"I don't know."

"Well, let's find out." He put his pen and pad down and stood up.

"How does it work?"

He opened a filing cabinet and started pulling packets from different folders. "Some interview, some questionnaire, and I'll send you to the lab for blood-work before you leave. It'll take about two hours."

I nodded.

"Alright, let's begin."

30

Sometimes it's Nice

Eleanor, 2020

I sat fully clothed in the empty tub, fabric no match against the cold porcelain on my legs and buttocks. I trembled as I rocked back and forth. I wrapped my arms tight around my torso, holding myself in a hug. I squeezed my eyes shut like I do during scary movies when I know something bad is about to happen.

I stayed like that for a few minutes, then carefully opened one eye to identify the faucet. I turned it, and water splashed onto the tub floor. It was icy at first, then gradually warmed. I lifted the knob that plugged the drain and kept one eye open, watching a small pool form around my feet. Water droplets splashed onto my sweatpants, darkening the navy-blue fabric for a few moments before absorbing further into the fibers. I closed my eye again. The pool of water crept up past my feet and began to soak through my underwear. Slowly, as the water rose, my clothes soaked it in further up my legs and torso. My eyes relaxed and I let them open. The bottoms of my pants were speckled with tiny air bubbles under the water, somehow making the fabric look like denim. My clothing clung to my body, weighted and heavy with the hot water like a compress soothing my muscles. I started to rock slower and less.

The bathroom door clicked open, and Danny quietly entered. I heard him move to the edge of the tub and kneel. I didn't look up, but I sensed him next to me. His arm crossed my line of vision as he turned off the faucet.

"Hey, honey," he whispered in his soft, baritone voice. He cautiously placed a hand on my shoulder. "Can you tell me what you're doing?"

Some bubbles broke free from my pant leg and rose to the surface of the water. They rested at the top for a moment before disappearing. I wished I could do the same. Float for a moment in pure weightlessness, then simply pop.

Danny moved his hand to my back, this time with more assurance. In the past I had sometimes recoiled from his touch during panic attacks. But this wasn't a panic attack. This was different. It was grief. I felt every bit of it deep in my bones, my blood, my soul.

"A bath will feel so much nicer without those clothes on. Can I help?"

I nodded.

Never in my life had I imagined a man removing my clothing with anything other than desire. But Danny undressed me like I was a child who fell asleep on a long car ride home before they had the chance to change into their PJs. The way he peeled off my shirt with my arms raised straight over my head, brought back a memory from when I was very young. Maybe five or six. My grandmother had woken me in the night. I'd been covered in sick. Mom had been out late that night, and I'd missed her, so I asked if I could sleep in her bed until she got home. When grandma woke me, Mom was back, next to me in the bed vomiting.

Grandpa stayed with her, helping her to her bathroom while Grandma carried me to the ensuite in her and grandpa's room. The lights were bright, and I kept my eyes closed as she placed me in the shower and turned on the faucet, rinsing the vomit off my PJs. She told me I could sit down if I liked, and I did. She then peeled the wet clothing off my body and gave me a good once over with a soapy loofa. A little vomit had found its way into my hair, and she took the strands in her fingers and ran them under the water with a little shampoo. She didn't make me wash all my hair, which I was glad about because I really hated washing my hair.

After I was rinsed off, she got me some clean PJs and put me down in her and grandpa's bed.

Danny finished undressing me, and I was naked in the tub, which despite being the usual way to bathe, left me feeling exposed and out of place. My muscles tremored.

"Are you cold?"

I shook my head.

"Do you want to get out?"

I nodded.

Danny reached in front of me again to lift the lever to the drain. The water rushed down into the pipes, gurgling as the level lowered. My body became heavier, but the worst thing was the stone that lay on my heart.

We sat in a church pew, Danny's arm wrapped around my shoulders, Marc in his lap. I wore a long, black, jersey-knit dress that I'd bought a few weeks ago when I'd accepted my body wasn't going to "bounce back" and began replacing my wardrobe with better fitting clothes. I wished my first time wearing the new dress was in better circumstances. Danny wore his suit and we'd put Marc in a tiny white polo shirt—the dressiest thing we had for him. The church was small and modest; the most ornate thing in the room was a wooden crucifix that hung on the wall behind the pulpit. The crucifix was decorated with delicate carvings, swirling around one another like leaves spinning in a wind.

Terrance stood at the pulpit giving his mother's eulogy.

I fixated on the crucifix. My grandma and grandpa were religious. Mom less so. She was spiritual, but when Grandma and Grandpa asked her to go to church with them, she would say she didn't subscribe to religion. She'd let us go though, my brother and me. I'd grown up with all the comfort and confusion that comes from putting everything in a being never seen. Danny's parents were very religious, and he grew up attending every Sunday as well. But now neither of us really went to church. I guess we'd never found a congregation we liked. Nothing could compare to my memory of Sundays with Grandma and Grandpa at their Alabama Baptist church. All the women would wear big hats and little dainty gloves. Everyone sat in the same pew each week and all the faces were familiar. The widow who sat in front of us, I think her name was Mrs. Simons, would sneak me butterscotch candies when the sermons went over. I realize now it wasn't really sneaky—Grandma knew.

When I was a teenager, I joined the youth Bible study and spent my Tuesday afternoons for four years reciting scripture and finding pride in being exactly the kind of child my grandparents wanted their granddaughter to be. But once I went to college, the motivation to worship faded. After a while, I wasn't so sure what I believed or if I had ever really believed at all. It was a culture, a community more than anything.

Terrance finished speaking and the small group of mourners in the congregation murmured scattered *amens*. Danny joined in the whispers, but my mouth was too dry to speak. The priest returned to the pulpit and announced a performance by the children's choir, which he said was one of Daisy's favorite parts of Sunday service.

My eyes drifted from the crucifix that had held my attention to the young faces that were gathering by the piano. There was only a dozen or so of them, but to me it sounded like a hundred voices.

Jesus conquered death,
He conquered death for me!
Because of Him I'll live again,
Because He died, I am free!

"Do you think it's true?" I asked Danny in the car when the service was over.

"What?"

"That Jesus conquered death. That we'll all live again after we die."

Danny checked the rearview mirror to look at Marc, asleep in his car seat. The service overlapped with his naptime, so he'd fallen quickly to sleep after we'd started driving.

"I don't know," Danny finally answered. "But it's a nice thought, anyway."

Outside the car window the sky was overcast, but with no indications of rain. I replayed the children's song in my head. They thought it was true. It was in their voices. Their voices that multiplied with their convictions. But it's so easy to believe when you're young.

"Does it really matter though," Danny spoke again. "If it's true?" He glanced over at me, taking in my expression. "I mean, if it gives people comfort, that's good enough, right?"

"My mom always says religion corrupts faith and belief."

Danny shrugged and made the left turn onto our street.

"But," I continued, "sometimes it's nice."

He nodded. "Yeah, it is."

31

A Hug

Rose, 1973

It was a regular day: I woke, showered, and dressed. Thomas kissed my cheek before leaving for work. I asked Eugene what he wanted for breakfast. He wanted eggs and toast. I made French scrambled eggs—his favorite, and mine. I got some oatmeal for Carol, and the three of us sat down to breakfast. Carol chirped and babbled, mixing in new words, like usual. Eugene helped her when she needed it, as usual. He took more responsibility for Carol than a nine-year-old should. A pang of guilt briefly shot through my chest, but I chased the thought away. I was learning. I needed to be more patient with myself. I read the paper over breakfast. There was an ad for an opening on the editorial team. I stared at it until Eugene told me it was eight-fifteen. Eugene asked where his book bag was, and I found it in his room. I told him to be safe walking to school. The same routine we followed every morning. The air was warm with the whispers of impending summer. I stood on the porch to see him off on his walk to school, like I always did. He put one foot on the porch steps then hesitated. Before I could ask what was wrong, he turned back and hugged me around my waist.

And all at once today was anything but usual.

When Eugene was gone, Carol and I went about our own routines. But now it felt different. Before her nap I read a couple stories. We read *Goodnight Moon*, which was Eugene's favorite when he was a toddler.

Eugene and I had been feeding off each other's emotions, living in parallel. We both lost the person most important to us in the world, were thrown into a new family, and grieved all in parallel. We went through the motions of living, struggled to bond with those around us, and harbored guilt all in parallel. We observed one another and failed to understand one another, while dancing a perfect, harmonious, parallel dance. We were more alike than I had ever realized, and he was my light at the end of this long, dark tunnel. Him and Carol.

After Carol was asleep, I went to the master bedroom and prayed. I couldn't just be their mom on paper. I had to choose it. I'd adopted these children in the eyes of the law, but for months had failed to adopt them into my heart. It was time to forgive myself for being alive and start making my life worthy of my sister's memory.

After praying I returned to the kitchen. The newspaper still sat on the table, folded to the page with the job advert. I read it again. And again. And again. Then I grabbed the phone.

That evening Thomas came home from work on time. I'd made beef bourguignon, teaching Eugene how to prepare it, and baked a fresh loaf of French bread. I brought out a bottle of wine for Thomas and me.

We all sat down to dinner. Thomas was tired, but as always asked me how my day was.

"I applied for a job."

Thomas stopped eating.

"Assistant editor for the Tuscaloosa News. They loved me so much over the phone they offered it to me already. I'm gonna be in charge of the food section."

Thomas beamed. "Rose, if I couldn't be any more in love with you."

"Just part time. I called Ma. She said she could watch Carol durin' the day. And I would leave after Eugene goes to school and be back before it lets out."

"You'll be great at that job, mama Rose," Eugene piped in. Then he smiled at me. A smile that said we shared something.

This was exactly where I needed to be.

32

Home

"We'll see you in a couple weeks." The nurse smiled as I left the exam room, handing me a brochure about timing contractions. This would be my last check up before the baby came.

Outside the clinic I sat on a bench to put the brochure in my purse. The letter was still inside. The one from the psychiatrist. I had read it over and over, but I still slid it out of the torn envelope and scanned it again. It was like reading an official notice that I was certifiably wacked.

My leg was bouncing up and down like a jackhammer. Finally, I stood up to use the payphone by the clinic entrance, fishing coins from a pouch in my bag. I picked up the receiver and dialed.

"Hello?" Her voice was exactly the same.

"Mom?" I whispered.

She gasped. "Lily?" Her voice cracked. The burden of the past few years reverberated in her voice.

We both cried for a few minutes without words, alone, but together. A woman stopped on her way out of the clinic to ask if I was ok. I nodded and mouthed, *hormones*. She nodded sympathetically before continuing to the parking lot.

"I'm sorry," I finally whispered into the receiver.

"Why didn't you tell us?" She didn't have to elaborate.

"Because even if you believed me, I was afraid you'd try to convince me divorce was worse."

She had stopped crying, and now her gentle breathing was the only noise between us.

"I'm glad you left the son-of-a-bitch," she finally said. The words hit me like baptismal waters.

"And Dad?"

She sighed heavily. "He wasn't happy when he found out you'd filed papers, but once your brother told him Don was beatin' you…"

I put another quarter in.

"He's your pa. He misses you. We all do."

I rested my forehead against the phone box. "Mom, I'm so sorry."

"I know." Strained emotion returned in her voice. "Don't worry your head anymore 'bout it, sweetie. I'm just glad you finally called."

My nose tickled, and I wiped it across the back of my hand.

"Can I come see ya'll?" she asked.

I breathed deeply and composed myself.

"Actually, that's why I'm calling. I'm having another baby, Mom. She's due in two weeks." I heard the quick intake of breath—surprise, and a hint of joy. I continued, "How soon can you get here? There's someone I want you to meet."

Mom flew in the day after I called. The reunion had been tearful and painful, but all at once her presence made everything feel right again. She held my hand when I went into labor, shouted at a doctor who made a flippant remark about my pain threshold, and cut the cord when her granddaughter was born. A month later, we all spent Christmas together at Grace's, and Mom made pastries and tarts and cooked an incredible Christmas feast. She showed no signs of returning to Alabama yet. Grace didn't mind in the least—she and Mom had become fast friends. And I was wondering how I could possibly say goodbye and separate from her again.

That author Grace liked was right to call the mind unquiet. I didn't know the mind could be anything but unquiet. What a strange revelation it was to discover that my head could be at rest. I found myself wondering about people: the clerk at the grocery store, my snobbish clients, the bank teller, the pharmacist—did they have quiet minds? What did their worlds look like? Did they sometimes feel that insatiable, clawing monster of impulsivity inside themselves, or did they always taste the sweetness of contentment? Did they periodically fall under the darkness that swallows everything whole, or were they always bathed in light? I didn't know what normal was. And it began to fascinate me.

Grace told me not to dwell on normal. *What even is normal?* she would say. But that's exactly what I wanted to know. What I hungered to know.

In my sessions with Dr. Reich, I would ask if something I thought or did was normal. She told me I had the passion of a neurologist. She would talk about brain chemicals and neural pathways. But I don't think I have the passion of a neurologist. I didn't care why my brain did what it did, I only wanted to know if everyone else's brains did the same things. I wanted to know just how abnormal I was.

I'd started medication as soon as the baby was born, which meant no breastfeeding. Dr. Reich and Dr. Roberts both agreed the risk of not starting medication would be worse than the risk of feeding my daughter exclusively formula. I didn't mind. I'd mostly hated breastfeeding with Niles, anyway.

Grace met me at the coffee shop. It was our new hang out after my official alcoholism diagnosis. It was the middle of a weekday and fairly quiet. I sat at one of those small two-person tables. My latte and Grace's book sat side by side on the tabletop in front of me. Christmas lights were still up in the window. It was that strange time between Christmas and the New Year when life was in limbo and existence felt like the end of a dream when you're now half-awake and reality starts to creep in.

Quiet jazz covers of pop songs played over the stereo. *How can anyone stand this stuff?* The juke box at the first bar Grace and I went to flitted across my memory. The 80s ballads and music good enough to move to, Cindy Lauper and Grace's awkward dance moves. I smiled to myself.

The chime of the bell hanging above the café door rang as Grace stepped into the shop. She waved at me before heading to the counter to order her drink. She was in her work clothes, having come straight from class. A couple minutes later she sat across from me with a black coffee. She poured in two Splenda packets and stirred.

She noticed the book next to me and smiled. "Did you actually read it?" Her tone betrayed her slight disbelief.

I nodded. "I learned a lot."

She sipped her coffee, never breaking eye contact as her cup lifted.

"I'd like you to sign it," I said.

Grace's eyes grew suspicious as she lowered her drink and cupped it with both hands. "Of course. Why the formality though?"

Across the tables the partial sun shone through the window in patterns through the clouds.

"My mom..." This was even harder than I'd imagined.

"Yes?"

"She asked me to come home."

Grace paused. She clearly already knew the answer to what she asked next. "To Alabama?"

I nodded.

Grace mirrored the nod. "It would be good for you."

I waited for her to show any signs of how she felt.

"What about your ex?"

"My dad helped me get a restraining order."

She nodded. "And Harry?"

"I had a lawyer reach out. He said as long as I don't go after him for child support we can consider him out of our lives. He doesn't care if I take El out of state."

"Well, it's really too bad. I'll have to find a new housekeeper."

We both laughed. I hadn't cleaned Grace's home in months, not since I moved in with her.

I reached into my pocket and pulled out the pink stone Amanda had given me that fateful day almost three years ago. I took her hand and placed it in her palm, wrapping her fingers around it. "For unconditional love."

Her eyes told me that her heart was broken. They always revealed her truths to me. The secrets of her heart. I'd wondered before if she was just easy to read, but now I knew—her eyes spoke to me, just to me.

I moved my hand to her face, brushing her hair behind her ear. The touch ignited something in her eyes. She returned it, leaning forward as she gently pulled my face towards hers. Our foreheads met first, and a tingling warmth swept through me. Then she lifted her face to mine and kissed me, our lips fitting together like two puzzle pieces. We didn't care who'd be watching. No one could hurt us. Not now. We'd been through too much.

"I'll miss you," she whispered. Pressing her forehead back on mine.

It would be the moment that haunted us both for years to come. A moment from another life.

33

Don't Make My Mistake

We started going to Daisy's church every Sunday. At first because her friends there had invited us, and we accepted out of respect for Daisy's memory. But after a while we'd become used to it. Danny believed. He may have never stopped believing. I wasn't sure if I believed in God or in Daisy, but either way the congregation soon felt like family. I enjoyed the community.

This Sunday Terrance was there. Danny asked if we should sit with him, and I shook my head. Throughout Daisy's funeral arrangements I hadn't known how to act around her three children. The twins, Bob and Sara, and Terrance. Apparently, Daisy had told them all about me, just as she told me about them. But it was like a movie being made of your favorite book—those characters are like your best friends, and you imagine them in a certain way, then the movie destroys those images, and the new versions are strangers. Not to mention the circumstance of our meeting made things tense.

But Terrance was waiting outside for me after the service.

"Eleanor, could I speak with you?"

Danny took Marc to the car, and I walked with Terrance out of the way of the socializing crowds.

"Here for a visit?" I asked, attempting polite conversation. Terrance lived in New York. None of Daisy's children had stayed close to their hometown.

"Just wrapping things up with the house."

Daisy's kids had gone through her things after the funeral, but most everything sentimental or of value she'd already mailed them. For bigger items, like her old piano, she'd arranged for ahead of time. Everything left over was being sold together with the house as an estate. Her kids would split the assets. Daisy's executor was a gentleman from church, a nice older widower who we came to suspect was the object of some playful, innocent romance.

"Eleanor, I need to talk to you about some of Daisy's medical records."

"I already told you, she didn't say anything to me about being sick," I replied, confused. "I'm sorry, but I had no idea."

"No, not her cancer. I hired a PI to dig up *all* her medical records. Since birth. After she hid her the cancer I needed to know if there was anything else. You know, anything hereditary."

I nodded, still unsure what help I could be in this area. It seemed extreme. But Daisy had mentioned once that Terrance was a bit of a hypochondriac.

"Eleanor, I need to know if she ever told you about a pregnancy. When she was thirteen."

My eyes widened.

"I take that as a no." He didn't try to mask the disappointment in his voice. He sighed, "The PI uncovered a record from an abortion clinic."

I avoided looking him in the eye. Daisy had lost a baby, too. She never indicated, never let on.

"I know it's a lot. I'm sorry." He sounded truly apologetic. He shuffled his feet.

"I do know something." I watched a small group of kids playing ring-around-the-rosie by the big maple tree.

Terrance froze, and I imagined he was holding his breath. I finally turned back to him.

"She was abused when she was twelve and thirteen. Multiple times, by a family friend."

Terrance looked down and wrapped his arms around his chest.

"She said her mom didn't believe her."

"Grandma must've made her get an abortion," Terrance spoke.

I didn't say anything. I didn't want to speculate, but it wasn't my place to tell Terrance not to.

"Thank you, Eleanor." He walked away. The encounter was abrupt, ending with so much uncertainty on both sides.

Don't make my mistake. Daisy's last advice to me reverberated in my head.

I turned and walked briskly to the car. I climbed into the passenger side.

"What was that about."

I looked back at Marc. He was watching a cartoon on Danny's phone. "I'll tell you later."

Danny started the car and pulled out of the parking spot.

"Danny?"

"Yeah?"

"I know what Daisy meant, now. About not making her mistakes. And I'm ready to talk about Ruth."

"This is the first step, Eleanor."

I sat in my usual spot in Aliza's office, on the edge of the sofa. She sat in her swivel chair. "You've already done one of the hardest parts."

"Daisy gave me the courage."

Aliza nodded. "What happened to your friend is devastating. But she shared about her past to help you heal, and that's a great gift. Just like her, you have the power to create meaning from this. No one can reframe the narrative for you, and sometimes the greatest meaning we get from life is the heaviest to carry. That's the weight of gold."

"I miss her."

Aliza smiled sympathetically. "Would you like to talk about Ruth now?"

I nodded.

I left Aliza's office with my soul light. Therapy was finally starting to make me feel better instead of worse. It was a transition I'd been through before, and experience had taught me there were brighter skies ahead. As if a manifestation of my breakthrough, the fall rainclouds from earlier that morning were parting for a bright sun.

When I got in the car, I pulled out my phone to check my messages. There were five missed calls and a text message from my mom.

Call me. Now.

Familiar anxiety fought to suck me down a spiral as I considered the reasons my mom would call so many times in the short hour I had silenced my phone. An ugly sort of nostalgia brought childhood fears to my mind's surface as I clicked the call back button.

The phone only rang once. "Where have you been? I've been trying to call."

"I was in therapy, Mom. What's wrong?"

"Your grandmother had a heart attack, El. We're at the hospital—she's in surgery, but it was bad. You need to get on the next flight."

34

Mothers and Daughters

2021

Eleanor stepped off the plane, Danny behind her, pushing Marc in a stroller. The humid Alabama heat immediately washed over her like a wall, familiar and inviting.

Danny wiped a hand across his brow. It was a warm October, even for Alabama. "Don't know how you enjoy this," he said.

Eleanor laughed. "Says the boy from Korea."

"I never enjoyed it there, either."

Outside security, her mom was waiting for them, pinching her fingers systematically.

"El, Danny!" she called out as they turned the corner into her line of sight.

They tearfully embraced, then Eleanor's mom unbuckled Marc from the stroller to carry him in her arms.

"Did you check any luggage?"

"No," Danny answered. "Just the carry-ons."

They made their way through the airport to the parking lot.

"How's Grandpa?" Eleanor asked.

Her mom gave her a flat smile that said more than words could have.

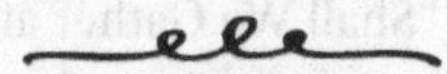

There was a vase of magnolia blossoms on a table next to the pulpit. Beside the vase, a photograph. She was young in the photo, with long, dark blonde hair in fat waves that curled away from her face. A single strand of pearls hung on her neck, the very same that Lillian wore now. Hymns played on the organ until the minister rose to begin the service.

"This afternoon we celebrate the life of Rose Whitfield Peavy who has returned to the loving embrace of God the Father. Rose's family has asked to participate as much as possible, today. Rose's daughter, Lillian Carol Howell, will offer the prelude." The minister sat down on the stage as Eleanor's mom rose from her seat and approached the pulpit.

"Welcome," she breathed shakily into the microphone. "Thank you so much for being here. To grieve, to comfort, to worship, and above all to honor my mom's life." Eleanor was mildly surprised her mother said *worship* so unironically. It was what her grandmother would've wanted, though.

Lillian continued, "I'm not much of a believer, so I'll leave the sermoning to Reverend Jones." Scattered chuckles moved through the congregation. "But I would like to say a few words about my mom. Because I didn't always act very grateful, and I want to thank her properly. There were a couple years when I was a new mom that I never even spoke to her. But when I came home," Lillian looked at Eleanor's grandfather, sitting in the front pew. "She and Dad welcomed me with open arms. They took me and my kids in. I wish I'd told her just how much that meant to me back then. Throughout my life, she would nurse me back to health during my lows. She taught me how to be a better parent." Lillian's voice became high and squeaky. "And how to be an independent woman. She was the strongest person I've ever known. I wish I was even half the woman she is—was." She cleared her throat and took control of her voice. "She never judged me. Her love was unconditional, and I hardly deserved it."

The minister handed Lillian a tissue and she dabbed her eyes, trying not to smear her makeup, but the eyeliner was already smudged. She turned to the photograph on the table next to her. "I miss you so much, Mom. Thank you. For everything." Lillian returned to her seat between Eleanor and Eleanor's brother Niles, taking their hands in each of hers and clutching them tight.

The organist began to play "Shall We Gather at the River?" Paper rustled as the congregation opened their programs to the hymn's lyrics. They sang quietly, with a few more confident voices rising above the others. Rose's family did not sing. They listened to the congregation, some of them praying in their hearts, others taking from the experience whatever was meaningful to them.

The hymn was followed by a reading. Eugene's wife, Tammy, recited verses from Ecclesiastes 3 about everything having a season. Afterward, the minister's wife, who had been friends with Rose, offered a prayer of gratitude and celebration for Rose's life.

The minister invited Eugene up to offer the eulogy. He stood up from his seat next to Eleanor's grandfather and approached the microphone. He gave a beautiful tribute depicting Rose's history and life story. He told a few of the stories his grandmother Annabel had told him about Rose's childhood and youth, one about her and her sister dumping eggs in someone's gym bag, which sparked true laughter among the mourners. Eugene said he loved that story the most, because it represented his two mothers' relationship with each other. As he moved into adulthood, her spoke about her successes, her accomplishments, and her influence on others. As she would've wanted, he spoke about her involvement in the church, specifically about her charity. For just a moment, eyes were dry as he recounted a life worth celebrating.

He ended with a quick word from his daughters: "My girls, Rose and Annabel, wish they could've been here today, but they asked me to express their love for Mama Rose and say that she inspired them both throughout their lives." He paused, looking around at the full pews. "She would've loved this. Seeing you all gathered here. Thank you. Thank you so much." He returned to his seat.

Eleanor's cousin Nathan did the next reading from his personal Bible, a passage from 1 Corinthians 15. Something about death as a transformation. Then the minister gave his sermon. Eleanor couldn't concentrate on these. She dwelled on everything said in her uncle's eulogy. There was a lot she'd never heard before. She felt guilty, like she hadn't asked the right questions while her grandmother was still alive to answer them. She was certain there were details of her grandmother's life that were now lost, forever.

The minister ended his sermon with prayer asking for God's comfort for Rose's family. Then he said, "Rose's granddaughter, Eleanor, has agreed to sing a verse from Rose's favorite hymn, 'How Great Thou Art.' Her husband Danny will accompany on the piano." Danny handed Marc to Lillian and helped Eleanor up.

Eleanor's voice cracked a few times as she tried to control her emotion. She tried to think about God the way her grandmother had—to convey Rose's love through the words of that hymn. And for a brief moment Eleanor felt something divine. Maybe the higher self her mom was always talking about. Or maybe the God that her grandmother had believed in. That Daisy had believed in. She looked at Danny to ground herself, and she saw belief in his eyes as he played.

When had he reconverted, anyway? Was it in a brief moment of clarity, or a slow build over time as they'd attended Daisy's church each week? Or had he never really stopped believing? She used his certainty to steady herself and ended the hymn strong in her voice, but still uncertain in her heart.

Danny wrapped his arm around her shoulders as they returned to their pew. They sat and Eleanor buried her face in Danny's shoulder. He kissed the top of her head and held her as she sobbed. Lillian rubbed Eleanor's back with her fingertips.

"Before we have our final reading and prayer, Rose's husband Thomas has asked to say a few words. After the prayer we will have forty minutes to gather at Hillside Cemetery for a brief graveside service. Before we part, I want to remind all in attendance to sign the newspaper in the foyer with Rose's first article she wrote for *Tuscaloosa Eats*." The minister looked at Eleanor's grandfather and nodded.

Thomas walked slowly from his seat in the front row to the pulpit. It was a short distance, but to everyone in the congregation it seemed a mile with Thomas's heavy footsteps. He held a cane in one hand, carved and polished from burl wood.

He approached the pulpit, no notes in hand. He scanned the crowd, taking in the faces who had come to honor his wife's memory. After a moment, he cleared his throat. "Gone too soon..." he hung his head. "I spoke my feelings the day Rose and I were married—when I made my vows. I feel I must do so again, now...I don't remember my mother very well, but I remember my father when she died. I now understand how he felt." He paused, breathing to compose himself. He still towered despite his hunched shoulders. "I don't know how long I'll last up here, so I'll be quick. Rose was strong. Stronger even than any of you know." He looked directly at Lillian, and then Eugene. "There was one thing that mattered to her more than almost everything else: honoring her sister's memory. I believe she was successful. I..." he paused, his voice catching. "I don't know what I'm going to do without her."

Lillian buried her face in one hand, sobbing. Niles took Marc and passed him to Tammy, then wrapped his arm around his mom.

"She was the love of my life. She never failed to surprise me with her tenacity and wit. My life had meaning because she was in it. My world is darker now. I'm afraid it always will be, until they day I see her again. But I will make another vow to her today. To live. To honor her, as she did her sister, by pushing aside the darkness to make way for light. For our children and grandchildren and great-grandchildren."

In the back of the chapel, a man about Thomas's age, maybe slightly older, stood unnoticed behind the pews. He listened to the widower's words, tears falling in a steady, silent stream down his leathery cheeks. He looked longingly at the row of family in the front. His dark eyes lingered on Eugene and Lillian. They were eyes filled with shame and regret.

Thomas paused. The mourners believed the silence was in overpowering emotion, stealing his words away. But Thomas had seen the man. They held one another's gaze, and there was understanding between them—two men who had lost what was dearest to them in the entire world. Decades of distance closed in a second, then the man turned and left.

The cemetery was hot. The mourners gathered under the golden canopy of the two trees near Rose's graveside to hide from the sun. Despite the temperature, some of the leaves had begun to fall, scattering the manicured lawn with red and brown.

A short graveside service reminded all that death was not the end. Niles gave a final prayer, then Eleanor watched as her grandmother was lowered into the ground by a row of green straps on a motorized pulley. As the casket disappeared, she felt a sudden urgency. It was too soon. She needed more time, more time to say goodbye. She looked around her, and everyone stood still and calm. Some tears and sniffles disrupted the silence, but no one seemed concerned that her grandmother's body was about to be covered in six feet of earth. Eleanor tried to remind herself this was normal—how it's done. But it all looked so out of place now, and panic pulsed painfully in her chest.

The family lined up to throw handfuls of dirt down onto the casket. Eleanor stayed behind, next to the cottonwood. Danny gave her a look and squeezed her hand. She shook her head. He moved forward without her, holding Marc with the same white polo on that he'd worn to Daisy's funeral. Danny helped

Marc grab some dirt and drop it down into the grave. After Danny and Marc finished, a tall, elderly Black woman in a suit approached the grave, removing a white glove before taking a handful dirt. Eleanor recognized the state senator—Great-Aunt Celiah as Eleanor had known her growing up—Grandmother's closest friend. Celiah kissed the top of her fist, then let the dirt trickle slowly between her fingers. She left the graveside and stood next to Grandfather, grasping his hand in both of hers.

Lillian approached Eleanor. "Come on, we'll do it together."

Eleanor looked at her mother, the panic and helplessness showing in her eyes.

Lillian took her arm. "Come, Eleanor. You'll regret it your whole life if you don't."

She led Eleanor to the graveside, picking up a handful of dirt, then nodded at her to do the same. Eleanor reached down and sunk her hand into the pile at their feet. It was cool and slightly damp, like fresh garden soil from the hardware store. It smelled like Daisy's garden. And Eleanor choked back a sob. As she opened her fingers over the hole in the ground, the dirt fell atop the pile that soiled the polished cherry wood of the casket lid.

Eleanor looked to her mother, but Lillian was focused on something beyond the gravesite. A petite, middle aged woman with greying blonde hair walked through the cemetery towards them. Lillian led Eleanor back to Danny and Marc, then almost ran to the woman, pulling her into an intimate embrace. Niles followed close behind his mother, hugging the woman after Lillian finally released her. The woman stroked his hair with affectionate familiarity.

Danny looked at Eleanor inquisitively. "Who is that?"

"I don't know," Eleanor answered.

A few more mourners stepped forward to add dirt to the casket, then Celiah, with her arm wrapped around Thomas's shoulders, announced there would be a reception at the Whitfield home for family and any friends who wished to pay their respects.

Lillian and Eleanor sat on the back porch of the old Whitfield house. Not much had changed about it in almost fifty years. The house had been in the family for generations now, inherited by Rose when her parents passed, and with

Rose's passing would be inherited by Lillian, since Eugene was Command Chief Master Sergeant at Mcclellan air force base in Sacramento, and had no plans to leave California. Lillian planned to sell her condo and move in with her father immediately, so he wouldn't be alone in that big house.

Close family friends mingled inside, nibbling on potluck dishes and exchanging tearful embraces. Outside, the leaves on the peach trees resisted changing their colors for fall. The familiar earthy warm scents of an Alabama October filled the Whitfield's small orchard.

"What did grandpa mean?" Eleanor sat down on the top step, holding a sweet tea that was still full. Her mother sat next to her, leaning against the porch beam and sipping her own tea.

"Mom didn't talk about it," Lillian answered. "But your grandfather told Eugene and I that she'd been really depressed for a couple years after Lily died. They didn't really know that's what it was back then. And you know, she never had kids of her own. I've only just learned that wasn't from lack of trying. She got pregnant a few times, as I understand. And almost died when she lost the last one. She didn't know how to get help back then, so she fought through it all on her own. But she didn't let that happen to me. When I had my first episode as a teenager, it was like she was on fire. She didn't stop until she knew I'd be ok."

"Sounds familiar."

Lillian smiled.

Both women stared out at the setting sun. The air was thick, and the elongated shadows didn't bring much relief.

"Were you ever diagnosed with anything, Mom?"

Lillian studied her daughter. "You know, when I look at you, all grown, I swear it's like photos of Lily come to life. You have her exact eyes, you know."

Eleanor turned to face her mother. "Please. You don't know how frustrating it's been to not know my own family history."

Lillian sighed and turned back to the sunset. The moon was high, reflecting the sun's golden colors as darkness pulled at the sky.

"Alcoholism, PTSD, and bipolar disorder."

Eleanor felt a rush of anger. "Bipolar? When—"

"I was diagnosed right before you were born."

"You knew my whole life? Why wouldn't you tell me this? Especially when I was doing all those evaluations?"

"I told your psychiatrist."

"You told my psychiatrist. And what, told him not to tell me?"

Lillian stared down into her tea.

"I was scared. My whole fucking childhood." It felt good to curse—like releasing the valve on a pressure cooker.

"I don't expect you to understand. Not yet. But someday you'll find that the people you are charged to love most, the ones you're responsible for protecting—there's pain you don't want them to ever know exists."

"I was still in pain."

"I know," Lillian looked at her, regret written across her face and deep in her eyes. "I'm sorry. Back then everyone encouraged people to keep that kind of stuff to themselves. Keep it from their kids. They still do." She sighed, deeply. "It's not an excuse. I just want you to know I was trying to do the right thing. I got it wrong, and I'm so sorry about that."

Eleanor looked into her mother's eyes. There was regret in them.

"But I did try to give you something better than what I had. Like your grandma did for me."

Eleanor's face softened. Her mom was wrong about one thing: She did understand. She was desperate to keep her darkness away from Marc. Maybe she couldn't forgive her mom quite yet, but she'd begin to try. She determined then and there she wouldn't make the same mistakes that her mom and Daisy's generation had made.

"Mom, there's something I need to tell you."

Lillian shifted, turning to face Eleanor better. The condensation on Eleanor's glass trickled down onto her hand.

"After Marc was born, I was diagnosed with post-partum OCD." Eleanor brought her gaze back up to the horizon, letting the tears go, not trying to stifle their intensity.

Lillian put down her tea and wrapped her arms around her daughter, resting her head against Eleanor's. Eleanor buried her face in her mom's neck.

"I'm ok now. It was temporary. But it's been a really hard few years. It's been hard having a baby after losing one. After losing...Ruth."

Lillian looked down at her daughter, surprised. "I didn't know you gave her a name." Ruth's gravestone read: *Baby Sun.*

Eleanor nodded.

"Do you want to talk about it?" Lillian whispered, softly.

Eleanor shook her head, her forehead rubbing against the fabric of Lillian's dress. They sat there for a few minutes while Eleanor's tears slowed. Then she remembered something.

"Mom, who was that woman at the cemetery?"

Lillian ran her fingers through her daughter's hair. "An old friend."

Eleanor sat up.

Lillian smiled, and something simultaneously sad and beautiful reflected in her eyes. "No. More than a friend, actually."

Eleanor's lower jaw opened just a bit, and she looked behind her through the glass porch door. The woman was standing by the kitchen sink, in seeming deep conversation with Eleanor's grandfather, her hand on his arm in a comforting gesture. Lillian followed Eleanor's gaze, her eyes sparkling at the sight of the woman.

Eleanor squeezed her mom's hand. "I didn't even know...I'm so happy for you, Mom."

Lillian turned back to Eleanor and nodded, smiling. "Her name's Grace. We met when I was living in St. Louis before you were born. Back then I was...too afraid. I pretended to not care what society thought of me, but truly I cared more than most. I was afraid of being outcast. And by the time I'd figured out that shit didn't matter, that we'd be fine if we faced it together, well...your grandmother had invited me back home, and it was the right thing for me. Truly I think if we'd been together back then it wouldn't have lasted anyway. I wasn't ready for a healthy relationship."

"Oh, Mom, I'm sure that's not—"

Lillian laughed. "Don't even try, El. You're a terrible liar." They both laughed, then Lillian continued. "Over the years, we lost touch. But we reconnected a year or so ago when I looked her up. I'm sorry I didn't tell you sooner, I didn't want to say anything until it was a sure thing. But she's going to retire early and come live with me here."

"That's okay. Thanks for telling me now."

Eleanor and Lillian sat in each of their own vulnerabilities, feeling a bond grow between them that was different than a child's and her mother's, but maybe only a different shape of the same thing. Eleanor put her arm around her mom, and they embraced as the sun dipped towards the horizon, it's orange light reflected in the glow of a sawdust moon.

Eleanor stepped off the plane, Danny behind her, pushing Marc in a stroller. The humid Alabama heat immediately washed over her like a wall, familiar and inviting.

Danny wiped a hand across his brow. It was a warm October, even for Alabama. "Don't know how you enjoy this," he said.

Eleanor laughed. "Says the boy from Korea."

"I never enjoyed it there, either."

Outside security, her mom was waiting for them, pinching her fingers systematically.

"El, Danny!" she called out as they turned the corner into her line of sight.

They tearfully embraced, then Eleanor's mom unbuckled Marc from the stroller to carry him in her arms.

"Did you check any luggage?"

"No," Danny answered. "Just the carry-ons."

They made their way through the airport to the parking lot.

"How's Grandpa?" Eleanor asked.

Her mom gave her a flat smile that said more than words could have.

There was a vase of magnolia blossoms on a table next to the pulpit. Beside the vase, a photograph. She was young in the photo, with long, dark blonde hair in fat waves that curled away from her face. A single strand of pearls hung on her neck, the very same that Lillian wore now. Hymns played on the organ until the minister rose to begin the service.

"This afternoon we celebrate the life of Rose Whitfield Peavy who has returned to the loving embrace of God the Father. Rose's family has asked to participate as much as possible, today. Rose's daughter, Lillian Carol Howell, will offer the prelude." The minister sat down on the stage as Eleanor's mom rose from her seat and approached the pulpit.

"Welcome," she breathed shakily into the microphone. "Thank you so much for being here. To grieve, to comfort, to worship, and above all to honor my mom's life." Eleanor was mildly surprised her mother said *worship* so unironically. It was what her grandmother would've wanted, though.

Lillian continued, "I'm not much of a believer, so I'll leave the sermoning to Reverend Jones." Scattered chuckles moved through the congregation. "But I would like to say a few words about my mom. Because I didn't always act very grateful, and I want to thank her properly. There were a couple years when I was a new mom that I never even spoke to her. But when I came home," Lillian looked at Eleanor's grandfather, sitting in the front pew. "She and Dad welcomed me with open arms. They took me and my kids in. I wish I'd told her just how much that meant to me back then. Throughout my life, she would nurse me back to health during my lows. She taught me how to be a better parent." Lillian's voice became high and squeaky. "And how to be an independent woman. She was the strongest person I've ever known. I wish I was even half the woman she is—was." She cleared her throat and took control of her voice. "She never judged me. Her love was unconditional, and I hardly deserved it."

The minister handed Lillian a tissue and she dabbed her eyes, trying not to smear her makeup, but the eyeliner was already smudged. She turned to the photograph on the table next to her. "I miss you so much, Mom. Thank you. For everything." Lillian returned to her seat between Eleanor and Eleanor's brother Niles, taking their hands in each of hers and clutching them tight.

The organist began to play "Shall We Gather at the River?" Paper rustled as the congregation opened their programs to the hymn's lyrics. They sang quietly, with a few more confident voices rising above the others. Rose's family did not sing. They listened to the congregation, some of them praying in their hearts, others taking from the experience whatever was meaningful to them.

The hymn was followed by a reading. Eugene's wife, Tammy, recited verses from Ecclesiastes 3 about everything having a season. Afterward, the minister's wife, who had been friends with Rose, offered a prayer of gratitude and celebration for Rose's life.

The minister invited Eugene up to offer the eulogy. He stood up from his seat next to Eleanor's grandfather and approached the microphone. He gave a beautiful tribute depicting Rose's history and life story. He told a few of the stories his grandmother Annabel had told him about Rose's childhood and youth, one about her and her sister dumping eggs in someone's gym bag, which sparked true laughter among the mourners. Eugene said he loved that story the most, because it represented his two mothers' relationship with each other. As he moved into adulthood, her spoke about her successes, her accomplishments, and her influence on others. As she would've wanted, he spoke about her involvement in the church, specifically about her charity. For just a moment, eyes were dry as he recounted a life worth celebrating.

He ended with a quick word from his daughters: "My girls, Rose and Annabel, wish they could've been here today, but they asked me to express their love for Mama Rose and say that she inspired them both throughout their lives." He paused, looking around at the full pews. "She would've loved this. Seeing you all gathered here. Thank you. Thank you so much." He returned to his seat.

Eleanor's cousin Nathan did the next reading from his personal Bible, a passage from 1 Corinthians 15. Something about death as a transformation. Then the minister gave his sermon. Eleanor couldn't concentrate on these. She dwelled on everything said in her uncle's eulogy. There was a lot she'd never heard before. She felt guilty, like she hadn't asked the right questions while her grandmother was still alive to answer them. She was certain there were details of her grandmother's life that were now lost, forever.

The minister ended his sermon with prayer asking for God's comfort for Rose's family. Then he said, "Rose's granddaughter, Eleanor, has agreed to sing a verse from Rose's favorite hymn, 'How Great Thou Art.' Her husband Danny will accompany on the piano." Danny handed Marc to Lillian and helped Eleanor up.

Eleanor's voice cracked a few times as she tried to control her emotion. She tried to think about God the way her grandmother had—to convey Rose's love through the words of that hymn. And for a brief moment Eleanor felt something divine. Maybe the higher self her mom was always talking about. Or maybe the God that her grandmother had believed in. That Daisy had believed in. She looked at Danny to ground herself, and she saw belief in his eyes as he played. When had he reconverted, anyway? Was it in a brief moment of clarity, or a slow build over time as they'd attended Daisy's church each week? Or had he never really stopped believing? She used his certainty to steady herself and ended the hymn strong in her voice, but still uncertain in her heart.

Danny wrapped his arm around her shoulders as they returned to their pew. They sat and Eleanor buried her face in Danny's shoulder. He kissed the top of her head and held her as she sobbed. Lillian rubbed Eleanor's back with her fingertips.

"Before we have our final reading and prayer, Rose's husband Thomas has asked to say a few words. After the prayer we will have forty minutes to gather at Hillside Cemetery for a brief graveside service. Before we part, I want to remind all in attendance to sign the newspaper in the foyer with Rose's first article she wrote for *Tuscaloosa Eats*." The minister looked at Eleanor's grandfather and nodded.

Thomas walked slowly from his seat in the front row to the pulpit. It was a short distance, but to everyone in the congregation it seemed a mile with Thomas's heavy footsteps. He held a cane in one hand, carved and polished from burl wood.

He approached the pulpit, no notes in hand. He scanned the crowd, taking in the faces who had come to honor his wife's memory. After a moment, he cleared his throat. "Gone too soon..." he hung his head. "I spoke my feelings the day Rose and I were married—when I made my vows. I feel I must do so again, now...I don't remember my mother very well, but I remember my father when she died. I now understand how he felt." He paused, breathing to compose himself. He still towered despite his hunched shoulders. "I don't know how long I'll last up here, so I'll be quick. Rose was strong. Stronger even than any of you know." He looked directly at Lillian, and then Eugene. "There was one thing that mattered to her more than almost everything else: honoring her sister's memory. I believe she was successful. I..." he paused, his voice catching. "I don't know what I'm going to do without her."

Lillian buried her face in one hand, sobbing. Niles took Marc and passed him to Tammy, then wrapped his arm around his mom.

"She was the love of my life. She never failed to surprise me with her tenacity and wit. My life had meaning because she was in it. My world is darker now. I'm afraid it always will be, until they day I see her again. But I will make another vow to her today. To live. To honor her, as she did her sister, by pushing aside the darkness to make way for light. For our children and grandchildren and great-grandchildren."

In the back of the chapel, a man about Thomas's age, maybe slightly older, stood behind the pews. He listened to the widower's words, tears falling in a steady, silent stream down his leathery cheeks. He looked longingly at the row of family in the front. His dark eyes lingered on Eugene and Lillian. They were eyes filled with shame and regret.

Thomas paused. The mourners believed the silence was in overpowering emotion, stealing his words away. But Thomas had seen the man. They held one another's gaze, and there was understanding between them—two men who had lost what was dearest to them in the entire world. Decades of distance closed in a second, then the man turned and left.

The cemetery was hot. The mourners gathered under the golden canopy of the two trees near Rose's graveside to hide from the sun. Despite the temperature, some of the leaves had begun to fall, scattering the manicured lawn with red and brown.

A short graveside service reminded all that death was not the end. Niles gave a final prayer, then Eleanor watched as her grandmother was lowered into the ground by a row of green straps on a motorized pulley. As the casket disappeared, she felt a sudden urgency. It was too soon. She needed more time, more time to say goodbye. She looked around her, and everyone stood still and calm. Some tears and sniffles disrupted the silence, but no one seemed concerned that her grandmother's body was about to be covered in six feet of earth. Eleanor tried to remind herself this was normal—how it's done. But it all looked so out of place now, and panic pulsed painfully in her chest.

The family lined up to throw handfuls of dirt down onto the casket. Eleanor stayed behind, next to the cottonwood. Danny gave her a look and squeezed her hand. She shook her head. He moved forward without her, holding Marc with the same white polo on that he'd worn to Daisy's funeral. Danny helped Marc grab some dirt and drop it down into the grave. After Danny and Marc finished, a tall, elderly Black woman in a suit approached the grave, removing a white glove before taking a handful dirt. Eleanor recognized the state senator—Great-Aunt Celiah as Eleanor had known her growing up—Grandmother's closest friend. Celiah kissed the top of her fist, then let the dirt trickle slowly between her fingers. She left the graveside and stood next to Grandfather, grasping his hand in both of hers.

Lillian approached Eleanor. "Come on, we'll do it together."

Eleanor looked at her mother, the panic and helplessness showing in her eyes.

Lillian took her arm. "Come, Eleanor. You'll regret it your whole life if you don't."

She led Eleanor to the graveside, picking up a handful of dirt, then nodded at her to do the same. Eleanor reached down and sunk her hand into the pile at their feet. It was cool and slightly damp, like fresh garden soil from the hardware store. It smelled like Daisy's garden. And Eleanor choked back a sob. As she opened her fingers over the hole in the ground, the dirt fell atop the pile that soiled the polished cherry wood of the casket lid.

Eleanor looked to her mother, but Lillian was focused on something beyond the gravesite. A petite, middle aged woman with greying blonde hair walked through the cemetery towards them. Lillian led Eleanor back to Danny and Marc, then almost ran to the woman, pulling her into an intimate embrace. Niles followed close behind his mother, hugging the woman after Lillian finally released her. The woman stroked his hair with affectionate familiarity.

Danny looked at Eleanor inquisitively. "Who is that?"

"I don't know," Eleanor answered.

A few more mourners stepped forward to add dirt to the casket, then Celiah, with her arm wrapped around Thomas's shoulders, announced there would be a reception at the Whitfield home for family and any friends who wished to pay their respects.

Lillian and Eleanor sat on the back porch of the old Whitfield house. Not much had changed about it in almost fifty years. The house had been in the family for generations now, inherited by Rose when her parents passed, and with Rose's passing would be inherited by Lillian, since Eugene was Command Chief Master Sergeant at Mcclellan air force base in Sacramento, and had no plans to leave California. Lillian planned to sell her condo and move in with her father immediately, so he wouldn't be alone in that big house.

Close family friends mingled inside, nibbling on potluck dishes and exchanging tearful embraces. Outside, the leaves on the peach trees resisted changing their colors for fall. The familiar earthy warm scents of an Alabama October filled the Whitfield's small orchard.

"What did grandpa mean?" Eleanor sat down on the top step, holding a sweet tea that was still full. Her mother sat next to her, leaning against the porch beam and sipping her own tea.

"Mom didn't talk about it," Lillian answered. "But your grandfather told Eugene and I that she'd been really depressed for a couple years after Lily died. They didn't really know that's what it was back then. And you know, she never had kids of her own. I've only just learned that wasn't from lack of trying. She got pregnant a few times, as I understand. And almost died when she lost the last one. She didn't know how to get help back then, so she fought through it all on her own. But she didn't let that happen to me. When I had my first episode as a teenager, it was like she was on fire. She didn't stop until she knew I'd be ok."

"Sounds familiar."

Lillian smiled.

Both women stared out at the setting sun. The air was thick, and the elongated shadows didn't bring much relief.

"Were you ever diagnosed with anything, Mom?"

Lillian studied her daughter. "You know, when I look at you, all grown, I swear it's like photos of Lily come to life. You have her exact eyes, you know."

Eleanor turned to face her mother. "Please. You don't know how frustrating it's been to not know my own family history."

Lillian sighed and turned back to the sunset. The moon was high, reflecting the sun's golden colors as darkness pulled at the sky.

"Alcoholism, PTSD, and bipolar disorder."

Eleanor felt a rush of anger. "Bipolar? When—"

"I was diagnosed right before you were born."

"You knew my whole life? Why wouldn't you tell me this? Especially when I was doing all those evaluations?"

"I told your psychiatrist."

"You told my psychiatrist. And what, told him not to tell me?"

Lillian stared down into her tea.

"I was scared. My whole fucking childhood." It felt good to curse—like releasing the valve on a pressure cooker.

"I don't expect you to understand. Not yet. But someday you'll find that the people you are charged to love most, the ones you're responsible for protecting—there's pain you don't want them to ever know exists."

"I was still in pain."

"I know," Lillian looked at her, regret written across her face and deep in her eyes. "I'm sorry. Back then everyone encouraged people to keep that kind of stuff to themselves. Keep it from their kids. They still do." She sighed, deeply. "It's not an excuse. I just want you to know I was trying to do the right thing. I got it wrong, and I'm so sorry about that."

Eleanor looked into her mother's eyes. There was regret in them.

"But I did try to give you something better than what I had. Like your grandma did for me."

Eleanor's face softened. Her mom was wrong about one thing: She did understand. She was desperate to keep her darkness away from Marc. Maybe she couldn't forgive her mom quite yet, but she'd begin to try. She determined then and there she wouldn't make the same mistakes that her mom and Daisy's generation had made.

"Mom, there's something I need to tell you."

Lillian shifted, turning to face Eleanor better. The condensation on Eleanor's glass trickled down onto her hand.

"After Marc was born, I was diagnosed with post-partum OCD." Eleanor brought her gaze back up to the horizon, letting the tears go, not trying to stifle their intensity.

Lillian put down her tea and wrapped her arms around her daughter, resting her head against Eleanor's. Eleanor buried her face in her mom's neck.

"I'm ok now. It was temporary. But it's been a really hard few years. It's been hard having a baby after losing one. After losing...Ruth."

Lillian looked down at her daughter, surprised. "I didn't know you gave her a name." Ruth's gravestone read: *Baby Sun*.

Eleanor nodded.

"Do you want to talk about it?" Lillian whispered, softly.

Eleanor shook her head, her forehead rubbing against the fabric of Lillian's dress. They sat there for a few minutes while Eleanor's tears slowed. Then she remembered something.

"Mom, who was that woman at the cemetery?"

Lillian ran her fingers through her daughter's hair. "An old friend."

Eleanor sat up.

Lillian smiled, and something simultaneously sad and beautiful reflected in her eyes. "No. More than a friend, actually."

Eleanor's lower jaw opened just a bit, and she looked behind her through the glass porch door. The woman was standing by the kitchen sink, in seeming deep conversation with Eleanor's grandfather, her hand on his arm in a comforting gesture. With her other hand, she fingered a pink-quartz pendant on her necklace. Lillian followed Eleanor's gaze, her eyes sparkling at the sight of the woman.

Eleanor squeezed her mom's hand. "I didn't even know...I'm so happy for you, Mom."

Lillian turned back to Eleanor and nodded, smiling. "Her name's Grace. We met when I was living in St. Louis before you were born. Back then I was...too afraid. I pretended to not care what society thought of me, but truly I cared more than most. I was afraid of being outcast. And by the time I'd figured out that shit didn't matter, that we'd be fine if we faced it together, well...your grandmother had invited me back home, and it was the right thing for me. Truly I think if we'd been together back then it wouldn't have lasted anyway. I wasn't ready for a healthy relationship."

"Oh, Mom, I'm sure that's not—"

Lillian laughed. "Don't even try, El. You're a terrible liar." They both laughed, then Lillian continued. "Over the years, we lost touch. But we reconnected a year or so ago when I looked her up. I'm sorry I didn't tell you sooner, I didn't want to say anything until it was a sure thing. But she's going to retire early and come live with me here."

"That's okay. Thanks for telling me now."

Eleanor and Lillian sat in each of their own vulnerabilities, feeling a bond grow between them that was different than a child's and her mother's, but maybe only a different shape of the same thing. Eleanor put her arm around her mom, and they embraced as the sun dipped towards the horizon, it's orange light reflected in the glow of a sawdust moon.

Acknowledgments

None of this would have been possible without my biggest supporter and best cheerleader, Max Gariety. Thank you for being my editor, tech support, and digital designer. Thank you for pushing me when I was on the brink of giving up. And thank you for giving me the time to accomplish my dreams.

Special thanks to my writing group and critique partners Madison Coffing, Jon Hermsen, and Amy Salazar who all read the first drafts of each chapter in this book. Thank you Madison for being my first ARC reviewer for the final product. And thank you Amy for my invaluable emotional support throughout this process.

Thanks to Ludlow Adams for jumping into the new world of podcasting with me, and for all the kind and beautiful praise you've given this work on that platform.

Huge thanks to my sensitivity reader Niesha Davis, and to *Ask a Korean* for cultural consultation.

I'd also like to thank the friends and family who graciously agreed to be my beta readers. Madison Coffing, Annemarie Henesy, Jon Hermsen, Jori Ellis, Amy Salazar, Amanda Skiles, Ashley Skiles, David Skiles, Nathaniel Skiles, Tammy Skiles, and Kimi Weldon. Your input helped me bring this novel to a new level. I hope you all enjoy the final version. I cannot mention them all here, but I'd also like to thank friends, family, and classmates who reviewed portions and chapters of early drafts.

And of course this book would not be reaching the hands of readers without the incredible cover. Thank you Kimi Weldon for the original art and beautiful, meaningful concept. And thank you again, Max, for executing our vision.

Finally, I'd like to thank my undergraduate and graduate professors for believing in me and giving me the confidence to pursue my goals.

Sponsors

A special thank you to my first supporters and patrons:

Tyler Cahoy
Lanae DHulst
Tara Sal
Tammy Skiles

About the Author

Fiction is truth observed through stained glass.

JS Gariety is an author of emotional, upmarket contemporary fiction and speculative fiction. She also writes creative nonfiction and flash fiction. She has a BA in English and creative writing and will complete her MFA in creative writing in the summer of 2023. She is certified in online teaching instruction and currently works in academic support for an online university. The Weight of Gold is her debut novel, but her flash fiction can also be found in Queer SciFi's 2022 anthology *Clarity*. Gariety is married with two kids. Her family enjoys camping and going on adventures together. When she's not reading or writing, Gariety enjoys pastry baking, snuggling her cats, and doing projects with her kids. Gariety hopes that her work will help people feel less alone in their struggles. You can find out more about Gariety and her work on her website: jsgariety.com

www.ingramcontent.com/pod-product-compliance
Lightning Source LLC
Chambersburg PA
CBHW010743310726
48971CB00010B/2919